Jerry

BILL

W9-BFN-027

ON JULY 4th MILLIONS OF
AMERICANS WOULD CELEBRATE
THEIR INDEPENDENCE.

ON THE SAME DAY, THE BOMBS,
THE POISONED WATER, AND
THE MASS SUICIDES WOULD
BEGIN . . .

Richard Condon
The Whisper
of the Axe

Also by Richard Condon
available from Ballantine Books:

MONEY IS LOVE

The
Whisper
of the Axe

Richard Condon

BALLANTINE BOOKS • **NEW YORK**

Library of Congress Catalog Card Number: 75-45310

ISBN 0-345-25662-X

This edition published by arrangement with The Dial Press

Manufactured in the United States of America

First Ballantine Books Edition: January 1978

"I was sitting so close I could hear the whisper of the axe."

Citizen Jacques Cerruti, at the execution of Marie-Antoinette, 16 October 1793

part
one

1

9:56 P.M., 27 June 1976

Agatha Teel's left shoulder had been shattered by a bullet fifty-one seconds ago. The man who shot her had just exited from the elevator two floors below her living room. She sat carefully in a chair and flicked on the light. She laid the open phone on the table and dialed.

"Jonas? Sis. Don't talk. We got about two hours to get me out of here. I got myself shot and I'm bleeding real good. No, *no!* Get me Pikow's surgeon and a big dark car. Then come get me. Okay? *Don't talk, baby!* Just do it."

She stood shakily. She moved slowly across the room, stepping over the body of a man lying on his back, working slowly around the body of a young woman. Agatha Teel went along a connecting corridor, leaving all doors open behind her, into her huge bathroom, which had once taken plumbers, decorators and jewelers two months to install: a fantasy of lapis lazuli and alabaster, Apulian marble and onyx. Gasping with pain, she shucked off her white beaver dressing gown. Her body, shining with blood, was picked up by six full-length mirrors in the walls around the room. She pulled gauze pads and bandages out of a cabinet and tried, with one hand, to improvise some way to pack the wound.

She was on the run. She looked into her eyes in the mirror. "You better believe it," she said thickly. "You on the run, girl. Maybe it's all over."

3

The wonders of her glorious life had been shut off like lights on a shimmering Christmas tree. She managed to fill a syringe with morphine and banged it into a trackless arm. She sat on the heated marble floor. Blood ran down across her satin skin into the coarse hairs of her lap.

If he made it, his people wouldn't arrest her and hold her for trial. They would hold her still right where they found her and blow her brains out; no questions. She made herself get up and move. She stopped for a last look into the mirror of the greatest room of her life and she saw herself framed by all the cunning lighting and semi-precious stones set so artfully into the eight walls above the white fur scatter rugs.

She made it to the closet in the front hall. Pulling at the hanger with one hand, she got the long sable coat over her nakedness. She thought that he could be lying in a lake of blood down there at the front door but more likely he could get through: that horror kept her moving. He was out on the deserted street moving himself across the night, bleeding like a broken dam and trying to find a phone booth.

She heard the elevator start at the main floor. She wondered dizzily who would get to her first: his people or her people? She leaned against the wall, faced the elevator door, and sweated the glory of the dead past.

2

January 1976

They held special "American-style" graduation exercises at the Guerrilla War College at Karlik Tagh in the eastern part of the Sinkiang Province, 80 miles south of the Mongolian frontier. It was New Year's Day 1976. Someone was playing "Oh, Promise Me" on the piano. Balloons in three colors were released from the ceiling as the last graduate was summoned to the stage and congratulated. Everyone in the class wore newly washed and pressed *p'u-fu* over fresh *ch'ao fu* and *chi-fu*. There was massed singing ("Show Me The Way To Go Home," "She Wore a Yellow Ribbon") and two valedictory addresses.

Sally Winn delivered the valedictory for the Women's Camp. A tall, strong, banana-colored woman with healed knife scars on the right side of her face, she gave a short, inspiring speech. Part of it included these words: "We learned plenty here. I used to listen to that shit like 'We Shall Overcome' and I figured— too bad. But I know different now. I mean—I understand now. I learned how to combine myself, to industrialize myself. Man, America industrializes everything—crime, sports, sex, religion—so we don't do one kidnap and wait. We don't do one hijack and wait. We don't rip off one bank at a time like little Mr. Lenin, no sir. We industrialize. We gone kidnap the famblies of twenty-five state governors on the same day. We gone take the money from the governors, then we gone kill those famblies of the twenty-five governors

5

by some Gr-is: we gonna throw them out the window. That's what I mean to industrialize. . . ."

Kranak made the valedictory for the Men's Camp because he was The Man in every way. He talked for twenty-eight minutes. In part of it he said, ". . . and I wonder how the great American people are going to adjust on the afternoon we detonate a fissionable device from an office in the Empire State Building in New York and take out that entire building and maybe eight square blocks around it and maybe waste forty or sixty thousand people." There was a roll of applause and a lot of whistling from the women. "I'll tell you how they are going to adjust," Kranak said, "they are going to learn that political violence is here to stay and that through political violence they will have the only possible way to ever get their own country back again."

The applause flapped and flared again. "Their country will fall. The people will pull it down themselves IF we break the people's backs, IF we scourge them and torment them until they overturn that Establishment as it stands. We will bring systematic terror against the people—killing, maiming and marking them. We will close our eyes and ears to their agony until justice is reborn in the United States of America. We will use American lives and American sanity as currency to buy a failure of the national will. Until our plan was born it was a textbook verity that no group could get popular support unless it explained its operations as something more than nihilistic violence and random criminal assaults . . . because the Mau Mau, the PLO, the Japanese Red Army and the Tupamaros were senti- mentalists. They kept telling themselves that they would, after all, one day be called upon to govern the nations they were fighting for and would need to remember how to imitate the dignity of the thieves and murderers who had governed before they were pulled down.

"Well—we are not sentimentalists. And we have no expectation nor desire ever to govern. When it is over—when we have done our work well—most of us will be dead. One third of America will be dead or dying and new leaders, now waiting, will take over the perfect state.

"We will rule from the streets until that day and our terror will bring that day—and salvation."

3

1968–1976

For a woman who planned the extermination of sixty million Americans, Agatha Teel was stable and amiable. Her even disposition was made possible by the certainty of her knowledge that she would have to kill a lot of Americans in order to lever the rest of them into saving themselves. She never talked about what was wrong with the American society or what she planned to do with it, beyond destruction, to put it right. Her focus was simply to make sure that all American institutions would be made to disintegrate. She considered it someone else's job to put it right after that, someone who would believe as much in the beautiful qualities of building as she believed in the healing qualities of destroying. She saw herself as being precisely and unselfishly fitted, as was no one else, to re-cast the American dream in annealing fire. She was sane. She used negatives to produce positives in her own explanation of herself to herself—such as "Kill them so they may live"—but she never spoke about why she would do what she was going to do. The power of the imagination of victims and torturers alike would produce, she knew, a collective vision far greater than her own. Also (no small thing) it was a personal challenge to surpass the power of the men leading the nations and the armies; to grind them into fine dust with her mind.

The conception of what she had willed herself to do was akin to Genesis with Teel as the Creator, but if she thought of herself as God no one ever knew that because no God had ever been as adorably amiable as Teel.

In 1968 Teel was thirty-five years old, with an IQ of 174, and commander of the still-as-yet (almost) unformed Freedom Fighters aka American Freedom Fighters aka FF/AFF, whose Eastern Action Area extended along the Atlantic seaboard from Boston to Miami, inland to 95°W which, roughly, made Milwaukee, Minneapolis, Chicago, St. Louis, Kansas City, Houston and New Orleans the western boundary of the command. Teel's Western Action Area would be smaller, operating only in the Pacific coastal cities plus Denver.

Urban guerrilla officers from Uruguay, the Middle East, Japan, Ireland, and China had been seconded to act as organizing Army Corps commanders until 1976, when the trained cadres of Teel's own native American officers would have finished their training. Some of these foreign officers were paid their salaries directly. Others preferred that their earnings go to their home organizations. They were all seasoned specialists: the Uruguayan, Enrique Jorge Molina, had been a divisional commander with the Tupamaros. He specialized in kidnapping, hijacking, and interrogations. Sato Koroshi was on a loan from the Japanese Red Army. His field was urban electrical systems, fuel gas storage, water treatment and sewage systems. Boohoo Gargan was a graduate engineer who had perfected car bomb design for the IRA and was a specialist in school and playground bombing. Together they covered the spectrum of Guerrilla Discipline, Materiel Storage, Compartmentalized Disbursement, Enemy Force Infiltration, Metropolitan Communications, Petrol Cannons, Torture, and Bribery. Teel had enriched the guerrilla technique with what she called Gr-1 (for Ground One), a plan for throwing people out of windows to simulate suicides and increase terror. Eventually, all Army Corps commands would be interchangeable. They would be fighting a new kind of war, i.e., to destroy people instead of troops, until the people, in their insane desperation, were driven to turn upon troops and government itself. Government would be even more impossible than it had been since the election of Richard Nixon, Teel figured, when the Rockefellers had planted Dr. Kissinger upon him.

Teel's General Staff was led by a Colonel Pikow, on loan from the Guerrilla Training Center of the People's Republic of China. The General Staff projected guerrilla operations in thirty American cities* as a simultaneous action in all-out, full-scale urban warfare. In 1968 Teel was still six years away from intensive recruitment. She had, however, begun specialist recruitment and specialist training. She was on her way to securing total financing.

Teel was as deliberate and as self-protective as Montgomery of Alamein. If she needed three of anything she laid away fifteen. She was going to refuse to allow any strike, small or enormous, until everything was prepared: weapons and munitions dumps; food; medical supplies; materiel caches and command hideouts; extraordinarily protected money-channelling so that precisely the right amount of money would be where it was needed but no chances would be taken that any great part of it could be lost without recovery. Her street hospital organization exceeded the efficiency of anything ever attempted by a contra-governmental force.

Teel demanded that everything interact on Corps, Division, Brigade and Regimental levels. She accepted only urban battle plans which would give her a 5 to 1 advantage of surprise. If a projected organizing span double-checked out to be a safe two years, four months and nine days, Teel insisted upon allowing—and then nailed down the provisions for—eight years of organizing and preparation. She could not be hurried. She carried the international operation of financing and training support in her head. She saw to it that guerrilla-organizing Corps Commanders, imported from the IRA, the Tupamaros and the PLO, learned to carry all details of urban guerrilla operations in their heads by a continual simplification and re-designing of the thirty city operations.

Teel's greatest need was to maintain her own invisibility as a revolutionary and as a revolutionary leader. She had no intention of going down in history as the female Lenin of the Second American Revolution. She believed in now and she believed in staying alive while it was still now. With the exception of her single liaison, Colonel Pikow, and her own brother, Jonas Teel, no one in the FF/AFF movement knew who she was. It was necessary that the revolutionary side of Teel remain invisible so that her visible side, like the moon, could loom larger and larger and fuller and fuller, as a "safe and sane, go-along, conservative American female leader" who sat on Presidential commissions, represented her country in the United States delegation to the United Nations, consulted with leaders of the Congress, the Pentagon, and Justices of the Supreme Court—a woman who was one of the three leading trial lawyers in the United States.

Teel had invented the source of financing for the Thirty Cities' War.* Her single financial problem was how to conceal the first half-billion dollars, how to hold back cash delivery from her multiple sources so that the money remained their problem, not hers, for as long as possible; how to launder and re-invest money; how to pay taxes on what part of what income; where to store the overages in places which would

---

* Boston, Providence, New Haven, The New York Metropolitan Area, Philadelphia, Baltimore, Pittsburgh, Washington, Charlotte, Atlanta, Jacksonville, Miami, New Orleans, Louisville, Memphis, Cleveland, Detroit, Cincinnati, Indianapolis, Chicago, Milwaukee, St. Louis, Kansas City, Dallas, Houston, Denver, LA, San Francisco, Portland and Seattle.

eventually deliver the money safely to individual commands at street-fighting level; how to pay for imported materiel in an untraceable manner.

Between 1968 and 1976, Teel established seven retail chains ranging from eight to fifty-one stores each, selling ordinary merchandise and making a good profit. She owned 209 businesses operating out of the Thirty Cities with a combined staff of 4,300 earning attractive profits. She owned a non-affiliated group of variously named personal finance companies with 151 retail outlets in the Thirty Cities which operated at splendid profits; sixty-seven wholly owned pawn shops, and forty-one used clothing and furniture stores. Teel operated these vast businesses as attorney for the non-existent other owners through management committees she appointed. Teel considered that she owned everything the way a bishop owns everything which seems to belong to the church within his diocese. For instant communications she owned 189 bars & grills, 219 newsstands, eleven taxi companies, the Rockrimmon Bank & Trust Company in Stamford, Connecticut, and a slightly smaller bank in Brussels. The organization could also communicate easily and quickly through direct courier access to 31,750 heroin pushers, 319 dope houses, 207,840 whores and 41,568 pimps; a formidable intelligence organization overall.

Because of her background as a criminal lawyer, Teel knew the heroin wholesalers across the country. They became a part of her planning because there was so much more money in shit than there had ever been in booze and beer during Prohibition. Also, the money in heroin had corrupted a lot of people across the board and it was easy for her to reach the people heroin had corrupted (not by their personal narcotics habit but as one more part of the hundreds of billions of dollars thrown off by the habit).

---

* This was the ultimate designation by the world history industry. The name was coined in a signed newspaper column by Thomas Buckley, *The New York Times*.

Teel could understand injustice and yet she couldn't.
She could feel what people might feel (she thought) as
she planned guerrilla operations, but she wasn't all
that sensitive and empathetic about what their feelings
would be when their children got blown through roofs,
or their wives got thrown out of twelfth-story windows
by fake firemen after an arson or when they looked
down to see their own left leg and it wasn't there
anymore. Teel was unable to remember that, throughout history, people had never felt militant about their
politics; habits were the order. Teel overlooked the
bodies, ignored the huge public mind which thought as
one, just as much as if it had been a creature of
Venusian science fiction, and settled down to make
sure that survivors of the second revolution—regardless
of race, creed, or color—were saved; their lot im-
proved. The last part was a necessary human corollary
in order to be forgiven the first part, because (throughout all of it in spite of all she did not understand) Teel
knew there was no charge for dying: she would sorely
resist her own chances to die as those chances came.

4

1933–1968

Publicly, Agatha Teel was one of the four leading black
women in the United States of her age group (35-55).
She was first among equals as a black leader at the
American bar according to all classified surveillance
on the computer reels of United States Government
investigative agencies. She was classified safely as
"leftish but not left" by the Federal Bureau of In-

vestigation, the Central Intelligence Agency, the National Security Agency, Air Force Intelligence, the White House Secret Service detail, Naval Intelligence, AEC Security, the Defense Department intelligence agency, the State Department's Bureau of Research & Intelligence, and the security unit of the Treasury Department. All other government security agencies cross-filed from these seminal sources.

Teel's parents were dead. Her younger brother, and only sibling, Jonas Teel, was an experimental and theoretical physicist. Historians were going to have a hard time figuring out what button of her lifetime conditioning Teel had pushed to get herself started as a terrorist. Teel was black in a white society, but so were 16,000,000 other Americans who had very few of the edges Teel had put together for herself and her brother. It was as if Teel had raised Jonas, so great was her influence on her younger brother. They had a mighty bond.

Teel had a summa cum laude degree from Barnard College and a co-editorship of the Columbia University Law Review. After passing her bar examinations in the top .3 percent of 1 percent of her class at law school, she was finally able to practice law after her twenty-third job interview. She had begun on Wall Street but ended successfully only with the firm of Rackin & Grady (in association with Turem, Schulz & Ortega) who specialized in criminal law practice and who shared offices with the Busy Bee Bail Bonding Company in a four-story cockroach farm near the courts on West 124th Street.

"I like what I see," Mr. Rackin, senior partner, told Teel after he had examined her exceptional credentials in his office where there was no room for Teel to sit unless she sat sideways on the end of the top of his desk like a gangster's moll in the Warner Brothers stock company studies of the thirties. The chairs, both of them, were piled high with canned food. The walls were lined with canned food. Mr. Rackin had had a terrible experience with food during the Great Depression and he had been unable to take the chance of not having plenty of it near him ever since.

"I'm not surprised," Teel said.

"You're not surprised?" Mr. Rackin responded with much surprise. "How many offers have you had from downtown? You are a black lawyer, Miss Teel and, believe me, there isn't another specialized practice in this whole town—although I except Brooklyn and the Bronx from that statement—who could use a specialist like you."

"A specialist at what, Mr. Rackin?"

"At being black. At being a black woman at the same time as being a lawyer. The division I would like you to take over for us is a practice which is loaded with a lot of black women and, believe it or not, whatever they did that got them in the court, they need a little human help, too. I mean, if I can do it, which isn't always, I'd like to give a little sympathy also for the fees because what they are always in court for is essentially a human condition."

"Like what?"

"Mostly they are whores—you know. Some are thieves—listen, a whole lot are thieves. Some are junkies, some are pushers, some are pimps. But, by and large, they are either hookers or hookers engaged in some other incriminating line."

"What the hell, Mr. Rackin! What do I know about all that? I've never seen a whore that I know of. You might just as well ask me to train lions in a cage."

"They ain't lions, Miss Teel. But they are in a cage, I admit you that. This isn't difficult law. You'll have it all figured out by the end of the first day. The clients are picked up in the streets and the bars and in a few raids on a police quota basis; then their pimps come to you with fifty dollars a girl. It's like an unofficial license fee which they pay every eleven or fifteen days to keep working. Out of the fifty, the cops get eighteen a head which they split with the two local political clubs. Eight goes to the boys in the courthouse, we get the twenty-four that is left and out of the twenty-four, you get eight, which is better money at the end of the year than anybody in your class will get downtown, believe me."

To get through the days, Teel began to remind herself that if she had been born white she might have been fat and dumb, but she couldn't sustain that consolation. She had no use in this law practice for the three other languages she spoke, except Spanish, or for her grasp of the subtle meanings of the law. She was unable to become aimlessly bitter so she became purposively, savagely bitter against her own skin color and the color of the people who had ignored her in the firms where she knew she should be practicing law. She saw that she was getting too emotional to remain objective and design ways to change it. So, she threw emotion out of her life. Emotion keeps people young with empathy, and when it goes it is a bad loss.

Teel moved into shrewdness, rejected that for hardness, then cut that away in token exchange for a year of despair while her clients told her about how the rats had run off with the baby. When she couldn't accept any more of it she told Mr. Rackin she was quitting. She liked Mr. Rackin. He was old, he wished everybody well, but he knew that couldn't be.

"Whatta you gonna do?" he asked Teel with concern. "You are a very good lawyer. That shows even in this kind of practice. But you are also a black woman lawyer and the promised land is late in arriving."

"I'm going to open my own office."

"That's crazy!"

"I got to find that out, Mr. Rackin."

"Where? Here? In Harlem? Miss Teel, believe me, no matter how it looks there is only so much business. The cops won't cooperate with you. And the political clubs? Listen, you won't be able to get a client. You are making a nice, steady forty thousand a year here. Why should you open your own office?"

"I got a gimmick, Mr. Rackin. I'm going downtown."

She rented weekly desk space on East 40th Street. The day before she opened she had a meeting at Chock Full O'Nuts with a former client who was a good thief and who was married to a great booster.

"Listen, Douglas," she said, "what I need is something nice in the ladies' two-hundred-and-eighty-nine-fifty line but I need it once a week. Can you do that?"

"You know it, baby."

"I would glom it if I had the time. But I don't. Just take stuff at around three hundred retail with good labels and give me a little variety every week. Like jewelry, maybe big perfumes, underwear. You know."

"What I don't know, Ethel knows. She has a good eye and she can keep every week matched up on an ensemble basis. Is it for you?"

"No, no," Teel said. "It's for the Area Billing Supervisor of the telephone company. She will be happy not to send me any bills, long distance or local, if I treat her right in the merchandise line."

Teel entered her own practice of law: the defense of the country's most publicized underdogs. Princely heroin wholesalers who owed her a few favors sent her the first clients. If Teel's clients were not nationally famous when they were dug up, they were household words by the time Teel had the jury tell them they were Not Guilty. Ghetto communities became so aroused, bleeding hearts hemorrhaged so heavily, that Teel's soon-heavy fees were put together on a national subscription basis. On a really good civil rights/criminal trial with the front pages working overtime, Teel was good for an average of sixty thousand dollars a case. She averaged three a year. What helped her was that she was a genius.

She was the sole trial lawyer, flashing her beauty and intelligence like a succoring lighthouse, for The San Antonio Two, The Aspen Six, The Winsted Nine, The Rockrimmon Twelve, and three sharp-looking black girls who had been charged with gang raping an Irish Tourist board representative in a Hilton Hotel in

Duluth. Teel was the most famous trial lawyer in the United States by the time she was twenty-eight years old. She could make a jury beg with their eyes to please stop the shame she made them feel and which they had not known they could feel. She looked so young and brave. She was the idol of every black man and woman who had ever felt the crunch—which included just about every black American except a very rich Jones wholesaler in south Chicago named Grunts Patterson.

Teel was decorated by the Government of the Democratic Republic of Congo, later Zaire, in a simple ceremony witnessed by 73,000 people inside and outside the Country Ballroom on 129th Street and Lenox. She was invited to convert to Islam and the Republican Party on the same evening. She was given an Agatha Teel Night at Shea Stadium before the start of a ballgame. The park sold out. That night they gave her the Mayor, two Senators, a Mercedes 450SL, a contract to model Blackglama® mink coats in the more established white magazines, $19,238 in cash, and a year's free supply of pot—all for the wildly popular reason that she had won an acquittal for two of the most admired Jones dealers in south Brooklyn; two men who, as revealed by Teel and confirmed by the jury, had been wrongfully accused of murder.

She went from triumph to triumph. She recorded "Shit, Baby, You My Man" for the Clef label and it sold 781,285 singles with "Moonlight in Kahlua" on the flip side. She taught labor law at Cornell University. She dined at the White House just as soon as displaying blacks became useful to politicians. After dinner with the Kennedys she attended an evening at Camelot of musical concert by Pablo Casals and Pat Boone. After dinner with the Johnsons she attended a "down home" evening in the East Room starring Pat Boone and Pablo Casals. She was invited by JFK to sit on her first two Presidential Commissions: The Presidential Commission for the Investigation of Civil Rights Horizons for Commercial Airlines Pilots and CRIME: UCDEEM

(The Presidential Commission for the Perspective Achievement Relative to Unauthorized Transient Canadians for American Employment Motivations Within the Publishing & Printing Industries).

By the time she was twenty-nine Teel's photograph had appeared regularly in the American press from *Women's Wear* to *The Messenger of the Sacred Heart,* 83 percent of the space having been nurtured by Shraderco, Teel's own public relations firm, based in the Bahamas.

By then Teel was earning two hundred-odd thousand dollars a year, but deep into the seams of her own mind, from an earlier season of believing that black people lived and worked apart from white people *by choice,* Teel now believed that the entire black world of the United States was a horde of broken reeds—addicts, prostitutes, skag merchants and habitual criminals; the amoral and the lost. The second conclusion was reached through her experience in the law and from the fact that everywhere she went or was invited to go outside her practice blacks were neither existent nor imagined. This conclusion also molded her eventual purpose.

To do what she would do, Teel needed big flaws. For example, her perspective prevented her from understanding that she knew only the most afflicted fringes of the black community. Teel had never had the opportunity to know more. Her grandfather had been the son of a slave who had been passed through the Underground Railway as far as Forestport, New York, and there he had stayed. His daughter had become the great and good friend of a white restauranteur in Utica who, dying, had passed Aunt Mewsie an envelope filled with $37,000 (to keep his wife from getting it). Aunt Mewsie never spent more than on sheet music, yard goods, and Caruso records, so the money went into a Utica savings bank.

Then Aunt Mewsie caught something which shook her all to pieces. She couldn't stop shaking and she felt bad. She transferred the money to Teel's father, a garage mechanic in a village that wouldn't have been able to figure out what a Negro was if it hadn't been for that runaway slave stopping over and starting a family with an imported wife from Gloriola, Canada (who had to be smuggled back into the United States under a wagon). Aunt Mewsie knew if she was shaking that much she couldn't live alone in Utica anymore, so they brought her back up to Forestport. She lived for twelve more years, was a comfort to everybody, most of all to Teel and her little brother; then she died.

Aunt Mewsie's money sent Agatha and Jonas off to college as each one's turn came. Teel went out into the world eight years before Jonas did. From the time she was a child Teel never had the chance to learn about black people. Then she practiced law and found out by too-close observation. If there were blacks on the streets, in the shops and on the subways around the Barnard campus, they had nothing to do with who she felt herself to be. From the day Teel entered the practice of law on West 124th Street, it was as though her entire chemical composition had changed, the way the chemical structure of food changes when it is deep-fried. Suddenly, she seemed to be composed of one part horror and two parts rage, on being lowered abruptly into that courthouse in Harlem.

The balance of affection in Teel's life had been sound from the day she was born. She came from people who knew how to love their children and pay heed to them. Teel never had a minute of loneliness. She never felt she had missed something other people had been given. What she felt, what turned her, was a reversal of that. Later, when she saw all those black people, as black as herself—so many of them—so many tens and tens of thousands of them after eighteen years of imagining that there were only a hazy kind of five of them in the world, the world of Forestport—her Father, Mamma, Aunt Mewsie, Jonas and herself— she decided forcibly, explodingly, that the balance of affection in the lives of all those many other blacks

moving in and out of that courtroom must have been
overthrown, that they had to be eaten away with loneliness and fear, that they had made themselves miss
everything to end up fifty-time whores in a urine-
smelling jailhouse, being dependent upon her. And she
blamed herself too, for embarrassing herself to herself
for being one of them. She blamed them for not having
what *nice* people had. A tilted conviction consumed
her that they had to be punished for cheating themselves just as *nice* people had to be punished for helping cheat them.

Devoutly, as an overbrilliant, depressed woman, she
got the fixation that her clients were all the black
people in the world beyond Forestport. It wasn't that
Teel, six years a New York lawyer, didn't know that
blacks had a different status, but she was never able
to close the gap between who she knew herself to be
and all the others and what they were—except by violence, and that was much later. She began to knit her
blind plans for the salvation of all through the punishment of everyone. She began to understand that people
never wanted to stand where they were told to stand.
They always wanted to go someplace else, do something else, whether they were white, black, or plaid.
Never mind them. Her job was to figure out what she
had been put there to do. She worked on herself, hardly
sleeping or resting, until she was convinced that she
must never allow herself to be viewed as black, not
as all those other blacks were seen by the world which
held them under—the way newborn puppies are
drowned in a pail of water.

She became obsessed and remained obsessed with
putting as much actual and psychological distance between herself and those broken people she served as
existed in all of outer space. However, deep in her
sense of self, and mother, and history—which is what
race is—she began to hate herself for what she felt.
She had the choice of either admitting that, becoming
one of them or, worse punishment because she knew
they were her family, of exiling herself from them.

Her perspective on these conditions altered, of course, as the angles from which she viewed things within the progressing tome of her life altered; she saw—though much later—that her clients back when she had practiced law in 124th Street were no different from her father, her brother, the Presidents of the United States, her favorite movie stars—they were only different from *her*. The condition had been a long time growing on her soul. Her sense of herself became as attached to her being as her physical, biological system.

She would talk it over with her brother Jonas.

"I am glad about certain things," she said. "I mean, don't go thinking I walk around singing the blues, holding the handkerchief on my head."

"Well, like, what certain things?" Jonas grinned.

"I'm glad you back in town. I am ecstatic you gone stay awhile. But mostly I am glad you come down to that court to see what the black world is like, you being a college boy in the heartland of the heartland."

"It was bad."

"Bet your ass."

"It was a freak-up. But, I mean, that ain't the black *world*."

"I been watchin' it a long time, baby. You been down on the farm. That's the black world. An' lemme tay you somethin' else. If there are any other black people who are different from my clients down there, then they are miserable ass-lickin' Toms. They are the fakey part of a society which deliberately lured them into non-revolutionary poses."

"How come?"

"And that ain't all, baby. If any *white* can't understand that, then *they* don't face up to what they owe their own children by pleading with the blacks to come in with them like the Constitution says—then they are enemies and their punishment, their destruction and the destruction of the brothers for not understanding that, is gone be the central goal of my revolution. You hear?"

"Well, okay," Jonas said stoutly. "I'm witchew. You the Momma. What else?"

"There is no other what-else," she said grimly. "Both sides got to be punished before I will even consider any what-else."

Nonetheless, Teel did have a secondary goal. She intended to amass more money than the richest of all the whiteys to prove to herself, with their own holy medals, that she was superior to them, that she had merely agreed to stay around them as an avenue to power, that since all of it was a society where *only* qualities of money one possessed had any meaning, she would make her revolution to punish both black and white for what they had done to her and if, later on, some kind of political formula was necessary to stabilize and solidify what would come after the revolution, she would have more money than all of them and she could buy herself a dozen professors of political science and sit them down in a locked room somewhere to figure all that out when she needed it.

It was the evolution of all past revolutions: first the agonizing psychological needs of the Leader. When that terrible pain was eased, his great political philosophy, which he hadn't known he had, would be revealed to change the world and to carry his memory onward into history.

"Blacks have to be punished," she told Jonas, "for waiting so long to lift their heads and see what they have been created to be. Not dirt on the ground, but air-breathers and space-fillers and ouch-yellers like everybody else."

Black and white had to be punished, she continued, for what they had done to themselves and to each other. When they had been punished, when they had suffered the same pain together, then they would understand each other and would be saved. Teel's revolution was never a political thing. Like Hitler's and Attila's, it was a personal matter.

When she had exchanged pain for money on West 124th Street and in the courtroom with the hordes of whores and the lamentations of junkies, she had continued to live in the apartment of a serene, white and spotless Christian Science couple, in the rented peace of her room on Riverside Drive, to descend each morning into the agony of a visit to Hell, to suffer its punishment, then to betray each day again by ascending each night unto another resurrection. Both black and white became her enemies; both her torturers. Refusing her own silently screamed demands to choose between black and white, she accepted neither. She hated them both but, vengefully, she began to teach herself to hate herself, or—not only because of her feelings—because she had become both of them. Her hatred turned inward; then, having energy, vision, and intelligence, she turned it outward and condemned herself to a world of terror.

"We are going to punish them and save them. You and me," she said to Jonas.

"Wherever you go, baby," Jonas said, "I am your man."

"First lesson. You are blood of my blood and flesh of my flesh but you are your own man, not mine."

"You're going to have to have some kind of a political line to lay down, baby. They all had one. Every one of them from Jesus to Lenin."

"Sure they did. But all that comes out afterward," Teel said. "The people will believe *anything* like that if you look like you is winnin' for them. But they won't believe one fuckin' thing if you lose for them." Teel often used street speech with Jonas—who had to listen hard to keep up with her—out of her bitterness and the balm of irony. Jonas's speech was like a Harvard physics professor's, unless he tried, and he did whenever his sister was in the mood, the way a man will try to look good in a tennis game with a crafty, pretty girl.

"So we gone do what all them othuh Big Winnuhs did," Teel said. "We gone win everything first or figure out how to make the people believe we did—*then* we'll pour noble political aspirations all over them."

Teel was only a great natural force. When lightning strikes and chars life, the lightning has neither a political message nor is it justice sent by the gods. Lightning, and earthquakes too, exist beyond these frames of reference. Teel had no Manifestos to turn their faces to when they were in doubt. She saw political dogma, before the fact, as alibi, and it never occurred to her that she would need an alibi along the way. Her task was a simple task: to punish, then to save. What happened after that would be the problems of the people she saved through her terrible punishment. Her crusade was for herself. It had three purposes: punishment, salvation and the continuing maintenance of her own invisibility.

5

1963

In the spring, Teel was invited to lunch at the Counting House Club in Dag Hammarskjold Plaza by Francis A. O'Connell, Jr., "The Elihu Root of Bronx Traction," and offered a junior partnership in Mr. O'Connell's discreet law firm of O'Connell, Carnaghi, Levin, Zendt & Sweeney. She laughed at him.

O'Connell, Carnaghi, Levin, Zendt & Sweeney were the powerbrokers who mattered. Their practice of law was sewing together deals: bankers with hustlers; labor union leaders with industries; regulatory agencies with anybody who had the scratch; realtors with The Church; show business and underwriters; organized sports with organized crime, into one hugely profitable quilt which would always keep

Frank O'Connell and his friends warm. The firm made New York mayors and governors the way a mint stamps out coins. The great movers—the fellows the voters thought shook everything—turned to O'Connell, Carnaghi, Levin, Zendt & Sweeney for instructions on how to shake it. Frank O'Connell was the unofficial leader of the *permanent* state and city government; a helluva living. And he could not be dislodged by crap like votes.

"Frank, I've been hacking out about two hundred thousand a year. What do you pay out to your junior partners?"

"It's real money, Miss Teel."

"Give me some numbers."

"Say we pay you fifteen thousand a year. That doesn't sound like much, but about once every three years, starting right now, the first year, you are going to get yourself a big closing. Maybe you don't know about closings, but the state and the city are always getting involved in multi-million-dollar projects which are financed out of their multi-billion-dollar pension funds. I had a closing myself last year—a gorgeous big housing development in northern New Jersey. It threw off a million nine. The Governor and the Mayor are tickled to let me assign these things and every three years I'm going to assign one to you."

"What's the smallest closing fee?" Teel asked.

"I'd never let you be stuck with anything less than eight-nine hundred thousand," O'Connell said solemnly. "That's my personal guarantee."

"Well—it's just that I can't hold still for any junior partnership."

"All right. A graded senior partnership, then, with your name in alphabetical order on the senior partners' listing on the letterhead. And listen—don't think the occasional closing fee is the end of it. The Governor asked me just a week ago to line up a solid citizen to serve on the State Medical Care Facilities Finance Agency. You are a natural because you'll be the first black member."

"Black is useful," Teel said. "What does that agency do?"

"Big things, Miss Teel. They are franchised to issue bonds and notes, for one thing, to provide funds to make mortgage loans to limited profit and non-profit nursing home companies and hospitals and medical corporations. I mean, it's a delicate post. A trial lawyer as good as you are can get real loaded real fast with a firm like ours."

"How are you on the Federal level?"

"Very strong."

"As strong as the Wall Street firms?"

"We are not statesmen," he said, biting off the end of his cigar and blowing it across the room to express his contempt. "We are litigators. And let me say if it takes a kick in the balls to win, we'll win. What do you want on the Federal end?"

"I'd just like to be appointed as a member of the U.S. delegation to the United Nations."

"You got it,"* O'Connell said. "When can you start with us?"

Teel became senior trial lawyer for the firm. Everyone prospered, mostly Frank O'Connell. Averaging out the closings and other emoluments, in sixteen months Teel was earning four hundred and eighteen thousand dollars a year in convenient packages that didn't shake her tax boat. She bought three connecting brownstone houses in Murray Hill, on East 38th Street. She began a social expansion of greeting the elite by giving them a place to meet, to connect where she calculated she ought to connect.

---

* Agatha Teel's appointment to the U.S. delegation to the United Nations was announced forty-seven days following her luncheon with O'Connell. She was immediately handed such agenda items as: "Status of the International Covenant on Economic, Social and Cultural Rights"; "Measures To Be Taken Against Ideologies and Practices Based on Terror or on Incitement to Racial Discrimination or Any Other Form of Group Hatred"; "Report of the Special Committee to Investigate Israeli Practices Affecting Human Rights of the Population of Occupied Territories."

This upward social mobility was a part of the second phase in the complex score of America's salvation through punishment that Teel was intent upon composing. Her implementation of revolution was expanding too. She had the concentration of a laser. She studied and absorbed the works of General Giap, Nasution, Marghela, Mao, Baljit Singh, Guevara and Ko-Wang Mei, slowly adapting these to fit American national character: masochism, refusal to reflect, hypnosis by self-interest, dependency upon instant gratification (as a way of life), passion to conform, and other finer points. As she began to work with increasing exhaustion on what finally became The Teel Plan, she was unable to understand that only about 2 percent of the American population, black and white, could see that they needed to be saved from their social system.

6

May 1966

"What have you written today?" Bart Simms asked his twin sister, Enid, kissing her ear as he entered the hotel suite after a sweaty day's work learning the Japanese martial arts at CIA training school. It was Enid's doting practice to begin a novel every day although she never took her novels further than their beginnings. She handed him the pages. He read them aloud.

I CALL FREEDOM LEROY
by
CARLOTTA YOU

"Dear Dad: I am living with a black guy in an illegal commune which is, well, different from Montclair. We had a baby. I gave it to some kids who wanted one. They are gone now but I named it after you even though it was a girl because I love you, Daddy."

Bart looked at her thoughtfully when he finished. "It won't animate," he said soberly. "Did you happen to notice what they had posted in the elevator for dinner?"

Enid recited one of the soups, three of the entrees, and two of the desserts. "What shall we have?" she asked.

"The minestrone and the noisette of pork."

"And wine."

"Oh, yes."

Enid Simms was in love with her twin brother because her father, the center of her life, had killed himself and her mother, the center of her psyche. She had lived in fear of being left alone ever since the April morning when she, thirteen years old, had run directly home from school and burst into a room to find the shotgun-ravaged bodies of her parents. Bart had never forgiven his father for plotting to do that to them, the survivors. He never forgave his mother for remaining with his father as the man grew more and more sorry for himself. Bart detested both of them as much as Enid loved them.

Bart was careful never to leave Enid alone for very long. With her father's brutal act her brother, too, had been rocketed far from the strange planet which was herself. But at the same time, he was also an introversion, incorporated within her. She had made Bart part of her soul even as she had catapulted him outside it. Bart loved her. Bart had patience with her terror and knew that they had to cling together, alone among all the millions of strangers. Six times she had tried to kill herself because she thought Bart had gone away. But she responded well to psychiatry.

Happily, she permitted all of her succession of psychiatrists to make love to her because they understood her deep need to have men love her. While Bart moved from preparatory school (Lawrenceville) to college (Princeton) to university (Wharton School of Business) to law school (Harvard) Enid moved with him; they lived off campus as day students do. Enid's psychiatrists paved the way for the ultimate understanding by the Central Intelligence Agency that Enid needed greatly to remain with Bart for the preservation of her life and sanity. To some of the finest minds of their generation, in the CIA, Enid came to be seen as the priceless hope of extraordinary opportunity; the structure of a new game plan; the remote, remoter, remotest possibility of somehow, some way getting an operative successfully inside China, the somewhat easier plan of creating, installing and controlling a future President of the United States. To achieve these things, Enid was planted as a double agent on her brother; an exquisitely functional psychological design.

Enid entered into a contract with the agency to assist Bart, as Bart's Desk Officer, who would travel with him and live with him when he was transferred abroad. During their two years as CIA trainees—Small Weapons use and the Martial Arts aside—their training began with light sedation followed by hypnosis, followed by de-briefing and reindoctrination, always working toward one fixed goal: the impossibility of any enemy of the CIA's de-briefing them, a common enough goal, but one which required inordinate amounts of time and care. The results obtained with the twins were the pride of the agency. A thrilling concept had been transformed into a pragmatic consequence.

Life on a campus wherever it is varies only with the sort of campus it is. For Bart and Enid, the campus was deep within their minds. Their faculty was the Behaviorial Activities Department of the Central Intelligence Agency under the Science and Technology Directorate, whose projects ranged from complex satellite systems to the development of miniature cameras to brainwashing through the use of psychological conditioning, radiation, electric shock, objective/subjective subtraction of self-esteem, harassment substances, sociology behavior-influencing drugs used for "induced reflection" by the institution of selected motion picture footage.

The CIA's Behavioral Activities Department, working with Bart and Enid (and others), could readily predict the likelihood of relation-change or concept-change on the basis of the nature of the cognitive structure in which an incongruous cognition is embedded (it is necessary that innovative psychologists use this phraseology in order to protect themselves from their own shame and guilt at devoting their gifts to such unexemplary mind bending. If they were to state directly that they had developed persuasion techniques which could make men voluntarily eat feces and enjoy that act they would find cumulative difficulties in living with themselves long enough to develop even greater degradations), which is only to say that it was a matter of no difficulty whatever to alter the morality of people. Morality, after all, is that which is applied by environment not something inherent: wife-swapping might be perfectly acceptable in Santa Barbara, for example, but shunned in Lawrence, Massachusetts. Bart and Enid had been raised by the ethics of their tribe-within-American-cultural-tribes and they had thusly been endowed with a massive sense of what was right and what was wrong as judged by those cultural divisions. Impersonal murder would be one of the things they would abhor reflexively but the Behavioral Activities Department competently coped with that, readily achieving, by hypnotic reversal of attitudinal effect, the amnesia for the hypnotic suggestion of affect-reversal which could be sustained, if necessary, for a period of six months, rather than the "usual" period of two hours. Furthermore this cognitive reorganization in response to hypnotic manipulation of attitudinal affect would *persist* until the removal of post-hypnotic amnesia.

The agency's Behavioral Activities Department of the Science and Technology Directorate could be said to have led the world in this most dramatic and intense form of persuasion because—as in the case of Bart and Enid—they had compliant subjects who, instead of having been conditioned for one or two months, were actually trained to a level of highest hypnotic competence over a full two-year period. All of this was achieved through a group of "Deverbalization" mechanisms, enhancing the Simmses' performance on a "learning without awareness" task in which reinforced triggers served as dependent variables.

The platform to support all this was simplicity itself. A person whose self-esteem is deliberately lowered by the operational techniques in experimental manipulation is thus instantly rendered prone to accept information contradicting his own opinions and moralities. Enid had very little self-esteem and was therefore a model subject for manipulation. But Bart began with a higher sense of self-esteem, so the first ten months were spent—simultaneous with electric shock, radiation, harassment-substances and behavior-influencing drugs to insure the most effective hypnosis—in the most degrading forms of humiliation, placing deeply within his psyche veritable land mines of self-doubt. The degrees of deprivation, isolation, degradation, overt threat and manipulation of guilt that he underwent would have been almost inhumanly deplorable had they not been so necessary to achieve results.

Both siblings had a rough course but were classical products of the greatest achievements in brainwashing, the "second signal system" made possible by bio-feedback concepts.

7

January 1971

The Mutual Security Tower soared over Manhattan like an upthrust middle finger. It was not the home office of a large insurance company. Its name came from what had been a traditional half-joke constituting the entire business policy of Joseph D. Palladino's late father: "Do like I tell you and we are going to have mutual security." The intent of the words was anachronistic in today's world. The whole concept of muscle had changed, the son thought. That gun shit was out twenty years ago.

It was J.D. Palladino, not his father, who had built the Mutual Security Tower, which had over six hundred tenants, a high-class book store which also sold symphony records, and a restaurant where the tenants could get bitten for forty-one dollars for lunch for two. J.D. Palladino's offices were in the tower of the Tower. It was a silent place. There were rugs on the carpets. The windows were double-glazed. The people who worked there either talked nice or they got thrown out on their ass.

J.D. Palladino walked to the four windows that faced north, clasped his hands behind his back and looked out and down at the city, counting seven buildings that he owned. His father had worked his whole life right on the street floor of the warehouse, which had smelled all the time like provolone, canestrato, casigiolu and provatura. Great smells, but times had to change. The blacks were going crazy trying to get their hands on all the Jones and all the blow. They would try to bust in if the Family worked right on the street floor. This was 1971, fahcrissake. Seven years ago the blacks had been begging for a little heroin to try to start a couple of Harlem dope houses. For fifteen years he had been making a fortune every week just by passing shit from his left hand to his right hand, then on to some spade. Now what the hell was happening here? They were driving the prices down.

Mary, the head secretary, came in. "Senator Karp is in the main reception area, J.D." she said.

Mr. Palladino looked at his watch and was pleased. "Let him wait," he said. "When is your vacation?"

"Two weeks."

"Where?"

"Florida."

"What am I? A dentist? Do I have to pull the facts out of your head?"

"Near Sarasota. It's very quiet. My father likes to see the circus winter quarters." Whenever she mentioned her father to Mr. Palladino, she was actually referring to her boyfriend, Harry, who was Mr. Palladino's chief collector. She knew Mr. Palladino would be shocked if he knew she was taking her vacation with a married man. "Just good food and plenty of quiet." Actually they were going to Vegas. She smiled at him like a hospital nurse.

"This is gonna be some upside down place when you're not here."

"Everything is organized the way you like it, Mr. P. Angela has trained for three months just for these three weeks."

"How is your mother?" He looked at his watch again. "Well, maybe you better send the senator in."

It was a fairly long walk from the main reception room. It went through two impressive rooms where Dom and Dino were always hanging around and where they frisked anybody who was less than a senator.

"Sit down, senator," Mr. Palladino said, not rising. "You want a cigar?"

"Too early, J.D."

"It cuts the appetite." Mr. Palladino bit the end off of a dark cigar and put fire to it. "What's up?" he asked.

Senator Karp had a divided face like a broken baked apple upon which some joker had dropped a false moustache. He was short and overweight yet actually wore sideburns. "The reason I called you yesterday to come up here today," Karp said, "was about a young man I'd like you to see because—"

"What?"

"He's getting set to leave the CIA and—"

"What?"

"He is Herbert Ryan Willmott's nephew. The only nephew."

"You couldn't tell me this on the phone? You couldn't put it in a letter? I didn't even feel like coming in today."

"His name is Hobart Willmott Simms."

"It sounds like a colored undertaker."

"Did you ever hear of Ataturk, J.D.? Or King Harold Godwin?"

"No."

"That's the whole point. Many vitally important people exist of whom neither of us has never heard."

"Important to you or important to me?"

"At present only to me. After you meet him, to you."

"Why?"

"He wants you to make a couple of hundred million dollars. Maybe more."

Mr. Palladino blew three perfect smoke rings. "Yeah?"

"He's a remarkable young fellow."

"What do I have to do?"

"You have to meet him on the nine-fifteen Staten Island ferry to St. George tomorrow morning. He'll know you."

"With a gorgeous layout like this I should meet him on a ferryboat?"

"He thinks you'll have a harder time bugging the conversation on a ferryboat."

"What kind of crap is that?"

"And if you don't want the couple of hundred million," Senator Karp said, "humor him anyway. He's —uh—very special CIA."

8

February–March 1971

In the winter of 1971 a Viet Cong courier made a routine stop for information at the back door of Happiness City, which had just closed for the night in Saigon. He accepted a funny cigarette from Big Lickie, the bar madam. The courier spoke Tonkinese. Lickie spoke Annamese. Their comprehension was about the same as in a conversation between a Vermonter and an Alabaman. After they had covered how much the courier's feet hurt, he said, "If you hear of anybody who has anything to do with Long Nose troop assignments, let me know."

"What's troop assignments?"

"You know—somebody who moves the grunts from one unit to the other."

"I have the man!" Lickie said with amazement.

"Who?"

"I have the master sergeant who is the Chief Clerk there, that's all."

"The *chief* clerk?"

"Absolutely."

"What does he like that he can't get so that we can get it for him and he'll owe us?"

"It's so easy you'll never believe it." Lickie chuckled out a St. Nicholas effect and shook when she laughed like a bowl full of jelly. "You'll *never* believe it—Soochow cunt."

"No kidding?"

"That's all he ever talks about. And he can never get close to the kind he really likes."

"What kind?"

"A top Soochow professional. I know—they all say they're from Soochow—but I mean a real old-fashioned mechanic with a hip line of chatter, thick with rice powder who is also a looker."

"You can't get that for him?"

"Of course I could get it for him. But this guy fucks all the time. Why should I let him tie up his money in one Soochow hooker when I got two dozen of my own little chicks around the bar depending on me? It wouldn't be worth it to fix him up."

"Well, that's great."

"When do you want him?"

"I'll have to find out. I'll tell you tomorrow night."

"It certainly ought to be worth ten thousand piastres. I'll be doing everything. I'll have to find the right hooker. I'll have to coach her. I'll have to lift the sergeant on. It won't be easy."

"I'll tell you tomorrow night."

The next night they settled on three thousand piastres as Lickie's fee. "How much time do we allow for the girl to break him in?" the courier said.

"Three months."

"Forget it."

"The girl has to build confidence. The sergeant has to have a chance to fall in love. The girl has to establish that he makes her ecstatically happy and so forth."

"I'll tell you tomorrow night."

The following night the courier told Lickie she could have two months.

"Okay. Give me the list of guys," Lickie demanded. "Now?"

"Of course now. This guy is on top of an operation where everybody in the fucking army wants to be his pal because he has the power to keep them alive, fahcrissake. The girl has to talk about these guys like they were friends of her sisters or something. Why is everything always an argument? It takes time so when the time comes to make the switches he'll be all set up."

"Okay. Tomorrow night."

The courier brought back the list of seven names. Lickie copied the list before she went to bed. At noon the next day she sent a note to an American colonel who was an old friend. The colonel, a man with busy eyes and noisy bones that snapped and popped with every move he made, came in through the side door at three peeyem. He looked like a Bedlington terrier. Lickie brought him two cold Cokes.

"I think I have something you'll want to buy, Colonel," she said.

"Show me."

Lickie told him the story about how the Cong wanted seven men shifted out of the Three Platoon, Bravo Company in the 414th, and seven other men switched in. The colonel's eyebrows shot up under his hairline.

"You wanna buy?" Lickie asked.

"I think so."

"Ten thousand piastres?"

"Nothing is worth that, Lickie, and you know it."

"How much?"

"Three."

They settled for forty-seven hundred. Lickie gave him the list. The colonel asked if Little Carmen from Ba Nihn was still around. "Oh, yes," Lickie said. "She talks about you all the time. Come on upstairs."

On his way back to Intelligence headquarters, the colonel was feeling so good that he stopped off for an aperitif at a large sidewalk café on the main boulevard.

He ordered a St. Raphael and sat soaking up the sun. A pedo came roaring past. The man on it threw a *plastique* into the crowd on the café terrace. Both the colonel's legs were blown off. He was DOA. The orderlies found the list in his tunic pocket, but it was meaningless to everyone in the Intelligence unit and was thrown away.

Master Sergeant Lamar Breitel did like a certain kind of Chinese woman. He sat with Lickie at the bar of Happiness City the next afternoon and said, "They have class, that's all. They are women, not girls. Shit, Lickie, I like Annamese women, you know that. But I am saying Chinese women—and I speak now about your top Soochow professional—they just happen to know where sex is."

"What they tole you?"

"They say sex isn't just a cheap thrill."

"Who?"

"I don't know her name."

"Thass shit. Chinese girl can't make it wit' you. They say you smell like a corpse, alla meat you eat."

"Me?" He rammed his forefinger into his chest and stepped back from the bar. She reached out with an arm like the Michelin tire trademark and pulled him back. "Not jes' you. Alla Long Noses. Chinese girl say you stink."

"Do *you* think I stink?" he demanded, uptight.

"How do I know? Now I eat meat all time. Now I stink."

"Well this certain Soochow professional certainly didn't think I stunk. Man, she loved it. She measured it out with her hands afterward how our guys had more length and strength and width and depth and heft. I mean—what is your itty-bitty Chinese guy next to your average American? I mean, we are *hung*. That is a natural fact. Jesus, I wish I could take you out to the Company shower room."

"Quit it, Sarge," Lickie said. "You gettin' me all hot." She yawned daintily. "Buy me a drink fahcris-

It was crowded, but he got a table in the front row.

sake." She licked out the inside of the shot glass with her famous silver tongue.

"You know how the Chinese people really know food?" Breitel asked. "Well, that's how a great Soochow hooker knows sex."

In a hapless, commercial kind of way Sergeant Breitel was a big stud. If he wasn't balling or talking about it he didn't know he was there. He spent every cent he could get lining up women. Lickie delivered the best, even if they all had a tendency to look alike to him.

"How much you pay?" Lickie asked.

"For a really highly trained, gorgeous Chinese woman, I mean trained in Soochow since childhood, who is capable of falling in love with me?" Sergeant Breitel was twenty-two.

"Yeah."

"I'd have to see her first."

"Okay."

"When?"

"Maybe tomorrow night."

Cholon, the Chinese quarter of Saigon, had been a city all by itself before the war. It was four miles away from the Happiness City Bar. Cholon was more Chinese than any treaty port. There were over nine hundred thousand Chinese in Cholon, all either first- or second-generation immigrants, nearly all of them from South China seaports. Since the Han emperors more than two thousand years ago, the Chinese south had been the home of lost causes and hot tempers; the cradle of political change.

Lickie sent a silent, white-haired Chinese man to take Sergeant Breitel to the restaurant in Cholon. They rode out together in a bus that had chicken wire over the windows to keep the grenades out. There were more chickens than passengers and three small piglets. They walked the last three blocks. The streets were packed with people, the men naked to the waist, the women in the black trousers and white short-sleeved jackets of South China. Breitel drew in his breath like warm soup through clenched teeth when a heavily painted concubine passed by under an umbrella held by her *mu-tsai,* a slave girl whose hair hung down her back. Coolies, naked except for loin cloths, shoved past him wearing wallets threaded to belts that held them to the small of the back where the skin is especially sensitive to touch.

The restaurant was a high Canton-style building in the rue des Mariniers. The lower floor was a café that smelled of dried fish and herbs. Upstairs there was a common dining room. On the floor above that the room had been partitioned halfway to the ceiling into *cabinets particuliers.* Each private room had half-height swinging doors like old-time American saloons.

She was the most gorgeous thing he had ever seen: rice powder, heavy makeup over that, the ceremonial hookers' costume, fan, everything in the total Soochow realism. He got an instant erection he could not lose. Her name was Alice Choy. Her English was better than Lickie's.

"Are you really Soochow-trained?" he asked eagerly, after the presentation.

"Oh, yes."

"Were you a child slave there? I mean—you know —from when you were a little kid or something?"

"Oh, yes."

"I mean, like did you have to let big, you know, men—like when you weren't practically old enough to go to school?"

"Oh, yes."

Late that night, after he had fallen in love, after she had demonstrated for all time that he had been absolutely right to hold out for a real Soochow hooker, she confided that her mother had been a famous Dutch cellist, Dame Maria van Slyke, who had given herself to Alice's father, a Manchurian war lord. Later, her mother and father had had a tragic argument after Alice was born, over whether Alice's feet should be bound or not. Winning the argument, Alice's mother had left China but had sold Alice to Soochow to be raised and trained in the oldest profession, just to embarrass the father. Lickie may have gone a little far in building that story, Alice had complained to her at first, but Lickie reassured her, "This is an *American,*" Lickie said. "They believe anything, particularly anything they want to believe." In fact, his new knowledge about Alice's parentage set Sergeant Breitel on fire. He was exultant. Exultant! A Eurasian princess! Her Dad was a war lord. And she had hands that were lovelier than any hands he had ever seen. Secretly, Sergeant Breitel was a hand man. Thirty-seven nights later, on a special family request from Alice, Sergeant Breitel transferred seven men out of the Third Platoon, Bravo Company, 414th Battalion, 2nd Regiment, 9th Light Infantry Brigade of the Colombio Division. In their place he dropped the seven men of Alice's choice. They were fiancés of Alice's stepsisters.

"But, baby," he protested, "if these guys are gonna be family, this is dangerous duty. Infantry is no place —I mean—that is where combat *is.*"

She tickled him softly along the bottom of his penis. "You know you're getting a Soochow accent?" she giggled.

A Tech Sergeant named John Kullers was doing the dullest of all Intelligence work, checking troop transfer reports out of Headquarters Company in Saigon. That was all he did, so he was used to it and he never got sleepy because he had nothing to contrast it with. He went over the rosters for Three Platoon, Bravo Company, 414th Battalion for the third time. After a while he thought he had figured out what was wrong, so he got up and took the previous week's rosters out of the file. When he had compared the two he went in to see Lieutenant Downs.

"I got a peculiar thing here, Lieutenant," Kullers said.

"What?"

"I got here seven men transferred out of Three Platoon, Bravo Company, 414th Battalion. Nothing unusual, right?"

"Right."

"But—hoHO!—where do the seven men come from who are transferred into that platoon? Lemme tell you. First, to answer my own question backwards. They are nothing but ordinary grunts who are gonna be moved out inna field. But—hoHO!—evvey one a these seven guys is bein' transferred out from Stateside installations."

"Were they *requested*? I mean did the Headquarters Company ask for them by name?"

"I gotta query that. I'll go look at the orders."

He left the lieutenant, but he returned in ten minutes, fairly excited because nothing unusual ever happened in his duty.

"Yes, sir. By name. Six dogfaces one officer. Each guy is *flown*—like some as far away as New York— to Saigon. What for? To do what five hundred thousand other guys already in Saigon could do—to get shot at."

"I don't get it."

"Well—mine not to figure it out. You know? But there is something fishy here, Lieutenant."

"Where did the guys go who were transferred out of Three Platoon?"

"Like next door. They're working, if you know what I mean. Guys get transferred out and guys get transferred in alla time, but nobody requests six dogfaces and a lieutenant from the East coast, if you know what I mean."

"Leave it with me." Kullers turned to go. "No, wait. Go down to the computer room and get me a profile on every man on that list."

"Yessir, Lieutenant."

Lieutenant Downs took the file in to see Captain Maas at 2:45 P.M., just three hours later. "I got a real puzzler here, Captain," he said. "I mean, nobody but Sergeant Kullers could even have stumbled on this, but he used to be a Skip Tracer and he is keen, I mean he is something."

"Whaddee git?" Captain Maas was short, slow and sometimes difficult to understand, especially when he lapsed into the speech of what he claimed was Lufkin, Texas.

"Seven men transferred out of a platoon of thirty-five men—that's a two-squad platoon?—all seven of them from the same squad—then their replacements were flown in from Stateside, five of them from as far away as New York?"

"No kiddin'?"

"So I run a check on these seven Stateside men and —funny thing—every one except two of them is an ex-convict. You know? I mean here are five guys all of who done time for armed robbery."

"Well, holy shit, Downs."

"Yeah."

"Any officers?"

"One."

"Well, he ain't no convict."

"Worse than that, Captain. I mean the implications. He's Academy."

"Well, for crissake."

"Yeah."

"Lemme tay yew Academy mixed up with a buncha convicts purely worries the *shit* outa me." He raised his voice to carry outside his office. "Sergeant Mount will you *please* do somepin about this air conditionin'?"

"It's worse than that, Captain."

"Worse?"

"There's a man Albert Cassebeer in this roster. Cassebeer's an experimental physicist. Now just how do we figure that out?"

"I donno whut it is, but you cain't beat it fer bayd," Maas said. "Gimme that file. I gotta take that inuh Colonel Purcell."

He took the file from Lieutenant Downs, shaking his head. He kept going right past Downs and walked out into the compound toward Colonel Purcell's dug-out.

They always identified things with World War I terms where they could because the Navy was always calling the walls "bulkheads" and toilets "the head."

"Be till tomorrow morning fore they can get a man in to fix this air conditioning, Captain," Sergeant Mount said.

"Shit!" Captain Maas said.

He laid the case out in front of Lieutenant-Colonel Lucius Purcell. He was the commander of the section and the only professional soldier, professional Intelligence wizard and career Army man on the floor. He was on his way to full colonel and he bragged that he would be sent right back to Asia to head up a combat regiment.

He studied the file.

"What is the recommended action, sir?" Maas said. He felt that if he didn't call Purcell "sir," Purcell would just whack him across the chops.

"This is the recommended action, Captain Maas," Purcell said. "We're going to fly Dr. Baum and the three colonels out there and we are going to have one of these seven men de-briefed."

"Oh, Jesus!"

"The situation warrants it."

"We'll be up the creek if that man doesn't survive it, Colonel," Maas said. "I am sayin' he hastuh survive it. If we gonna find out anything here all seven men got to stay intact."

"That's all right with me. I'm no sadist. Run those seven men through the computer and tell me who is the most rugged and that is the man we will give to Dr. Baum for de-briefing."

"I mean like if this is a conspiracy or somepin like that, thin iffen one a the seven dis'pears, the othuh six is gunna fade on us."

"Oh, come on, Maas. If a man has to disappear we can arrange a very convincing accident. Go find me the man. I'll get Dr. Baum."

The most rugged of the seven transferees was flown

from the touch down of his MATS flight from Illinois Air Base at Saigon. He was a powerfully built man who had once done two years of service in 1957–58, had mustered out in Illinois and, within three months, had been sentenced to one and a half to three years at Joliet for simple assault upon a policewoman. He was the only Illinois convict of the five convicts. He had been intercepted just before his transfer to join the other men in the Third Platoon.

The transferee was flown to a base hospital at Quang Tri where he was prepared for de-briefing with three injections of Dr. Baum's own preparations and strapped tightly to a chair that was bolted into the floor. He was strapped at ankle, knee, hips, chest, neck, forearm and wrist facing a nine-foot-square rear projection screen. At 7:09 A.M. on a Friday, Dr. Baum and the three colonels entered the small room and began de-briefing procedures that had been developed by Dr. Baum in eastern Europe during the last years of World War II when he had been employed under a different management.

At 14:27 on the following Sunday Dr. Baum extracted the last available scrap of information from the rugged transferee regarding the mission of all seven men, but Baum did not bother to seal over the man's memory stacks because he had, in fact, died at the termination of his questioning.

Lieutenant-Colonel Purcell flew to Quang Tri to await Dr. Baum's report. Baum's gay colonel had transferred all the rough notes into a typescript of 117 pages that laid out everything the man had known about his mission.

What the man knew, by his own confession to Dr. Baum, was both a little bit and a great lot at the same time. All he knew was that he would be part of a unit of seven GIs (whom he did not know but who would reveal themselves at the proper time), that with them he was to desert from his Army unit and travel northward along the north–south cordillera to make a ren-

dezvous in North Vietnam, where they would be delivered detailed orders as to the operations that would
follow. What he did not know or would not tell was
who had recruited him for this action. He had, in fact,
died while Dr. Baum was insisting that he reveal this
information.

Purcell flew the report to Washington. Baum remained in Quang Tri to de-brief three North Vietnamese. Purcell's direct superior, General Marek, was
waiting for him. Fifty minutes later they were both
before an *ad hoc* committee of the Joint Chiefs of
Staff presided over by its Chairman's deputy, Lieutenant General Ludlow "Petey" Doncaster.

Marek made the report on Dr. Baum's findings. He
introduced Colonel Purcell as the man responsible for
the brilliant work of uncovering the plot. Purcell
undertook to explain where the unit would need to
be placed, as Three Platoon, before they could take
off into the cordillera and make their way north toward what Purcell and Marek assumed must be the
Chinese frontier. The others agreed. What else could
it be? He said, in the nature of military operations,
there would be no way of predicting when the Three
Platoon would be in such a position, if ever; the seven
men might have been transferred into Three Platoon
to wait years for the chance at finding themselves
conveniently at the farthest northwest of the war zone.

General Doncaster asked for Colonel Purcell's rec-
ommendations. Colonel Purcell recommended that
they wait until all six of the transferees were in place
inside Three Platoon in Saigon and then rearrange
operations so that Three Platoon was part of a strike
by the 9th Infantry Brigade of the Colombio Division
to be made to the farthest north and northwest. He
further recommended that an Army Intelligence agent
be chosen immediately to take the dead man's place,
to be escorted, they hoped, inside China with official
Chinese sanction. Finally, he recommended that his
own unit undertake an analysis of the records of all
seven men who had been ticketed for the rendezvous

and that nothing be spared to run down their origins, backgrounds, and recent contacts to uncover who in the United States had recruited them and for what reason. When the Army Intelligence plant came out of China, his report would coincide with the evidence they must find to stop the plot—whatever it was—from ever reaching fruition.

"The CIA has been trying for twenty-seven years to get a man inside China," General Doncaster said. "They failed so many times it could have filled Arlington Cemetery. This is the biggest chance we've ever had. We've got to give it everything we've got."

Everyone at the table agreed enthusiastically. General Doncaster directed General Marek to handpick a volunteer for the "China" assignment. "Find a tough one, General. Probably better if it isn't an officer. We want an agent who can live the way ex-convicts live and talk the way they talk. But smart! The agent has to be one of the best anywhere in Army Intelligence today. Put your personnel computers on overtime, give them the most detailed profile you can build for this agent and bring whoever you choose into Quang Tri from wherever in the world you have to for a briefing by Dr. Baum."

Everyone at the table involuntarily dropped his eyes at the mention of Dr. Baum's name. Marek's eyes were shocked at the idea of sending one of his own people into that. "Dr. Baum, General?"

Doncaster chuckled a fake chuckle that convinced no one. "Baum isn't rough on his *briefings*. A lot of men—the greater percentage, I would say—have survived them. It is his *de*-briefings that take their toll. Anyway, Dr. Baum has updated his techniques to include hypnosis, narco-hypnosis, bio-feedback, and behavior modification processes like the 'second signal' system. He is considerably in advance of Asian methods of human programming."

"Yes, sir." Marek relaxed. Chillingly cold science had taken over.

"This man, whoever he is, is going to need to be

made over into the psychological image of the dead transferee. Get moving, General. There's no time to spare." Hurrying away from the meeting Colonel Purcell asked General Marek, "Why the hell does the agent need to be made over into the psychological image of the dead man? Who is going to be with him that will know who he was, what he was like, how he thought—and things like that? I mean, what the hell, the old man wasn't talking about any cosmetic surgery here, was he?"

"No, no, no," Marek said irritably. "What the hell, you can figure it out. Suppose this agent the computers find for us was once a dress designer or a tap dancer? He's going to be thrown in with a lot of convicts and he's got to think like a convict—he's got to get that criminal kink put into his mind to be able to live with them, swap stories, keep his place and be believed by them, that's all."

"Oh. Yes," Colonel Purcell muttered, wishing he had thought the thing through before he opened his mouth. He didn't want any dumb attitudes to go on his service record. He wanted to make full colonel, get out into leading some combat, then keep moving up as a general officer until the time came to retire.

In April, the month the war in Vietnam cost the people of the United States thirty million dollars a day, Task Force Headquarters were set up at Landing Zone Margie, southwest of Hué, where Able, Bravo and Charlie Companies of the 414th Battalion were assembled. Their strike areas had been located for them by ARVN because ARVN was Vietnamese and able to infiltrate to find out where Charley was hiding. It was never reliable information. A lot of Americans were lost that way but this was a different kind of war the Americans were fighting.

Bravo and Charlie Companies were ferried out by nine troop transport helicopters accompanied by two gunships. Bravo Company was flown farthest west to a target area that was almost at the Laos frontier. Three Platoon was ordered farthest west of Bravo Company. Three went almost to the base of the cordillera.

Bravo didn't reach the target area until 7:47 A.M., which was thirty-two minutes after Charley Company had started to search out and destroy anything that moved at Khe Thong, thirty-one miles east of the Bravo target. The men were told that large numbers of Cong would be waiting for them. According to the official rationale of the mission, surprise was the key factor. Once the helicopters put them down, it took twelve minutes to form the men, with officers yelling. The men were bug-eyed. They expected to be blown apart by BAR as they came off, but nothing happened. ARVN had fucked up again. The guys milled around a couple of minutes, then began to move out, splitting into platoons and dividing the target area. It was a very hot day.

The Three Platoon moved across the wet plain and the myriad canals, some with bridges, others just with slippery poles to sidle over. The whole country was one big box of Uncle Ben's Quick Rice. It was so flat, so hot, and so monotonous that a man stuck out there, even if he expected to get shot any minute, got bored. It was just a boring country. Nobody could figure out how they had gotten the people to fight for it.

Lieutenant Orin Dawes led the Third Platoon west for about twelve hundred yards. Their mission was to make it to a spit of land holding a small hamlet, then to search it and destroy it and everything living in it. They had done it many times before, but none of them could get used to the women who all looked seventy when they were maybe thirty, dragging their babies and trying to run ahead of the Armalites as they were cut in half at the rate of 750 bullets a minute traveling 3,250 feet a second.

The hamlet was screened by a thick hedge and was densely guarded by booby traps. Three mines were tripped at the same time. Everybody in the platoon heard the screams. A sergeant was killed and four GIs were badly hurt. Helicopters were called in to evacuate the wounded men. As the platoon moved forward again, booby traps killed three more men. After the second set of booby traps, the GIs who were left passed the word that they were not going to continue the mission. Colonel Braden, leading the Task Force, flew in himself to see the evacuation of the wounded. Rather than bring up the Second Platoon he canceled Bravo Company's order. After Braden flew away, Lieutenant Dawes was frantic to find a substitute target. What was left of the Third Platoon followed him in an aimless struggle in the general direction of west by northwest. The pine-covered slopes of the 6,000-foot-high Annamese Chain loomed ahead, retreating north into Laos, then back farther into China. Before they had gone 300 yards they could see, through heavy brush and trees, a collection of straw and mud houses. They could see only women, children and old men.

"Okay, men," the lieutenant said, "there's your Cong. Blow them away!"

Two machine gunners set up the M60E1s on tripods and put on asbestos gloves for the barrel changes. The barrels got hot but they were still great machines, using a feed system of the German MG42 because imitation is the sincerest form of flattery. Dawes ordered the gunners to open fire.

When the gun handlers had finished, four point men went into the village street with Armalites to shoot civilians still skulking in their straw houses. The noises of the rapid fire, grenades exploding, the screams of the dying, and Dawes's shouts to kill the fucking Cong all blended into a hot threnody. Ninety Vietnamese were dead almost instantly. Surviving women, lifting or dragging children, had run out of the village toward the hamlet's system of bunkers and tunnels, which was well out of sight about 110 yards away. Dawes took two point men and four GIs and set out after them, yelling back at the radio operator to tell the CP to fly in more explosives.

When the seven soldiers got into position near the mouths of the tunnels, they were isolated from the rest of the platoon. Everything changed. The frantic urgency was replaced by cool.

"This is the shape-up," Dawes said to the men. "Show your slips." Each man unbuttoned his blouse pocket and produced a blue piece of paper with a number on it. "Who has the map?" Dawes said.

Sergeant Kranak had the map. He spread it on the ground and they made a circle around him. It was a Lambert conformal conic projection of northern Laos, Tonkin, and lower China. It showed Ho Chi Minh trails marked as Road Routes 8, 12, 23, and 122. It indicated numbered paths through the mountains along the Xe Bangfair and the Na Oa La rivers where the greatest opium crop in the world was harvested.

Kranak looked very nervous; as if he thought nobody was going to believe him. "You know what it means, I got the map?" Kranak asked them.

"It means you're in command," Dawes said.

"How come him?" Lurky Anderson said.

"We're going through those mountains to the north," Kranak said. "I was Special Forces in those mountains."

"I'm not complaining," Dawes said. "I believe in discipline."

They heard someone running toward them. They turned. It was Flash Vorshuta, the youngest grunt in the platoon. "What are you doing here, Vorshuta?" Dawes yelled at him with shrill irritation.

"I couldn't stay back there, Lieutenant," Vorshuta said. "It's too much. Our guys are shooting at dead bodies now. Jesus. Lemme stay here."

Dawes looked at Kranak. The men looked at Kranak. "Gimme your sidearm," Kranak said to Dawes. Dawes jerked his automatic pistol out of its holster and handed it to Kranak. It was an M1911A1, the most successful combat pistol ever developed; sweetly crafted by the Singer Sewing Machine Company with a muzzle capacity of 860 feet per second. It took most of the top of Vorshuta's head off at that range and knocked him about sixteen feet backward.

"Okay," Kranak said to Dolly Fingus, a skinny black GI. "Get his rifle, his canteen, any Mars bars, and we'll move out."

The seven men went toward the mountains at a steady pace, Kranak in the lead. They were off the plain and under the evergreen shelter before the helicopter bringing up the dynamite Dawes had sent for appeared far back in the sky.

9

1967

Teel was a great cook. A writer for *Gourmet* who had been hanging around pretending to ask her about the origins of Soul Food (he was convinced that it had been brought to the Gulf Coast by the Sumerians who had ridden the Atlantic currents past Nigeria 9900 years before) was actually there just to eat the way he liked to eat. The third time, he brought Dr. Kung. Dr. Kung was in the United States "from Korea" to study Theological Administration & Funding under a two-year scholarship from the China Lobby.

Dr. Kung and Teel met in the spring of 1967. Orientals merely look bland. In the hay, Dr. Kung was a ball of fire.

Despite their intimacies, and the fact that Dr. Kung was actually a subversive agent of the Chinese government sent to the United States to *teach* Revolutionary Administration & Funding to underground Presbyterian Maoist groups (in cities of more than two million population), it was some time before he saw Teel as a possible extension of himself, someone who could continue his work when he was recalled. She was black. Like all revolutionaries Kung believed that all blacks seethed with impatience to overthrow the white yoke. Having completed her Plan, Teel actually was seething with impatience. Aside from fielding a few hundred orgasms for Dr. Kung, Teel was unable to think of much else beyond her urban guerrilla miracle. After his first confidence about himself, however, she stayed cool. She talked to him about her ideas, but only peripherally.

Slowly, he began to understand how unique was this mechanism which lay under him (and frequently all over him). As he locked his mind into that conclusion he began to talk about what was on his mind.

"Teel?"

"Yeah?"

"We are friends."

"Right."

"You are black."

"No doubt about it."

"I trust you."

"What the hell is this?"

"Teel, listen—I am a revolutionary."

"So was George Washington."

"No! Listen. I am not really a Korean. I am Chinese. My government has sent me to the United States to take up one small part in the fomenting of revolution."

"What do you do?"

"I teach Revolutionary Administration and Funding to Presbyterian groups in cities of over two million."

"Whaaaat?"

"You are shocked. I thought, because you were black, you would understand everything."

"Shit, Kung—I am shocked that the Chinese would send a perfectly good man all this way to teach a fucking college course. What is this Administration and Funding? You want to break the back of this country? It would only take a handful of experienced saboteurs, if they were fanatical enough and if they were so trained for urban guerrilla war that they couldn't think about anything else, to tie up the key cities of this country for months, even years, Kung, to scare the people themselves so shitless they wouldn't even leave their houses. The economy would evaporate. That's administration. That's revolutionary funding."

"No, no. That is tactics, Teel. Administration and Funding are entirely different things which altogether——"

"Revolution isn't *all* talk, Kung. And what is urban guerrilla war if it isn't the weak against the strong until the strong become weak and the weak strong?"

"All that is entirely out of my field," Kung said. "We have all that behind us."

"Oh, horseshit! You people fought a running war across a lot of mountains and out in the fucking snow. I am talking about war in cities—more complicated than anything China ever knew. You know anything about the wiring in an eighty-story skyscraper, what a metropolitan water supply is like, with all that pumping necessary? Do you have any idea what it takes just to get food into complexes like that? This is a new kind of guerrilla war I'm talking about. Inferior, more lightly equipped forces harassing conventional armies —sure. But inside gigantic cities so that the light force *always* holds the surprise, and can never be found when the conventional force tries to strike back. If they strike back they murder their own people—and, man, are they ever going to murder a lot of their own people. Cities are the kind of terrain that gives guerrillas absolute insurance when it comes to total revolutionary victory. Remember Carlos Marghela: 'It is necessary to turn political crisis into armed conflict by performing violent actions to force those in power to transform the political situation into a military situation. That will alienate the masses who, from then on, will revolt against the army and the police and blame them for this state of things.' Now—that is a scenario for a civil war in American cities, Kung."

She made him drag the Plan out of her. In the weeks to come she permitted him to draw her further and further into discussions of her ideas of American revolution. When she knew he was ready, she took him through the volumes of the Teel Plan.

Kung was startled, then horrified; then afire with admiration and enthusiasm. He told her *all* about himself, his cell within the organization of the Revolutionary Export Division of the People's Republic of China; who, what, why, when, where.

"How come you people are so big in Africa?" Teel asked him over the best Chinese meal he had ever eaten and she had ever cooked.

"Why not?"

"Why not? What is more racist, more anti-black than the People's Republic of China?"

"That is tradi*t*ional, not poli*t*ical! We are the only people we ever saw for three thousand years of absolute continuity. Naturally, it will take three or four centuries for our leaders and our people to get used to blacks. Look how long it took us to get used to whites. No, no—you are mistaken. There is nothing racist about it."

"Your government isn't anti-black?"

"My *gov*ernment is anti-black, yes. But my revolutionary leaders, the entire Revolutionary Export Division is absolutely most certainly not anti-black. Quite to the contrary. We are brainwashed out of it, it is impossible for us to be anti-black if we are assigned to this work or if we lead this kind of work."

"That's nice. I sure do feel a whole lot better now."

Not that Dr. Kung was a quick study of the Teel Plan. He would protest, "It has yet to be proved that urban guerrilla fighters by themselves are capable of bringing about revolution. They are political catalysts, yes. They can break down the fabric of democracy and change the political climate within a society, as in Weimar Germany and right now in Uruguay. But urban guerrilla warfare has its severely restricted limits."

"War is the tool!" Teel yelled. "The irresistible political tool! We can drive the people backward, step by step, then we can drive them backward crawling on their bellies, and when they see themselves at last, their babies blown apart, their houses burned to the ground, all food gone, all help gone, they will turn on the government that failed to protect them and they will bring it down forever."

"Why do you hate these people?"

"Hate? Who? The government?"

"Not the government. The people with the dead children and the houses burned down."

"*H*ate them? Are you crazy? I'm going to save them."

"But they will suffer so much it might be generations before the special changes you want can really do anyone any good. What we did in China we did in —almost—one generation because *we* did not hurt people. The people loved us and they love us still. If we had hurt them—which is inconceivable—we could not have governed them just as Chiang and the other war lords who hurt them could not govern them."

"Say—Kung—what is this—a bragging session?"

"Anyway, remember, Teel, there has never been a successful revolution in an industrial society."

"Will you forget those textbook theories? Never mind that. Tell me something—how can you think I hate the people?" Teel was seriously concerned. "I love the people. That is what a humanist is, Kung. A person who loves the people—and I am, first and foremost, a humanist. And if you want to know why there has never been a successful revolution in an industrial society, I'll tell you why. No movement like mine— no war like mine—was ever properly funded before. They all tried to do on fifty thousand dollars what I'm going to do on five hundred million."

After she knew she had locked him in, Teel concentrated on getting Kung back to China with a copy of the Teel Plan. "Listen to Mama, Kung, this is the greatest opportunity they'll ever have to overthrow the government of the United States and establish a prime place in this tremendous market. This is the chicken-in-every-pot shtik, baby."

Kung was impressed with Teel as a woman, a leader, a trial lawyer, a Washington figure, a U.N. delegate; he was impressed with her access to the White House, her wealth, her enormous social acceptance, her beauty and her intelligence. He was really hung up on Teel because he saw her as moving everything right. *("When I get the war going here, I will form two separate revolutionary groups. The big group will be the fighters. The second group—while extolling the need for change—will abhor the fighters. Yes, sir. When the fighters force the people to destroy the establishment and the government, the people will have only my second group—the reasonable group—to turn to to make things run again.")*

For a fleeting instant he thought of asking her to fly to China with him, but he realized that would be out of the question. A respecting Chinese son could hardly bring a black woman into his father's house. Teel was way ahead of him: she moved him around and turned him inside out until he pleaded with her (instead) to be allowed to smuggle a copy of the Teel Plan to China via Quito and Hong Kong. Graciously, when he asked, Teel did not demur too much. Her timetable had been advanced by a few years. This fortuitous accident of a *Gourmet* writer who was a soul-food addict having dragged Kung into her life was just that, an accident. But, a good planner allows for accidents just as he allows for rain. Now she could shorten her lead time. She wouldn't have to spend the time at the U.N. and in Washington, discreetly sorting out the men from the boys among the agents the Chinese had paid for so long in the government. And it was possible she would have gotten nowhere there, so she might have had to follow the threads of the paths of the opium business in the Golden Triangle of Asia that would ultimately have brought her to the Chinese leaders she sought. But now this little accident might just do all that for her and take her straight into the hard-nose revolutionary councils in Peking. It had to be the Chinese. First, it took big money and only the Chinese and the Russians, among America's enemies, had that kind of money. And the Russians were no use to her. They had crossed the line into unit capitalism, into Them and Us, designating their own people just as the owners designated the people in the United States of America. The Chinese were shits. They were the absolute totem-pole-top of all the racists in the world but—what the hell. Pull them in now and screw them later. She wasn't in this to help the fucking Chinese. So she handed Kung the Teel Plan.

The Plan was total in its strategic, tactical, anthropological, social and economic realizations. The mechanics of its essence would make American life untenable. The Plan would create material and psychological hardship, destroy populations, cities, the past; the face and energy of America. Teel set down one irrevocable condition: to make it work her Plan had to be underwritten by not less than $500 million a year on a rock-bottom basis for a minimum of five years (but more likely for eight and a half). The average cost per day for the shorter period would be $1,350,000. If the war were won within the minimum period, the total cost would be about $2.5 billion. If they needed to fight longer—not specified as maximum —the costs would be around $3 billion or only 37 percent of the gross sales of pornography in the United States or 25 percent of the cost of U.S. Air Force Intelligence for one year.

Peking studied the Plan. Dr. Kung was recalled to China. He and Teel exchanged their last operatic embrace. Not the last until they would meet again, but the very last because Kung was killed in the overflow of a riot outside a San Francisco supermarket. Ironically, it was a demonstration riot, part of the graduation exercises for the senior classes of the Presbyterian Maoists Dr. Kung had been training. Too bad for Kung, she thought, in passing, when she got the news, but he did his work for all scientific socialists everywhere and no one can say better words than that over a dead helper. She made a mental note to name a street after him somewhere like in Grosse Pointe. He might be useful someday as a martyr, she thought for a minute or two; the first casualty of the second American revolution, knowing as she did that some of the best minds of the scientific socialist generation in China had ordered old Kung's death, figuring that negotiations could proceed on a much better basis with him out of the way.

10

January 1964--1966

Bart and Enid's CIA contracts were negotiated by their distinguished uncle, Herbert Ryan Willmott, to everyone's satisfaction. In January 1960, when Bart and Enid were twenty-six years old, Bart began introductory courses at the agency's facility in the Broyhill Building in Arlington, Virginia. After Arlington, Bart was sent to The Farm, near Williamsburg, Virginia, for his operational training. He and Enid lived at a hotel in town. At The Farm, which operated under the U.S. Army cover name of Camp Peary, Bart got his light-weapons training, his backgrounding in explosives and parachuting, and his skills in the Japanese martial arts. He was a fine karate player. Because of his superiority in one-to-one confrontations he was not sent along to Fort Gulick in the Canal Zone with the paramilitary group, which formed most of Special Operations, for heavy weapons training and guerrilla warfare exercises. Instead he was held out from the rest of the class and drilled even more intensively with small weapons.

Bart's special Psy profile and his skills at face-to-face killing saved him from serving the usual year at Langley as an assistant to a Desk Officer backing up requests for information from the field. He was allowed to work on the development of his cover, which was astronomy. Bart had advanced mathematical skills. Astronomy had always fascinated him. He had a real interest in universal concepts, made possible, perhaps, by his own somewhat cold and distant objectivity. He had always enjoyed the intimacy of deep space and knowledge of the relative sizes of bunched galaxies because these seemed to discredit religious dogma so ably.

Bart was chosen to be one of the few *American* CIA agents in Europe. The U.S. Army and Air Force Intelligence maintained agents there and so did the FBI, Naval Intelligence, State and Treasury. But the CIA believed in recruiting their agents in the country where they were to work since, as natives, they are always "inside" the country so that everything they do makes them that much more difficult to detect. These agents are usually run by a "Resident," always an American, who usually lives across the border in an adjacent country and who receives *his* instructions from an American Case Officer usually operating from the embassy in the same country as the agent.

However, Bart's work was out of the ordinary. In 1966 he was assigned, with Enid, to live in Switzerland (but not to work there) on general European assassination duty. They were based in Locarno, close to the Italian frontier. His Resident was an American dentist who practiced in Milan. Bart's Case Officer was in

Langley, Virginia, because Bart's work was supra-policy.

Enid loved Locarno and when she was happy, Bart was happy. In 1966 Locarno was still a country town of about 11,000 people. The climate was charming. They had the chance to speak Italian and German. Their house was on the side of a mountain above the village of Monte della Trinità, 1,100 feet above the lake where, from a forty-one-yard-long balcony, they could look down to where Lieutenant Henry had rowed Catherine across the lake to her death in *A Farewell to Arms*. Bart was interviewed by the Zurich and the Ticino press as an amateur astronomer and became a local celebrity. Locarno schoolchildren and students from as far as Bellinzona came to see his observatory, which the agency had furnished with superlative equipment. His cover was lavish and complete in every detail, neither cent nor scruple being spared from CIA funds.

On the long balcony Enid grew basil for making *pesto* and raised cannabis in three large tubs. Enid had a green thumb for growing pot. They would sit in canvas deck chairs, side by side, blowing grass and holding hands, supremely content to be together. They were $\male$ and $\female$ of the same pattern. They were twins in size, features, expression and projected spiritual texture. Enid was nearly a beautiful woman. Or she was beautiful except for her emotional frailty. As in photographs of Virginia Woolf, Enid always appeared to be on the very verge of imploding because of deteriorating inner structures as well as certain curses from the past. Delicately featured, ectomorphic but full-breasted, she had the sort of body that should not be required to wear anything but a *tanga,* that wonderful Brazilian string bikini. She had long, perfect legs—legs sculptors create, Bart said (ruling out Henry Moore and Epstein).

The twins were tall. Bart was a cold-faced wand of a man who might have been too inwardly focused for anyone, except Enid, to be aware that he was a quite handsome man. It is said (by jockeys and film producers) that women do not care whether men are handsome or ugly but look for something else such as money or a complaisance. Although Bart knew other women, beyond Enid, he knew them only briefly, as if his life were spent in a singles bar, possibly because, looking for that something else in men, whatever it might be, no woman could find it in Bart. It could have been the quality of seeing them when he looked at them. Women like that. Bart never seemed to see people, although he looked. Bart had the permanent expression of Woodrow Wilson at his coldest, most somber: not always typical of Wilson but entirely typical of Bart.

His heavy mouth triangulated with heavy cheekbones but, instead of accentuating his sensuality, it made capital of his wariness and preoccupation, which can add up to an extensive social error. Despite Bart's negative façades and Enid's signals of hopeless despair, they were copies of each other; strongly molded people of instant distinction with passionate, bony noses and good, white teeth. Most interesting, under thick, sorrel hair and tall foreheads were their well-spaced eyes: Enid's lime-green, Bart's distant sky-blue; all four amygdaline. Their faces had character that emerged from their self-congratulatory arrogance. They had raised themselves from earliest teens and were, therefore, their own people, beholden to no one. They knew they were beating the system even though they didn't know what the system was. They were Willmott-Simmses. The Willmott told of a great heritage in American roofing materials. Bart had been named for Garret Hobart, his mother's grandfather's second cousin who had been McKinley's vice-president at a time when the best people were chosen for that office. Bart and Enid had always felt that they were a part of an American peer group that stretched from the Bohemian Grove to Harold Pratt House, even if Uncle Herbert had all the family's money.

Enid said, "Bart?"

"Mmm?"

"I have a very, very important suggestion to make." It was the trigger phrase she had been taught at Langley. It made Bart more rigid. At least, his languor dropped away. He stared at her.

"I want you to run for the Senate, darling."

"Baby, that takes a *pile* of money."

"I bet."

"Where would I get that kind of money?"

"You'll find a way. You're the smartest boy who ever was. And after you're in the Senate I want you to start a run for the White House."

"Sweetheart, *no*body can think how to get the kind of money that takes."

"You can."

Enid's sudden suggestions, wishing to make Bart an American leader, were all phrases and in-puts that had been poured into her daily in Virginia by some of the greatest minds of their generation. For its own reasons the CIA had decided Bart could do well for them in politics and Enid was well trained to persuade him. Enid had been triggered by a phone call that afternoon. Bart responded well.

"How?"

"You are a highly trained business executive. You're a Wharton honors man and a Harvard lawyer. When our two-year tour is up here, Uncle Herbert has to make sure that you are transferred to the agency's big business operation in Thailand." She swung her long, brown legs off the deck chair so she could stare into his face and demonstrate the seriousness of what she was saying.

"What big business operation?"

"Two whole airlines. One of them, the one you should be managing, they call Air Opium and, man, it's a *big* deal."

"How come you know that?"

"Around Langley."

"But—what's the advantage?"

"I just have an idea that's where we can find the money to put you into the Senate."

"How?"

"Honey, *I* don't know how. You're the one who has to figure it out." She slid off the deck chair and knelt beside him. "Are you going to do that for me?" she asked him huskily, whispering close to his face. He could smell her. She leaned over him and covered his mouth with her mouth as his hands moved out to find her.

11

1968

Late in the summer, Teel went to Geneva, thence by Swiss National Railways to Domodossola, in Italy, at the far side of the Simplon Pass, thence by mountain tram to Ascona on Lake Maggiore. On the second day she took the bus two and a half miles to Locarno and seated herself on the terrace of the Hotel du Lac café facing the Piazza Grande where, on schedule, she was greeted by a Miss Norma Engelson.

"I'm the courier," Engelson said.

"I'm listening," Teel said.

"They want to see you."

"Here?"

"Peking."

"Not me."

"Why not?"

"Because there is a CIA man with a camera at every door to China."

"These people don't plan things that way. They don't want to blow the deal any more than you do."

"We haven't made a deal yet. I am very, very black. I would stand out in Peking. The British or the Canadians would pass the word to Washington."

"Will you quit it? You're with the wily Chinese. You book for Hong Kong. Everybody goes to Hong Kong for markdowns. You lay over for local color in Bangkok but you'll never leave the Don Muang airport because the CIA will meet you and fly you straight into Lashio in Burma. My people will zoom you straight into Peking from there."

"The CIA?"

"A different part. The Air Opium part. They do a lot of business with my people. They'll think you are a heroin buyer from some big department store in the States. They are glad to do a little favor now and then."

"Crazee."

"Normal."

"Better let your people come out here."

"Too many. This is a high-echelon committee thing. They don't assimilate either. Try palming fifteen Chinese guys in Switzerland and you'll have newspaper headlines like the World Series."

They shared a demi of Fendant while Teel thought everything over. Finally she spoke. "Okay. I'll leave from Zurich for Bangkok three days from today but— one thing—no names and no passports. Dig?"

"Sure."

There was no passport examination at Bangkok. Teel came down the ramp from the SwissAir jet and was greeted by a gorgeous blond guy—no names— who guided her across the tarmac to a Dassault Falcon ten-seater fan jet. There was no delay. They just took off. Teel decided the cabin had been decorated to look like a Colonel Sanders fried chicken joint. There was a bar so she made herself a Dr Pepper and vodka. Lashio was even more so than Bangkok. She was walked from the Falcon to a huge, four-engined Russian Myasishchev strategic bomber by an elderly English-speaking Chinese who tried to get her to talk about soccer. She was strapped into a bucket seat. The engines were turning over. She yelled, "Hey! Is this thing pressurized?" He nodded.

They were airborne for about three hours. The plane came down at the almost-deserted Nan-Yuän military airport nine miles out of Peking.

Two women and three men were waiting at the ladder. The men did not speak. The smaller woman was the interpreter, Tan Wen-sheng, born in Brooklyn. The other woman was Wang Hai-jung, a slight, bespectacled woman who was identified as being assistant to the Foreign Minister but who was also a niece of Mao Tse-tung. They were driven away in a limousine that was veiled with thin silk curtains. Teel could see out but no one could see in. They rode to Taio Tu Tai, the government guest-house compound, beside a lake in a Peking suburb. The three silent men were representative of the Social Affairs Department, which was the Intelligence Unit of the Central Committee of the Communist Party, which corresponded to the Soviet KGB; an agent from the Foreign Intelligence Department in the Ministry of Foreign Affairs, which corresponded to the American CIA; and a man from the Political Department of the Defense Ministry; all cops.

The next day Teel faced thirteen bone-weary bureaucrats who had been arguing since the night before. A Management Statistics Commissar chaired the meeting. Speaking P'u-t'ung-hua, as if to make it easier for the visitor, he said, "We feel an awesome regard for your beautifully conceived plan, Miss Teel." The interpreter translated. Teel, being a lawyer, did not answer.

The commissar said, "The drawback is the cost." This was translated. Teel remained silent.

"However," the chairman said, "it is a question of correct funding. We have voted and have secured approvals for a willingness to support your plan with 38 percent of its requirement, providing Libya, Albania, Algeria, and Uganda will jointly supply the rest. In fact, now that France is disengaging herself from the West to join the Third World, I am sure France would want to contribute to your great struggle."

"No."

"No? Why?"

"Listen," Teel said, "when the smoke clears and the government of the United States, as it exists today, is overthrown and finished, I am going to owe you—right?"

He shrugged daintily.

"Right. So—I don't also intend to owe Libya, Albania, Algeria, Uganda and France."

"We don't see how else you can raise that kind of money."

Teel stared individually at each of the thirteen faces across the table. She stared most of them down. Over three minutes of silence passed. The Management Statistics Commissar said, "The Chairman of our Republic teaches thrift and lives thrift. It would be ungrateful if we were to agree to spend the entire amount ourselves, even if we could agree to spend the entire amount."

"Then why did you make me fly my ass all the way out here?"

"Ass?" the interpreter inquired.

"Rephrase," Teel told her.

"Because—mainly because—we considered you to be so advanced and enlightened with regard to the development of the plan itself, we felt certain you would have advanced ideas on funding as well."

"Maybe I have," Teel said. "But if I did, your country's position would have to be negotiated way downward."

"We would like to hear your ideas for raising three billion dollars," the chairman said.

"We will finance it ourselves with a minimum

amount of help from you. So little help from you that your equities in this entire revolution are going to drop from a possible fifty-percent position to something close to five to seven percent."

"Very well. Since we will not fund you, but are willing to help you, we will accept the reduced equities—as you call them—and rely on your good will." He turned in each direction at the table to get confirmation. Everyone agreed while the interpreter broke it down for Teel.

"I can finance the whole thing with opium," Teel said flatly, not concealing that this had been the way she had always intended to finance her war. "You find me the raw opium and set up six Number Four heroin processing plants, get me a great chemist like Joseph Cesari or his half-brother, Dom Albertini, and the people of the United States will buy the heroin from me and shoot it and we'll save them in the promised land." She looked away from them sadly as the interpreter translated.

The Deputy Foreign Minister spoke in English with the faintest accent of San Mateo, California, from the far left end of the table. "May I say, Miss Teel," with a voice big enough to have been produced by an opera singer, "that we have certain international agreements? That is, China has become a co-guarantor, with the United States, that the government of Taiwan will be allowed to receive all Number Four heroin manufactured in Laos and northern Thailand. We don't allow opium inside China except to produce medicinal morphine, but heroin has become the most important export of Taiwan, and opium is the only cash crop for the mountain peasants of Laos, Thailand, Burma, and our own Yunnan Province. These countries and Taiwan are at our borders. Of the four, two are poor but two are financed and armed by your country. Therefore, since we will not allow opium in China, we are agreeable to allowing these countries to grow it and sell it. In that way we keep the peace. In that way, the American CIA, which is sort of a

Waffen SS, is pleased to transport the opium, with the help of the Military Advisory Command of Vietnam, because, in return, they gain the cooperation of everyone in Southeast Asia for the plans of conquest they have."

"Amen," Teel said. "If Taiwan takes the Laotian and Thai production, that leaves plenty for us in Burma and Yunnan."

"Yes."

"Okay. Then build me six Number Four plants. But, please—French chemists. The Chinese chemists out of Hong Kong only understand Number Three. We can't sell Number Three. Only the French know how to make the pure and a man like Cesari can turn out forty kilos of Number Four a week, per plant. A Hong Kong man is lucky if he can produce fifteen."

"How much will these Number Four heroin plants cost?" the Management Statistics Commissar asked prissily.

Teel seemed to look at him when she answered but it could have been that she wasn't seeing him. "It's a big price, baby," she said. "The highest. It's gonna cost my own soul and the bodies of a few million brothers. Shit takes its toll, baby. Shit takes its toll."

The second meeting convened at eight fifteen the next morning. The membership of the committee had shifted to an entirety of four military men. The agenda called for a discussion of guerrilla officer training. Teel wanted seven men and five women trained in every aspect of urban guerrilla warfare toward the specific execution of her plan for the Thirty Cities.

The Chinese explained that they had established two guerrilla training camps for foreign guerrillas in the Tsinghai Province. These had every facility of faculty and equipment. Fourteen countries were at present participating in the indoctrination of officers.

"On a generalized guerrilla training program?" Teel said.

"Oh, yes."

"I don't want that for my people. I want them trained to execute *this* plan." She slapped the Plan on the table in front of her. "How long is the present course?"

"Two years, four months."

"No good for my plan."

"My colleagues have already agreed that your people should stay with us for three years."

"I want the course programmed for four full years," Teel said. "These people will appreciate it more if it comes out to the equivalent of an American college education."

The officer made a note. "When will you want them to begin?"

"I'm gonna let you know about that. And how much help I'm going to need from you to get them inside China."

"The best way to bring the men in is through the war zone in South Vietnam. It is an easy matter to get Americans as far as Saigon. We can take over from there."

"Good," Teel said. "That's great."

"We'll probably have to move the women differently. We could include your women with the trainee candidates from Latin America."

The third meeting convened at one twenty that afternoon for a discussion of Chinese representation in Teel's command.

"We want to have our own man there to liaise with you. Immediately."

"That's reasonable," Teel said.

"He is qualified to be your chief of staff."

"That's good. Who is he? I want to meet him first and, if I like him, we'll make a deal. But I agree to the principle."

The Chinese choice was Colonel Pikow (the only name Teel ever got for him), the former director of the Guerrilla Training Camp and Guerrilla War College Studies for the People's Republic. He was a tall man next to his compatriots. He was unusually silent. He looked Mongolian but that was mostly western Chinese. (The Tsinghai Province was populated largely by Tibetans and Mongolians.) His most impressive strength (for a soldier) was his intelligence. Teel liked him after the first hour with him; he was a born second-in-command who knew that was as high as he wanted to go. Teel innovated; Pikow implemented. In later years Teel would tell Jonas, her brother, that Pikow had meant more to the movement than any other factor she could name, excluding herself. During that first hour, Teel told Colonel Pikow that she wanted China to approach the guerrilla movements of Uruguay, Japan, Ireland, Palestine and Vietnam to second experienced specialists to her command in the United States. She would pay them on whatever basis they chose. "When our leaders graduate in China, I want them to enter a finished organization—everything done and established, everything—so that they can realize instantly that what they had been taught for four years was not a lot of makeshift theories but a program for an army they were taking over—an army as ready to fight, as impatient to kill as they were."

Pikow agreed. He said he agreed with her ideas, all of them, and that whereas he was to liaise with her organization to provide information for the People's Republic, he was, first and foremost, her man, and he would clear all signals with her before they went out. He said he knew all international guerrilla organizations because he had taught most of them. He would contact them. It was not something that they should need to take up with the Defense Ministry. He would choose the men she needed for the jobs they would be required to fit within the Teel Plan. He held out his hand. "We will make a good war," he said. Teel and he shook hands earnestly.

12

1966–1968

Bart Simms was given only five European assignments
in their two-year tour in Locarno. He wasn't away
from home much, which was best for Enid's and his
own happiness. He never knew the people involved,
not even as public newspaper figures. There were
only three men and two women whom he was required
to kill. Enid told him, at the beginning, to reassure
him: "You know these people must deserve to get it.
When a government of the importance and wisdom of
the United States, and the freedom for which it stands,
decides that a man must be liquidated with extreme
prejudice, you simply have to know he has it coming."

"I suppose so," Bart said.

The jobs were straight duty assignments within the
work for which he had been trained at considerable
expense. With the exception of a single instance, he
completed all the assignments successfully with a
single-shot Liberator M1942 pistol, the agency's preference for assassination work. It was a good weapon,
manufactured by the Guide Lamp Corporation, a part
of General Motors, proving that what was good for
General Motors wasn't necessarily good for everybody
else. Actually, the weapon was a sentimental carry-
over from the days when "the old boys" at the agency
had used it in the OSS for the same work. Its short,
smooth-bore barrel was very accurate. Its simple twist-
and-pull breechblock opened so that the round could
be placed in the chamber. However, the shooter did

have to be good, and work up as close as possible because if the shot missed, it was a complicated business to reload, the pistol requiring that some suitable implement be pushed down the barrel to eject the used cartridge case. The agency had lost relatively good men because of that feature but those men had been assumed to be sure shots so it was their own fault, not the Liberator's, Langley reasoned.

The actual on-the-spot work was a lot different from the training, Bart told Enid when he got back from completing the first assignment. He explained how he had asked himself at the moment before he was sure he was going to murder for the first time (a) isn't this extraordinary work for a Harvard man to be doing? (b) how had Evel Knievel felt about his first gigantic jump?

"He must have been scared witless," Enid said, "and so must you have. Weren't you?"

"Correcto profundo."

"That is an entirely normal feel," Enid said.

Getting nerved up to carry through the first two assignments was rough, but after that he knew in his heart he had it made. He knew he had made the right choice because the agency had shown him what realism was.

"I'll tell you one thing, hon," Bart said to Enid, "I know what realism is now."

"A viewpoint most Americans sorely lack," Enid reassured him.

Other lawyers, businessmen, even politicians who voted for death every day were a bunch of helpless idealists compared to what the agency had made him, Bart told Enid. Realism? Jesus, *yes!* It was so real it could make him weep. He couldn't bear to upset Enid so he tried to control it and to weep only when he was alone, like in the loo, but if he had had too many uppers he could lose control and there was nothing he could do about the weeping. He had looked straight into Reality—right at it. He knew what reality was and he detested it. *Jesus!* People talked about being realists. They didn't know what they were talking about. Because someone had to live in a rathole in a slum, that didn't make that person a realist, for Christ's sake. Because Uncle Herbert had to own some of those slums as part of his overall portfolio, that didn't make Uncle Herbert a *realist*. Realism was when a young girl, say a nice-looking, decent-looking girl who happened to have a lot of crazy political ideas that ran against the grain of the power pattern—not some reject who was shooting shit or some kind of a crazy, acid-dropping dyke or something—just a young girl with a lot of wrong ideas about how people should be housed or something, with a sweet face—not pretty, not anything he could go for, not anything like that —but, well, a nice girl but a boat rocker, kind of a troublemaker—and you had to end her life for her. Well, *shit*. You sat right across from her on the stone floor, holding her long hair in your left hand and pulling her head back with it and she pretended that she thought you were just threatening her. Her eyes told that she knew it was no threat, that this was it, but she wasn't scared as much as she should be. She was able to talk without breaking or screaming. You had to admire her. For just a few moments you even thought maybe it shouldn't happen to her, that you should let her go if you could only think of what kind of deal you could make with her.

Then the young girl began to talk to him as if she were teaching him something important, he tried to explain to Enid, sobbing in her arms. The young girl's eyes filled up as she saw that she knew something he would never know. She said it was going to bother him much later if he killed her. She said he was some kind of talking dog who didn't know what he was doing at all. Then—unfairly—suddenly and unfairly— she told him her name—Louisa. That was unfair because nothing was impersonal anymore. He had to kill her. He and Enid had figured out the route to the top of the mountain. But if he didn't kill her, then back to the salt mines in some Wall Street law firm. Good-

bye Senate and other plans. *Louisa!* He pushed on the
razor and pulled it across her throat until it stopped
at the vertebrae as he jerked downward on her hair.
It had to be done this way, the Resident said, for its
effect on her people when they found her. Son-of-a-
bitch!

When Bart and Enid finished their two-year tour in
Locarno, Bart was replaced by a young Swiss woman.
Bart was instructed by the Resident to advertise the
house for rent in the local paper and to rent it only to
a woman who would be wearing a yellow hat. The
girl in the yellow hat was called Signora Marton-Hess.
She paid him a deposit of Sw. Fr. 400. He told her she
would be welcome to occupy the house on the first of
the month. He was amazed and dismayed that such a
superior type of young woman was to take over liq-
uidation services; she seemed so, well, *Swiss.* Eleven
hours after he had rented the house another woman
rang at the gate saying she had come to rent the
house. He explained that the house had been rented.
The woman pointed to her hat, a yellow hat, and said
it was impossible that the house had been rented. Even
asleep she would have been a grim-looking woman.
Bart realized that a mistake had been made but, very
stiffly, he told the woman that the house had been
rented and clanged the gate shut. "That's the trouble
with those old fuckers at Langley," he told Enid.
"They are so committed to cloak-and-dagger nonsense
that they naturally foul up."

Uncle Herbert's influence and Bart's record brought
in the assignment Bart and Enid had dreamed about
—the top management job at Air Opium. They were
transferred to northern Thailand. They had a lovely
house that had been built by the agency. The second
night they were there, as they sat on the screened
verandah and blew grass, Enid told him about Spider.

Spider, Enid said, was a colossal, computerized,
personalized library maintained at Langley of viciously
vital information on every leading man and woman in

the world. "I mean—every fact every one of these people has broken his back to hide forever—well, those facts are in Spider, Bart. And the fact is, these Spider files are going to make your fame and fortune."

"How?"

"You'll come up with the answers. All I thought was that when we finish our tour here, if Uncle Herbert could get you transferred in as Assistant Curator at Spider, and if you could really start training your memory while we're out here, you could bring home a part of the Spider files in your head every night. We could work up some kind of code to store them, so that when the time comes for you to make your move to get big campaign financing to put you in the Senate, you are going to know exactly who the moneybags is that you are going to slam it to to make him sign those checks to pay for your campaign."

"Slam it to whom?"

"Whomever you pick out of the Spider files. Whoever is the most vulnerable, honey, if you know what I mean."

"Dynamite. Really dynamite."

"It sure is."

"Let me think about it."

"You're the brain."

Totally certain that Enid had solved the problem of the gigantic costs of running for public office, Bart laid out the work program he must follow during his off hours away from airline management tasks. He settled down into intensive memory training, working with Enid for five hours every night he could be home. They worked with English language newspapers and short-wave radio broadcasts. They used columns of drone from *The Congressional Record* because Enid felt that memorizing anything interesting after memorizing the *Record* would seem like the easiest thing in the world.

During his two years of training and two years in the field, Bart and Enid had never asked for any leave so, when they knew this memory thing was going to work, they applied for three weeks of R&R in Europe. The request was granted. They slurped up Paris restaurants, then they rented a car and set out for the champagne country so they could motor on to Strasbourg, then cross into Germany, then to Dusseldorf where Bart paid a mathematics professor the DM equivalent of $8,000 to develop a mathematical code. It was the only kind of code that could protect him from agency surveillance. Having used astronomy as his cover from the beginning, Bart had spent a considerable amount of time with mathematics and the agency's staff surveillance people no longer paid any attention to the sheaves of mathematical notes Bart left lying around. Mathematical codes held so many possibilities for permutation that even a bank of on-line computers used by the best cryptanalysts in the world couldn't break down such a code in hundreds of years. Bart had come to feel a great deal of respect for the tiny German mathematics professor whom he had known during the two years of his European assignment, but the man simply had to be liquidated with most extreme prejudice because he was the only other person who held the code's keys. Enid had to agree with Bart's decision and felt just as sad as he did about it.

While he treated mnemonics as a hobby by night, Bart pursued the agency's work just as thoroughly during the day. He really ran that airline, jacking up its net profit by 12.079 percent. He viewed opium as another payload just as if he were engaged in flying shoes out of Endicott, New York.

Bart's excellence was a tradition of the service. Although the higher military grades of the MACV and the South Vietnamese forces were heavily involved in the narcotics traffic out of the Golden Triangle of Laos, Thailand and Burma, the CIA's severe exception to personal corruption among its officers kept most of them from being stained. There was the occasional rotten apple, but by and large CIA management personnel observed a strict code against profiting personally from the narcotics trade. Not that Bart ever questioned things like that. He was so irreproachably stainless himself that he simply assumed that anyone else privileged to serve The Agency in Asia or anywhere else was just goshdarned lucky.

13

Spring 1969

When Teel got it all figured out about how to spread the pure and how to launder the money so she could drop it into the accounts of the several hundred companies she had spent so much time forming, she telephoned New York's leading black wholesaler of shit, an evil, expressionless dark brown man named William Buffalo, and asked him to please call at her office.

Buffalo was a hard man who had made it to the top of the metropolitan narcotics trade without too much strain. He had been cut up and shot, but nothing permanent. He had known Teel since back on 124th Street when he had been a dealer ambitious to expand. Teel had won him the street again on a murder charge three years before. He believed in Teel just as everyone did who had ever talked to her. His bodyguards waited in the outer office and kidded around with Teel's banana-skinned secretary who wore a turtleneck sweater with the word PEACHES sewn across it. Buffalo went into Teel's office, *taking his hat off,* and sitting down while he smiled his terrible smile, unable to do anything about his eyes which might have seen too many people in bad trouble. Teel grinned at him.

"How's it, William B.?"

"I'm winnin'."

"I don't want anything. I'm gone give to you."

"What you givin' today?"

"Would you believe fifty kilos of the pure, purer, purest?"

"*FIFTY?* Jesus Christ, Miss Teel. Did you say fifty?"

"That's right."

"I been around all my life. I never saw fifty. I never saw more'n seven."

"Can you move it?"

"Shit, yes. At what price?"

"I want this load to go at five percent under the street price."

"You mean the import price or the wholesale price?"

"You tell me."

"Is it cut? Will you take the first cut? Thassa difference between import and wholesale."

"No cut, Will. Total pure. The highest."

"Then why knock off five percent?"

"I'll talk about that. How much can you handle?"

"All you can shovel at me."

"For cash money?"

"I think so."

"How about a hundred keyes?"

"Nobody, not even the Rockefeller boys, can shake up the cash for a hunnert keyes. If it wasn't you sayin' it, I wouldn't even believe there was a hunnert keyes of H all in one place."

"I want the five percent off to start a price war and make more users," Teel said. "I want you to case the country where the Sicilians control it and where the brothers are working. Then I want you to pick out the black wholesalers and dealers you can trust and pass along the five percent to them. And if it turns out all of a sudden you can't trust them, I want them killed the day you find out."

"I dig. A little bit. But mostly I ask you—why?"

"In a little while I want to stop the black whole-salers and dealers from buying from the Sicilians."

Buffalo whistled.

"Then," Teel went on, "when you got your deals set with the pure going out and the cash coming back on maybe two hundred keyes a month, then I'll run it and you and I will work out the split."

"All right. But what about the Sicilians?"

Teel smiled broadly. "Well, they got to go sooner or later anyhow, don't they?"

He grinned back at her. "That's the truth."

"Suppose we go to a man like Grunts Patterson in South Chicago and we offer him five points under the Sicilian price. Then what?"

"He take it."

"Okay. When he takes it you know how to tell the rest of the people in Chicago they can have the same deal. Then what?"

"Well—a little time passes, right?"

Teel nodded.

"Then the Sicilians go to war."

"And if we back up our customers, city for city, with more muscle than they could ever get together themselves, and we blow the Sicilians right into the lake—then we own Chicago. Right?"

"Thass right."

"That's what I want and that's what I'll give."

"And I'm the middleman on all this?"

"If it ain't too rich, William."

"When do we start?"

"We start this summer but we start slow. We won't really hit them till seventy."

14

December 1970

Teel told Frank O'Connell, the head of her law firm, that she was going to need a closing pretty fast. He set her with a large housing development and shopping mall in northern Virginia. Her fees for the closing came to $891,000. When she had the cash in hand she called Buffalo, who remained in awe of her as he probably was of no one else alive. "How are we on prison information?" Teel asked.

"What kind?"

"I want six men and five women who have done time for armed robbery. Can you do it?"

"Shit, yes."

"But it's got a little twist. I need those same people who did the time for armed robbery to have Army or Marine Corps combat experience."

"Well, sure—the men. But not the women."

"Just get me women who were in the Army or the Marines. Okay? That plus about five years in the women's wing of some state pen will toughen them up just about right. But they all got to have a military background and an armed robbery on their sheet."

"I'll go right on it."

"When you get them, I want you to talk to them for me, one at a time."

"Is this all about the pure we got comin' in?"

"Indirectly."

Buffalo's top man was a crazy, coffee-colored bookkeeper who could make those ledgers tell the tax creeps anything Buffalo wanted to pay. His name was Dawes and Buffalo knew he was crazy because Dawes was an anarchist. Dawes was actually in the heroin business not for any large score but because he wanted to waste society as fast as it could be flaked away. "They is too many people," he told Buffalo, "and they is fuckin' each other up."

Dawes was crazy but he was smart. He gave out good advice. He'd been working for Buffalo for eleven years, on the down ramps and on the upswings, and Buffalo knew that little Binchy Dawes had a head on his shoulders. So, when Buffalo wanted to think out loud, he thought out loud all over Binchy. Binchy was how William Buffalo pronounced the nickname for Benjamin. Dawes's full name was Benjamin Disraeli Dawes.

"You know my big connection, Binchy?"

"I know you got it."

"You know what she ask me today?"

"Whut she ast you?"

"She ask me can I find her six dudes and five foxes who done time for armed robbery one."

"No kiddin'?"

"The fact."

"Then she got to be a woman to go with. She got to be an anarchist."

"She the most. You know what she want them folks for?"

"What for?"

"She want the men to join the army."

"Join the *army?* With a *war* on?" Binchy chuckled. "I got a son in the army, Bill. He a *real* anarchist. No shit. Went all the way thoo West Point. Number six in his class. He a lieutenant now. Someday he gone be in a real position to fuck up that army for good. What she want them to join the army for?"

"She doin' something big. A fox like that don't collect no eleven robbers to work unless it somethin' very, very big. She gone pay out twenty-fi' grand to ever one a them—thass three hunnert thou, Binchy—she think *big*."

Dawes became very serious. "You got to get my boy in on that, Buffie. We don't care about the twenny-fi' gee. My boy is a trained officer of the Army of the United States, an Academy man, an' there ain't nothin' any armed robber can do my boy cain't do—besides he an *officer*. She see that inna minute when you tell her. I mean—ever'body know that one devout anarchist worth two bank robbers no matter what."

Binchy Dawes flew to Washington early the next morning. He rented a car and drove out to Fort Sissons. He sent in word that Lieutenant Orin Dawes's father had come up from New York to see him on urgent family business. After a twenty-five-minute wait Orin came out. He was a fine-looking boy; brown with caramel eyes like his mother. He had a smart look, like an interesting man, just the way he had always been an interesting little boy. And—Jesus!—he sure looked great in that uniform.

"Let's take a little spin," Binchy said. "I won't take much time." They got into the rented Plymouth and drove along at an easy pace. The son waited for his father to talk.

"Well—it come just like I always said it would," Binchy said. "The big chance has come. We can strike the blow."

"The blow?"

"The chance is here to git to the place where we can bust the government and the army by doing what we know the best to do."

"What happened, Pa?"

"Something big. Eleven of the messiest cats you ever saw are gonna enlist under orders from the top."

"What top?"

"We don't need to know that, Orin. After they in, they report back to my boss. Then they take over and turn the whole fuckin' army upside-down and I got an okay from William Buffalo to have you lead that buncha weirdoes."

"That's pretty hazy, Pa." He looked glum.

"It's gotta be hazy! What kinda anarchist outfit would we be runnin' if ever' man with a job to do knew the whole thing, step by step of the way? You jes' let us do the thinkin', Orin. You get the action part."

"I don't know, Pa."

"Whatta you mean, you don't know?"

"It's just that—well, I got picked over everybody else for a big Army assignment, Pa."

"What assignment?"

"I can't talk about it."

"You don't need to talk about it. You can forget it. After a lifetime of plannin' and trainin' since you Momma died, we right at the brink, baby. Everything we been plannin' for."

"Okay, Pa. What do I do?"

"You just stay right here till we can get you transferred out. If they move you, jes' tell me where. That's all you got to do, Orin."

"Okay, Pa."

"We ain't never gone look back, son. This the biggest."

It took eleven days for Buffalo to line up the convicts. Teel accepted Lieutenant Dawes. She listened to Buffalo read off the prison records, then she said, "Somebody who goes in for armed robbery is only reckless in a certain way. He is an achiever. He knows he's going to win—or forget it. That's his whole thing, William. He is an artist so he hates authority. He hates the rules. He grabs at being the most dangerous kind of piece man there is. But, at the same time, he doesn't want to lose. He wants to go on defying everybody and he can't do that inside any prison. So mostly he's smart. He is the very prime of the primest. Okay. The instructions are in the money envelopes. You can read them. All they got to do is agree to join the U.S. Army and we take care of the rest, like the governors' pardons and that kinda jazz. As soon as they get stationed somewhere you tell them to tell you where they are. Then you tell me and we get it all on the road. But that ain't all, William. For every day over ninety days they are still in that army, every one of those cats is gonna get a thousand a day from you. Okay?"

"Well, sure. Okay. I was just wonderin' 'bout me. You think it's good for business if one a them cats should—uh—like crack open and talk, maybe say it was me recruited them for the Army?"

"Buffie, no way. Not a way for anybody to tell one of *them* dudes from five hundred other thousand grunts."

She got home at three o'clock in the afternoon to make her brother Jonas one of the last of the high French meals he was going to have for a long, long time—and he was a boy who liked to eat.

She was going to start him off with a salad of Louisiana crawfish tails with Beluga caviar on top of a lemony mayonnaise with heavy cream folded into it. Then would come sea bass in puff pastry, then some roast woodcock on croutons followed by fat duck's liver in a truffle salad.

She would let him rest a little, then, maybe drink a little mineral water to be ready to eat some more, but with Jonas that was one issue which was never in doubt. A lot of the most of the rest of the world was in doubt for Jonas. She couldn't figure how the two of them could have been raised in the same very special way, in their very special isolation from the slings and arrows, and have it turn out with her being so sure and he being so unsure. After they had had their farewell talk—Jonas was the one human it was so hard for Teel to say farewell to—she would stoke him up again with a green salad, some prime ribs, then grilled lobster and a crawfish "bush" with all those bitter-tasting veins removed. But she decided she couldn't do that. Instead she soaked the little shellfish in a milk bath for two hours. They didn't like the taste of the milk. They wiggled around and purged themselves of all the bitterness without losing any of the taste. She would finish him off with a mousseline of apples and walnuts, polishing its perfection with *noyau* liqueur, the French almond liqueur known as Noyau de Poissy. If he was still hungry after all of that, she'd crown him with a pot.

They talked all through the meal, not just at the break between. Jonas was about the handsomest black man she had ever seen and that was more beautiful than any man has a right to be. He was as black as she was but twice her size; a huge gentle man with quizzical eyes. In a way he was her little boy.

"The best thing is that you know just what the other men in Three Platoon know—and that's all. Except you also gone know I am the mover behind it. But— it goes without sayin', baby, even the wild horses can't drag *that* out of you. Okay. Tomorrow you gone in the army for a while but it all comes up roses at the other end. You gone get the finest training in the production of nuclear energy that any experimental physicist at your level ever had, you hear?"

"How you gone do that, Ag?"

"Never mind. Just trust. Say your sister Aggie told you that so it's gone happen." She smiled at him tenderly. "Just like everything else I ever said is gone happen, happens. Now you just save yourself. Get along with them six other guys. You got to. But just be friendly; don't mix in with them. Save yourself so that when all of you get where you're goin' your mind will be wide open so you can easy walk away from them without feeling blue and lonesome and settle down to learn everything you got to learn about that nuclear power and how to design it to fit packages our people will be able to walk around with. Okay?"

"Yes, ma'am. What food! But where we gone that I find out all this here?"

"I'm gone tell you so, all over again, just like it

was the first time, you gone know I trust you. You
gone to China. You gone study with them crafty Chinese."

"I shouldn't have asked you."

"We're walkin' up toward the edge now, baby. We
gone make it right to the edge—then we gone jump
in."

"Does it make any mind where I check into this
army?"

"How do you mean?"

"If I'm gone to China I got to get to Washington
first."

"How come?"

He shrugged clumsily. "A girl."

"You never said a thing!"

"Not much to say, Ag. Jessa girl."

"You want to say good-bye?"

He grinned, "Sometimes good-byes can be nice. They
can get you results you might not get otherwise."

Teel smiled back at him. "No, then it doesn't matter
where you enlist. Just remember to tell me where they
station you after they take you in.

"One other thing, baby," she added. "I got you a
brand-new birth certificate. You gone enlist under the
name of Albert Cassebeer."

Jonas, who was to be his own man, smiled weakly.

15

March 1969

"Nations," Bart explained to Enid while they rested happily on the large double bed one night, "have come to prize and protect their rights to profit from opium and heroin just as sincerely as they prize and protect their interests in copper, oil, uranium and coffee."

"Balance of payments—don't forget that," Enid said.

"But not entirely. Political leaders guard heroin with the lives of their people because it is so much more profitable than, for example, some resource such as oil."

"And everybody knows oil people are always making money so they are always throwing rocks at oil people. We hardly ever see people throw rocks at politicians."

"Profits from heroin drench politicians, hon. Heroin could not get itself sold anywhere without earnest cooperation from politicians. The greater the market —like the United States—the greater the political involvement on every level from the corner cop to the White House."

"I honestly don't know how people can shoot chemicals into their bloodstream. It is disgusting. But they certainly do it. I mean, more every day."

"The profits are almost beyond man's ability to count. If every man has a price, then heroin brings ten thousand times the price of any man."

"That scans, Bart. I mean, that could like be a line from Polonius."

"Exactly—as follows night and day the gross annual income from heroin sales in the United States alone is sixteen billion two hundred million dollars. The street price for one kilogram of heroin is one million two hundred thousand dollars."

"It's like buying a Rolls. The time to get one is when you are, say, twenty-one. The car lasts for seventy years so the twenty-five thousand you pay comes out to about three hundred and fifty a year."

"How do you mean?"

"Well, the thing to do is to buy your kilo of heroin when you're—say fourteen. That should last you for at least twenty years—if you can last twenty years with your arms and your head in shreds," Enid explained, "so it brings down the unit cost of your fixes."

"If you do that, buy wholesale, because the raw material from which the kilo was made—that is ten kilos of raw opium—cost six hundred dollars. From maker to wearer, the cost of the product goes up two thousand times."

"No industry could be that greedy."

"It isn't the industry, it's the politicians and police and enforcers who are so greedy. They want such a big cut that the sale price of heroin at entry in New York has risen from twelve thousand dollars a kilo to twenty-six thousand. Jesus, hon, the re-sale price to the first wholesaler in New York is thirty-five thousand dollars—or forty-two thousand in Chicago. He cuts his kilo with lactose and the wholesaler has two kilos, then he sells each one for forty-eight thousand a kilo in order to be able to afford to pay the politicians."

"How much *is* a kilo, sweetheart?"

"Two point two pounds."

"That's not much—I mean not if you had King Kong on your back."

He looked blank.

"I made a joke," Enid said.

"The thing is that the kilo is cut and re-cut, then cut

again until its value, in five-dollar bags, reaches a million two. Then what did they do, for Christ's sake? The dealers lowered the content of each five-dollar bag from twelve to five milligrams."

"I read the book."

"What book?"

"Panic in Needle Park."

"They got a book out of the weight drop in five-dollar bags?"

"What a book!"

"Well, it takes a lot of heroin to fill all the little bags they sell. Fifteen tons a year, the United States needs. That's thirteen thousand five hundred kilos. At a million two a kilo. No wonder lawyers' fees are so high when politicians get into trouble."

"Those terrible men," Enid said. "And I lapped up Mr. Deeds on television."

"How do you mean?"

.."*Mr. Deeds Goes to Washington*—to get rich on protection money."

"Well there's just so *much* heroin money. Anybody can make heroin. The processing costs nothing. It's the splits that cost so much."

"How do they make it, darling?"

"Heroin is only diacetylmorphine, an alkaloid obtained by heating a mixture of morphine and acetic acid. Heroin was first produced by the German firm of Bayer in 1898. They thought they had developed a miracle drug."

"What a drug! And it's a miracle that anybody survives it."

"Politicians survive it. That's what it's sold for. It can be made in the bathtub at home like Prohibition citizens used to make gin. You just start out with impure heroin—a mixture of base morphine and acetic acid heated for six hours in a double boiler at a temperature of eighty-five degrees centigrade. To make base morphine out of opium all you do is let the raw opium simmer in water, then precipitate it with quick lime to separate all the vegetable elements and isolate the morphine and codeine."

"Mama used to give us codeine a long time ago. Do you wish those times were back, Bart?"

"No."

"Funny that Mama should give us *co*deine."

Bart was wound up. He wanted to keep talking like Tom Swift. "Then you strain away the impurities you can see, add a pinch or so of ammonium chloride and you have base morphine. It's crystallized powder. The color of milk chocolate. Of course, making heroin can be dangerous work. It can all blow up if the temperatures are wrong or it can come out less pure than eighty percent, which would mean the American market won't touch it and the American market is the name of the game."

"Times they are a-changin' " Enid said. "Whatever happened to martinis on the rocks with an olive? I tell you, doll, the only things that last are the habit-forming things. Like love and fear."

"And heroin. Given these kinds of profits, the politicians will see to it that forty percent of the population will be hooked by the year two thousand. And we're not about to run out of opium to make the stuff. Right where we are now, the Golden Triangle of Southeast Asia, ships twelve hundred tons of opium a year. And they did very effective merchandising from here for the American market. In 1964 the bar girls of Saigon were put on sales promotion to turn the GIs off booze and beer and on to heroin. There are seven processing plants operating in the Golden Triangle. Then our airline, Air Opium, flies it out to Vientiane where US military aircraft take it into Saigon. The American Army command and the ARVN provide protection and transport for the Five Passport Chinese racketeers who provide the financing, conversion and collection of the crop. Everybody gets rich. A lot of kids' lives are ruined but everybody gets rich."

"There must be a Greater Consciousness and a Higher Scheme behind all that, Bart. I mean—the friendly neighborhood padre has explained away much more than heroin in his time. Why should we wince?"

"Hon, I don't wince. We're here to get a job done for The Agency, and I'm doing it."

"It just seems so screwy that The Agency would get mixed up in stuff like heroin."

"Well! Defense! National security! In 1949 the remnants of Chiang Kai-shek's Kuomintang army— they call them the KMT, the people's national party —one of the few parties made up entirely of politicians with no constituency—was driven out of what had suddenly become Communist China into Burma, twelve kilometers from the Thai border. The KMT troops settled in. They took Shan or Yao or Lahu wives. They overthrew the local chieftains. When they were beefed up by the locals they were a fighting force of almost fourteen thousand men."

"A gang. A gang of crooked Chinks."

"In the early fifties they caught the imagination of the CIA."

"I bet."

"The Agency saw the KMT as preventing Communist filtration in Southeast Asia."

"Oh, God."

"They even saw it as invading and pinning down a part of China itself, so they supported the KMT with weapons and materiel."

"While the KMT went into the dope business."

"Exactly! This year the KMT has control of eighty percent of the traffic in the largest opium-producing area of the world."

"But——?"

"Well," Bart grinned, "they had the opium and if they could get it to Taiwan they could get big money. The Agency had the transport. So a deal was made because The Agency figured out that it wouldn't cost them a cent out of their secret appropriations anymore —to support the KMT, that is—so they agreed to transport."

"That's all," Enid said mockingly, "just transport."

"Well, in the best construction on that—yes. But when the USAID built ninety-one landing strips to move the opium and heroin out of the high mountains, it was just that a lot of irrelevant people got rich, the Taiwanese and the American high command in Vietnam and a lot of greasy criminals."

16

April 1971

Moving north along the ridges and high valleys of the cordillera, Kranak ran everything. Lurky Anderson asked him as they moved along, "Hey, Kranak. How come they make you the boss?"

"You wanna lead the way?" Kranak said. "Be my guest. Go ahead. Lead the way."

"I din' say that. Don' put shit in my mouth, man. I ass you how come they pick you."

"Because if they picked you we'd be up shit creek," Kranak said. "I spent nearly three fuckin' years in these mountains in Special Forces. I speak the languages—Meo, Viet and Chinee. Now what the fuck do you thinka that, shithead?"

He had the six men dig sleeping trenches which were snowflake-shaped. They slept with their heads together, their feet at the perimeter; rifles beside them. Kranak knew how to live off the land. He held command easily.

"You musta done plenty of soldiering," Orin Dawes said. "You sure know how to move these guys around."

"What the hell, Lieutenant, I was an A Team Sergeant. This is nothing."

"Well, just the same. It's a pleasure. I'm learning as I go along," Dawes said.

"That's the name of the game, Lieutenant."

Of the seven men four were black: the officer, Lieutenant Dawes, Jonas Teel, Lurky Anderson and Dolly Fingus. Fingus was almost as mean-looking as Kranak. Lurky Anderson was a big, ugly man with a cut-up face and chips all over his shoulders. Reyes was a Puerto Rican with a happy disposition. He was happiest when he was making trouble. He wished a happy life to anybody who would throw rocks at a cop. Buckley was a big city Mick. It didn't matter what city. He waved the IRA flag and refused to take a bath wherever he was.

"'Hey, Kranak," Lurky Anderson said, always hoping for a little friction. "Whatta you? You ain't no Spic and you ain't no Wop."

"I ain't no fuckin' nigger either, baby."

"Watch yo'seff!"

"In your hat, black boy."

"Well—what *are* you?"

"I am a Lipan Apache."

"Wassat?"

"I am a North American Indian. My people made America with their hands. And one other thing, baby."

"Wassat, Tonto?"

"I hate niggers."

Kranak was maybe forty. Fingus and Buckley were in their middle thirties. Dawes and Teel were late twenties. The rest were kids.

Kranak told them to keep their mouths shut on the trail. "You think we're all alone up here," he said. "But you don't know nothing. This is like a main street. Cong and Montagnards and traders are moving north and south all around us all the time."

"Nobody gone tell me to keep my mouth shut," Anderson snarled.

"Hey, Anderson!" Buckley said in a low voice.

"You want the shit kicked outa you? You know what is six guys all kickin' you inna head the same time? No more head, that's what it is. So keep your mout' shut, you hear?"

On the second day they lay flat and quiet when a long party of either merchants or Cong went along the narrow trail moving southward with rifles hung across their backs and high, heavy packs on their heads.

They were high up and it was cool. Kranak kept them moving at about twenty-nine miles a day. They were hard men, very fit men. There were 368 miles to go to the rendezvous point, he told everybody on the second night while they were lying over.

"Whatta we gone do when we gits *there*?" Fingus asked in a whisper.

"What the hell you care?" Reyes answered in the darkness. "You got twenny-fi' grand, ri'?"

"Yeah, sure," Fingus said, "but who wants to be a fuckin' grunt for twenty-fi' grand? I wanna know where we *goin'*."

'We're goin' north. What else? Wait'll you get hit before you start cryin'."

"Whose cryin,' man? I *ask*in'."

"You know where we goin,' Kranak," Buckley said. "I mean, like, if you know it's three hunnert and some miles, then you know where we're goin'."

"Listen—every guy here—now get this straight for once an' for all. This is what I know. Nothing else— all right? We are going to a river. You guys ever see a river? We are gonna get in some fuckin' canoes and some fuckin' natives are gonna paddle us someplace. That's all."

"What do you figure from that, Kranak?" Dawes said.

"Well, I figure when the fuckin' natives get us there, somebody will be waitin' there. And whoever is waitin' there will tell us what they paid us the twenty-five grand to do. What else can it happen on us, fahcris-sake, Lieutenant?"

"Listen, Kranak," Buckley whispered. "You know the territory. Many little broads around here?"

"Plenty."

"Sensational!"

"Listen, you know how long it took the guys in my outfit—healthy, strong guys—to screw one of these little broads?"

"How long? What you mean? Like a haffa hour, five minutes or something?" Buckley said.

"No, no! I mean how long before they could get themselves to screw these broads. The broads climb all over you. You got to hold a gun on them they want it so bad."

"I don't get it. I should guess how long and I win? Three seconds, I guess," Buckley whispered.

"The shortest was eighteen days."

"How come? Are they *that* ugly or are they female impersonators?" Buckley asked.

"Because they *stink*, baby. They don't believe in washing like nobody you ever smelled."

"I bet it won't take me any eighteen days," Buckley said. "I bet you twenty dollars I can do it in twelve days.

"I bet you I can do it in three," Reyes said.

They trailed through very high country, sometimes stopping at Meo villages to rest, watching the opium crop being brought in from as far as nine miles away. And smelling the women. Dawes had to wrap shorts around his head the stench was so bad.

"Twenty bucks," Kranak said to Buckley.

"Maybe I better pay you now," Buckley said. "I don't think I'm gonna make it."

Kranak knew what the Meo liked and, in exchange for information, money, or presents, the party was made welcome—but only at two villages where Kranak had once lived and beside whose men he had fought. The Meo women were ever ready to scrag any one of the American party, even after the kind of day's work they had to put in dragging the opium crop up the mountains, but the seven men asked the headman to protect them and settled for a little skull-pop and sleep. Everybody knew Kranak would have them off and moving fast before dawn the next day.

Kranak was a big man with wary eyes. Both his parents had been Lipan Apaches but, early in Kranak's life, his father had come into some money and moved the whole family out of the southwest into New Jersey where he had died of booze. Kranak rarely told anyone he was a Lipan. Since the 1830s there hadn't been any blacks to lean on worth a damn in the whole Southwest Territory and, as soon as the Indians were herded into reservations, they had become the niggers of the region. All his life Kranak carried the fear that people might somehow confuse the idea that being a full-blooded Lipan Apache Indian—the bravest, most resourceful, and cruelest of any North American Indian tribe—was somehow mixed up with being a nigger. For that reason Kranak abominated niggers.

Every third day Kranak gave the men a rest while they did their laundry. He felt it was the best thing for morale and discipline to make them do their laundry. "You guys wanna smell nice to them little Meo chicks, right?" he said.

He washed himself and his clothes first. Then, while the men washed, Kranak sat with his back to them, the Armalite 18 across his lap, his chitinous eyes never seeming to blink as he watched everything move around them.

"Where you figure they got us doin', man?" Anderson asked Teel, beside him.

"Just like the Army. You know the army."

"*He* know the Stockade," Fingus giggled. "Man, did he ever know the *Stock*ade."

"I never fuck around wit' them MPs," Reyes said. "My two years inna army, I play eet rill cool till I rape that lady and everybody dump on me."

"Four more days," Kranak said over his shoulder. "Then we get into the home stretch for the big time."

"What kinda big time you think that is?" Fingus asked.

"Well since I am obviously the only fucking idiot here who has a brain in his head—in charge of a pack of fucking talking chimps, fahcrissake—I will tell you my guess. My guess is that the CIA hired us to knock off some North Viet *capo*—maybe old Ho, ho, ho Chi Minh himself."

"You think they want us for *that?*" Buckley said. "For a lousy twenty-five grand? Shit—they're gonna hafta move that old fucker into some bargain basement like in some Hanoi department store before I help kill the little prick for that kinda money."

"Yeah." Anderson snarled, instantly ready to make trouble. "What kinda rip-off is this?"

"Easy, easy, easy!" Lieutenant Dawes said.

"Listen, you guys," Teel explained reasonably, "Kranak only tellin' us his *guess*. Kranak ain't gone know any more than you or me till we all see The Man, so don't get your balls in an uproar."

"Well, shit," Anderson said. "This is just too fuckin' much like bein' in the fuckin' army. Man, I *hate* the army."

"Anyhow," Fingus said, "how come William Buffalo in this? William Buffalo get me in this. Who got you guys in this?"

"Buffalo . . . Buffalo . . . Buffalo," so many different men said that it sounded like a hunting party of hungry Sioux out scouting for meat on the Great Plains.

"What's wrong with that?" Dawes asked hotly. "If William Buffalo puts a hundred and seventy-five thousand dollars into a down payment for something, then you got to know there is going to be a *big* payday for everybody. William Buffalo is the *cool*est."

"Nobody said nothin' to me 'bout no payday," Anderson growled.

"Why, sure. This got to be the Big Deal. Now you *know* it. William B. is The Man of all the men. Why, now it all come clear to me. We out here to take over a gigantic pile a skag, git it out and git it back to William B. You bet your ass there's gone be a *BIG* pay-day."

"Don't be a sheethead, Fingus," Reyes said. "We de solchurs. We do de durty work."

"*Sol*diers?" Fingus said in such a comical way that all the men laughed. "I don't see no soldiers. Maybe I sees some once soldiers but all I kin see now is a lotta piece men and bank robbers."

"Come on wit' this soldier shit!" Buckley said. "Show me where the money is, show me who ta shoot ta get it, and I'll handle it for you. The name a William Buffalo is good enough fa me."

"Where you from, Lieutenant?" Teel asked pleasantly.

"Idaho."

"This is a funny place to find a West Point guy. I see your ring."

"My old man is a big anarchist. He never let up on me from the time I could talk. He even got me in this outfit."

"What's a anarchist?" Lurky Anderson asked suspiciously.

"We think all government is harmful and unnecessary. Some of us work to destroy all existing governments and one or two think we should change how people behave first."

"No keedeen?" Reyes asked. "People actually theenk like thod? You mean, first you read the book, then you throw the bomb?"

"What the fuck you guys talkin' about?" Dolly Fingus asked. "Is your Daddy happen to be William Buffalo?"

"My father works for William Buffalo," Lieutenant Dawes said proudly. "As an anarchist he believes heroin is a classical way to overthrow the government."

"What gummint?" Lurky Anderson said. "What kinda shit talk is that? Whatta you—some kinda Commie freak?"

"I just told you," Dawes said quietly. "I am here because I am an anarchist."

"An' you say anarchists gone throw over the gummint? You think they git alla us here to throw over the *gummint?*"

"What you care what we here for?" Reyes said. "It's money in the bank, ri'? Sheet, I deen come all the way ott hirr to talk a lotta politics witchew guys. Come on. Who got the cards? We got time."

"Where you from, Cassebeer? What kinda name is Cassebeer?" Fingus asked.

"New York."

"What was your West Point?" Dawes asked.

Teel grinned. "MIT. I'm an experimental physicist."

"You mean you know how to make a nuke?" Dawes asked, eyes wider.

"I kinda know your face from somewhere," Fingus said.

"All you got to know to make a nuke is that a tunable laser excites the two thirty-five, then the ultraviolet radiation knocks the electrons off the atoms and gives them an electric charge."

"Say, Cassebeer," Fingus repeated. "Like how come I know your face?"

"You don't know *my* face. You know my *sister's* face."

"Who dat?"

"Agatha Teel."

"You 'bout the sixth cat who come up an' say he Agatha Teel's brothuh," Anderson said nastily. "Evuhbody Agatha Teel's brothuh—how come she don't send two?"

"She makes out like she's with the poor man," Kranak said from the tree, "but look in the papers and she's always with the rich man."

"You outa you mind, Kranak. She the best. I git a little tahrd of all this shit you peddle," Anderson yelled.

Kranak stood up and threw the Armalite with two hands to Dawes. "Take my duty, Lieutenant," he said. He turned to face Lurky Anderson. "Now I'm just gonna beat the crap outa you so you unnastan' who you're workin' for."

Anderson stood up to his six feet four inches, moving his two hundred and twenty pounds lightly, and towering over Kranak.

"Now you just go ahead an' try that, you poor little fucker," he said, moving fast toward Kranak.

Kranak hit Anderson so hard that he knocked him right across the stream. Only the feet lay in the water.

"Bring him around," Kranak ordered. Buckley and Reyes jumped across the brook and began to slap Anderson's unconscious face. "Wha' hoppen?" Anderson said after two or three minutes.

"Come on, come on!" Kranak snarled at him.

Anderson shook his head, roared with rage and came up from the ground sprinting at Kranak. In about six or seven minutes Kranak had him all cut up.

"Man, you sure can mix it," Dolly Fingus said admiringly. "Lurky tough. Lurky usta fight in prelims."

"He was probably a dressmaker," Kranak said. Everybody enjoyed that noisily. "All right!" Kranak snarled at them. "Pack it up and get it outa here!"

They made the rendezvous without incident, seven hours ahead of schedule. They were deep in North Vietnamese territory. They waited near the Black River for the headman of the Muong to get there with his boatmen. There were about sixty thousand Muong in the Black River region. Their language was an archaic form of Annamese. Kranak could handle it.

The Muong wore Annamite clothes (although they insisted they were Thai), but instead of the male dress being brown it was indigo blue. They were farmers who lived in houses on stilts. They had an aristocratic social organization and an indifference to sexual promiscuity.

Seven light boats came, each with a talisman in the bow: a live cockerel in a cage attached to the prow.

The Muong knew that it was the presence of the cock that got the boats through the rough water. When the boat reached smooth water, the cock was killed and eaten. They didn't need him anymore.

The river course was enclosed by mountains. The heights of the mountain forest turned to deep blue against the light-blue haze in the high sinuous crevices. The river narrowed until they got to the Cho-Bo barrage where the rough water began. The Muong boatmen shot the rapids as if they were all birds seated on flying spears. They made it with the greatest of ease (excepting for the sensation of heart failure among the soldiers) into the Red River. They got to Lao-Kay early in the morning and made a bad breakfast. Buckley said it was worse than Florida prison food. Fingus asked him if he ever tasted French Foreign Legion food. Buckley said, "How the fuck would I taste French Foreign Legion food? Anyways, everybody knows the French make great food."

Fingus spat. "I am tellin' you this. That food, this mornin', was worse than French Foreign Legion food."

Lao-Kay was crowded into a narrow valley that was one of the natural entrances to China. The entrance itself was high up—far up from Mat-son at sea level. They were at the base of a wall of rock that soared like a city skyscraper. China lay more than a mile higher up.

A smiling Hanoi government official came to find them at Lao-Kay. He brought them identical suits of Chinese clothing. He spoke excellent English. He told them how happy he was to have their uniforms for re-indoctrinated American prisoners of war to accomplish many tricks in and out of combat.

"Where we go from here, hombre?" Reyes asked directly.

"You board that train." The official pointed.

"Where do the train goes?" Reyes asked.

"Where? China. Where else?"

"China!" Five men said the same word. Dawes and

Teel kept their cool, but the others were incredulous.

"That's what you're here for, isn't it?" the official asked.

"We don't know what we here for, man," Anderson said. "You tell us what we here for."

"I assure you, sir," the official said, "no information about your destination or your work was passed to me. I am here to apologize for your bad breakfast and to see you aboard the train."

They boarded. The seven men wore A-18s slung over their shoulders. Dawes carried two rifles, his own and Vorshuta's, the GI Kranak had murdered. The Hanoi official issued them plastic identification cards printed in Chinese, carrying their individual pictures, which had been made on the spot. The cards were signed by high Chinese authority and stated their destination so that they also served the purpose of railway tickets.

The train rumbled slowly over the old international bridge built by the French seventy-six years before. Although the journey had hardly begun, they changed trains on the Chinese side, at the Ho-k'u station, 250 feet above sea level. The Chinese customs men and army teams glanced at the plastic cards with boredom.

The seven Americans sat in the long, low Michelin train with a diesel engine. It was packed with Tonkinese and Chinese, many elegant Chinese women. The train climbed swiftly over the road built by the French under a concession granted as one of the last gasps of the Chinese Imperial Government. The railway, one of the great engineering feats of railroading outside Switzerland and Peru, linked the harbor of Haiphong on the South China Sea with Kunming, the capital city of the Yunnan Province, 540 miles away.

The tawny hillsides glowed in the morning light out of tangles of banana trees, palms, and shrubs of castor. Far, far below—down starkly abrupt precipices—

the green waters of the Nam-ti raced, with sapphire-blue birds skimming the surface.

"Where's the fuckin' war?" Kranak asked contentedly.

The train climbed 6,000 feet in thirty-five miles, in and out of tunnels. Rhododendron bushes had taken over from the banana trees. The air was cool. They passed mud-walled villages where hundreds of human figures in every shade of blue moved in preoccupation. Bleak mountains and broad valleys succeeded one another. As the afternoon faded, the train reached the highest point on the railway, at 7,000 feet, before it began its descent into the heart of the Yunnan Province. The train flowed down the mountain to the wide, crowded valley, which had nine months of spring and one of the densest crops of people in the world.

Kunming was in sight ahead of them. Its walls rose unchanged since Marco Polo had arrived as emissary of the Great Khan. They were in the cradle of China. They had completed the second leg of their journey.

17

1968–1969

Before the CIA established Air Opium, the KMT had been able to get only 7 percent of the total Meo opium crop to market. Between March and June the great KMT caravans would begin their massive, slow descent from the heights of the north; a gorgeous ele-

phant train carrying twenty tons of raw opium under
the guard of five hundred troops.

When Bart Simms was put in charge of reorgan-
izing the opium arm of the huge CIA airline in Asia
called Air America, it was already one of the largest
publicly or privately owned airlines in the world (in
combination with its other airline labels—Air Asia,
the Pacific Corporation, and Southern Air Transport).
The entire CIA facility was an airline and maintenance service with 160 heavy transport planes and
20,000 employees—3,500 employees more than the
CIA itself. The maintenance company was larger than
any military facility. It was based on Taiwan.

Air Opium, Bart's operation, was by far the most
complex of the four agency units because it involved
agricultural supervision of the opium (growing it to
U.S. Department of Agriculture standards), the collection of the crop at the ninety-one USAID airstrips
in five countries of Southeast Asia, and the operation
of seven heroin conversion plants. Air Opium traveled
from coordination of the primary work of the Meo
tribesmen in high, burnt-out mountain clearings right
down into the veins of American youth itself.

Bart worked out of a company that existed behind
a door marked G. Wherry and Company in Ta Pae
Street in Muang Phayao. The war continued in Vietnam, Laos, and Cambodia, but Bart moved freely
across all inimical boundaries, tending the world's
opium patch for his government. He made fast friend-
ships in China and in Hanoi. One of his closest friends
in Asia was Lieutenant General Franklin Marx Heller,
the bag man for the MACV command's share of the
heroin industry. Heller was based in Taiwan, the stag-
ing area for distribution. Heller was a fabulous host. He
had the Air Force working for him and he put that
organization to a lot of trouble when he entertained
Bart in Taipeh. General Heller had all his own and his
entertainment food cooked in the States because he
said the fucking Chinks didn't know anything about
real food. With Heller, Bart would eat baked beans

and clam chowder and codfish cakes straight from Boston. He was served *schnitz un knepp:* apples, dumplings, and ham from the Pennsylvania Dutch. Every time Bart flew into Taipeh they had something different: Kentucky burgoo made with squirrel meat; chicken and lamb with plenty of red peppers; Alabama fried pies filled with peach butter; catfish fry; and Milwaukee cheesecake flavored with lemon rind. Heller was such a stickler for the American Way that he got his hot dogs directly from the Sheboygan Bratwurst Festival and his *kalbwurst* straight from the Wurstfest at New Braunfels in the Hill Country of Texas. For a highly placed narcotics executive General Heller was an affable, pseudo-kindly man, but then, he was making a tremendous amount of money while still protecting his Army pension. Bart always hated to leave when the time came to go back to Muang Phayao. He made the trip to Taiwan after each delivery by his airline of one hundred tons of opium or ten tons of heroin, whichever had been invoiced.

"There are an awful lot of people who haven't bothered to find out the facts," Bart told Enid. "I mean people who prefer to frown on The Agency's operating in the narcotics business. My operation is making possible an enormous saving in foreign aid to those greedy Chinese ruling families on Formosa. By helping the Gissimo and the Soongs we are actually helping the American taxpayer. Just look at the facts. Taiwan is about the greediest country for foreign aid anywhere today. In World War Two, General Heller says, they ripped off eight hundred and eighty million in gold *bullion,* for heaven's sake. I mean—*shit.*"

"Try to watch the swearing, hon," Enid said.

What enabled Bart to fly in and out of China and North Vietnam was that his plane carried special identification status (OPI-1) because of the economic importance of his work. He had to be away from Enid for an average of two days and one night a week while he traveled among the Meo farmers. No amount of Enid's wheedling could get him to consent to take her along with him. It was too dangerous flying across those downdrafts in the mountain passes and there was also a war on.

The Meo tribespeople were the last primitives to arrive in the Golden Triangle from the south of China. In upper Tonkin, Bart worked with opium-growing tribal resources of 40,000 Meo. He supervised the crops and crop delivery of 20,000 more on the Tranninh plateau of northern Laos. In Thailand he coordinated 30,000 Akha and Lahu. The Shan grew the crop for him in Burma.

Because the Meo had come into the region only two or three centuries before, they had found the fertile valley bottoms occupied by Thai tribes and the lower mountainous slopes inhabited by Man tribesmen up to an altitude of about 3,000 feet. The Meo had had to accept the steep higher slopes. Opium was the only crop that would grow for them at altitudes of about 4,500 feet. They practiced *ray,* or forest clearing, by felling all growth, then reducing it to burnt ashes. The ashes produced good fertilizer for a year or two, but after that the soil became sterile and was abandoned. The method had disastrous consequences in the gradual deforestration of the country, but it made rich opium crops. Bart nursed along the industry of post-Stone Age people who toiled at the crop that was destroying western civilization to a greater degree than any plague or famine, shepherding his flock from a Chinook helicopter with payload capacity of seven tons over a mission radius of 140 miles with 907 kilograms of bolted-on, built-in armor protection. Bart traveled with his own bodyguard of thirty Thai troops. His flying office ranged from the Yunnan Province of China down through Bun Thai and Pak Seng in North Vietnam to Xieng Mi and Muong Ki in Laos.

On the morning of the seventeenth of March, while the St. Patrick's Day parade was raging in New York and Boston, after twelve marvelous days of R&R with

Enid in Hong Kong, Bart's special identification status aircraft was ambushed by a band of ignorant Pathet Lao guerrillas who had never taken the trouble to understand special identification status. As Bart stepped down from his Chinook onto USAID Strip No. 42. at Nam Kheum, *after* the Thai troops had been deployed to make sure everything was secure, Bart's left kneecap was shattered by a Pathet Lao bullet. "I swear you'd think they were waiting for me," he told Enid much later.

"But why should they be waiting to shoot *you*," Enid asked indignantly, "the only CIA manager who ever brought real prosperity to this region?"

The Chinook left the Thai troops at Nam Kheum and flew Bart out immediately to the nearest U.S. Army Base Hospital at Quang Tri in South Vietnam. The hospital was deep within the war zone but, as per their contract with the Simmses, the agency flew Enid across the mountains from Muang Phayao to be with her brother.

The pain was bad. Enid held his hand tightly, staring desperately into his eyes, pleading with her eyes not to feel the pain or, somehow, to transfer the pain to herself. After the first operation (there would be twenty-three), because she was there to make him feel safe and because of the salvation in the morphine of his own manufacture, Bart relaxed into some limbo while Enid read Jane Austen aloud to him.

"Did you get word to Uncle Herbert?" he whispered.

"Yes, darling."

"Is he working on moving me into Spider?"

"Everything is being taken care of, darling."

"Those Pathet Lao solved everything," Bart murmured.

"Those Pathet Lao may have transferred you right into the White House, sweetheart," Enid said. She kissed him softly on the temple, the forehead, then on the lips. "We're going back to Langley, dear," she said.

The agency flew Bart and Enid back to Washington as soon as the doctors would allow it. Bart spent a ghastly year at Walter Reed in surgery and rehabilitation, with a CIA substitute surgeon and anesthetist standing by in the operating rooms in case the patient began to "talk deliriously," at which point all other personnel would have to leave the room regardless of the stage of the operation. Bart would walk stiff-legged for the rest of his life but, as Enid told him earnestly, that would give him a certain novelty, a distinction as a politician. Sometimes the pain was quite bearable. It depended on the weather, Enid told him, but the very best day for his knee was when Enid marched Uncle Herbert into the hospital room and Bart listened to Uncle Herbert say that he had just come from seeing Mr. Ehrlichman at the White House where final arrangements had been made for Bart's transfer to the job as Assistant Curator at Spider. "The plain fact, Bart," Uncle Herbert said, "is that the agency indicated they'll be darned glad to have you there."

Bart and Enid spent the last two weeks before he reported to Langley at White Sulphur Springs. They had a *marvelous* time. When they got back to Washington, they discovered that Uncle Herbert had arranged to get them a really sweet little house in Georgetown. Although Uncle Herbert sort of pretended he was lending them the house, it wasn't really his. It was government property, a CIA laboratory house, wired for tape recording and sound transmission, equipped with still and sound motion picture cameras that worked behind one-way mirrors or through apertures in all rooms throughout the house. During the time Bart worked at Spider, and he and Enid lived in the house, they were under the agency's surveillance every minute.

Bart's imagination of what the Spider archive must be like had fallen short by 70 percent. The files were the most protean, personal, preternaturally prying records ever assembled on the most deeply concealed and regretted deeds of the foremost men and women of the time. Each day Bart pored over them, committing them to memory. Each night he typed out the information he had carried back to the little house, within his head, on a mathematical symbols typewriter. In the history of the agency he became the only CIA employee who had ever seen this archive from AA to ZZZ. The Curator of Spider was always busy on Admin problems. No one else in the agency, including the Director of Central Intelligence, was allowed to see more than fractional parts of the files because the overall functioning policy of the agency was based upon the "need to know." If the need to know wasn't justified, no Spider information could be released.

Bart accumulated and recorded in mathematical symbols information on terrorists, presidents, educators, actresses, generals, organized criminals, conglomerate operators, bankers, journalists, cardinals, pornographers, philanthropists, politicians and movers and shakers all across the board.

On the eighty-seventh night of their work, Enid leaned across the table and rested her hands lightly on his on the typewriter keyboard. "I think you've found it," she said. "This looks like it."

"Which?"

"That last card."

He picked it up and studied it. "Why?"

"Because he needs you. Maybe to these other people you'd just be a blackmailer and they'd find a way to get rid of you. But not this one. He is very greedy and you can make him richer and richer and richer."

"This fellow? He's a hoodlum in narcotics."

"So?"

"Ah! Aaaaaahhhh!"

"Of course."

"It will take a lot of refining."

"You have the time."

"But you're right. How did I miss him? We've found our angel. We have found the seven million bucks it takes to make an instant senator."

Enid hugged him from behind his chair. "And I

think we've found the fifty million it takes to be nominated as president. Oh, Bart! Now how will you get to him?"

"Love will find a way," Bart said.

"Get out the vice-president's cards. Have him call this man for you."

"That would be using a shotgun on an ant."

"Then lay it out for that kinky senator in the K file. The one from Pennsylvania."

"That's just right. I'll call him tomorrow and explain the facts of life."

In January 1971, Bart was happy that the CIA phase of his life was almost over. In two more days, after his meeting with this leading criminal in New York, he would resign from the agency on medical grounds. He certainly wouldn't have to lie about the trouble his leg was giving him. He was ready, and exhausted by pain, to move up and out into national politics. He and Enid had hated killing just as much as they hated heroin and blackmail, but sacrifices had to be made if one had purpose. And, as Enid said, the plain fact was that there would always be people who had to be killed by some control representing the common good because people like that just lived cross-ways. And what is dope? Enid had asked. Dope is alcohol, a narcotic in a different form. But no one had too much objection to alcohol, did they? When you came right down to it, alcohol and heroin were merely culture-cushions, weren't they? Bart had to agree. He thought about it: "I will hold up my end of the bargain with the American people and do my best to serve them as well as every other statesman."

"I know you will, darling," Enid said.

18

January 1971

J.D. Palladino boarded the 9:15 Staten Island ferry
and sat on the open rear deck so that he could look
at the receding skyline when the boat got underway.
Dom was carrying the suitcase that would record whatever the transmitter in the feather in the band of
Mr. Palladino's hat broadcast while he and this CIA
man had their meeting.

Dom and J.D. had not boarded the ferry together.
They were too smart for that. But they had arrived
in the same car. Bart watched them go into the ferry
building separately. He followed them in with his stiff-
legged walk, taking his time. When the ferry was well
out into the harbor and Mr. Palladino was swiveling
his head, becoming offended by the possibility that he
had been stood up, Bart came up behind him and
tapped him on the shoulder. Mr. Palladino wheeled
in place.

"I am Hobart Simms," Bart said. "Senator Karp
spoke to you about me."

"All right," Mr. Palladino said. He led the way to
the aft bench that encircled the bulkhead facing Dom's
back thirty feet away at the boat's rail. Mr. Palladino
played the heavy hood to the hilt. "What can I do for
you?"

"You can begin by telling your man to bring over
that tape recorder so I can dismantle it or you can't do
anything for me."

"What tape recorder?"

112

Bart didn't answer. He stared with his cold blue eyes, as expressionless as a leopard.

"Dom! Bring the suitcase."

Dom was bewildered, but he did as he was told. Bart opened the case and removed the cassette.

"What the hell is this?" Dom demanded in his tough, occupational way.

"Go look at the buildings," Mr. Palladino told him. Dom moved away.

"All right!" Mr. Palladino snarled at Bart.

"I am not saying that Turkish opium isn't going to make a big comeback," Bart said, "but it is going to be very expensive. What you are buying from Pierre Weill in Marseilles now is heroin made from the Turkish reserve, but the delivery is unreliable. The Bureau really have the French cased and the French hate to pay. So—in our mutual interest—I am here to offer you either a thousand kilos of raw opium or a hundred kilos of the purest but if you take the heroin you are crazy."

"What the fuck can I do wit' raw opium?"

"Take the opium and I will offer you a thousand-percent safe place to convert it to heroin so that, instead of paying twenty-seven thousand a keye to import it, you'll be converting to heroin at a cost of six thousand a keye for the highest quality heroin—with guaranteed, one-hundred-percent safe delivery."

Mr. Palladino blinked.

What Bart had said went into Mr. Palladino's hat feather transmitter, then into a receiver-recorder in a cardboard carton which Dino had beside him on the continuous bench around the corner along the bulkhead, out of sight. Dino could not see the receding skyline as well, but otherwise he was placed pretty good. Not like Dom.

"If anybody can do that, why ain't you doing it?" Mr. Palladino asked. "What is this—giving away heroin for six thousand a kilo?"

Bart didn't answer. He puffed on a foul pipe. Gulls

cawked. Tugs tooted. Dino watched the Statue of Liberty.

"Where do you get the opium?"

"Asia."

"Where is this hundred-percent safe place to convert?"

"Haiti."

"Who guarantees it?"

"The President of Haiti."

"What would I need you for after I had a deal like that?"

"You would take the best kind of care of me, Mr. Palladino, because I know you turned in the Sesteros. And I know you gave them Abramo Viseggi for the Comanti killing."

Mr. Palladino got to his feet immediately and rushed unsteadily to the ferry rail and vomited over the side. He leaned against the rail for a few minutes, then he went directly to the cardboard box on the bench at Dino's side, picked it up and flung it into the Upper Bay. Weakly, he went back to the seat on the bench beside Bart.

"You doubled up on tape machines?" Bart asked with admiration.

Mr. Palladino nodded. "Let's talk about your deal," he said hoarsely. "How you gonna move it?"

"The vice-president will call President Duvalier for an appointment for you. You will go to Haiti to set the deal with him and he will grab it. When you have it set I'll go to Asia and set the opium shipments from Taiwan to Port au Prince."

"What is your end?"

"In a minute. To sweeten Duvalier for you, Senator Karp is going to arrange for Education and Potable Water Loans for Haiti from the Inter-American Bank which will apply when he agrees to our plan."

"How do you know he'll take the deal?"

"Because he's been cut off from foreign aid for seven years and we're going to get it back for him."

"I can't say anything until I know what your end is."

"I don't want any split if that's what you're worrying about. I want to be elected United States Senator from Maryland. That takes a lot of money but still not the kind of money that would even dent the kind of deal I am handing you."

"How much?"

"Out of this deal—and I have only told you part of it, I have other, bigger angles—I want seven million five hundred thousand dollars to be paid directly into my campaign in a way I'll lay out when the time comes. Then, every year for the next four years you pay seven million five directly into another campaign fund in the same way."

"What other campaign fund?"

"From the day I make it into the Senate, I'll be running for President. When I run, I'll need more money because a lot of money has to be spread around. But you'll never miss it. And you'll have a friend in the White House."

Mr. Palladino felt an enormous surge of pride. If his father had ever thought that his own son would be in a position like this he would have kissed his feet. His father! A man who thought a big political contract was like Frank Costello, fahcrissake! He couldn't believe what was happening. He would be J.D. Palladino: kingmaker! A *king*maker! He took a pale lavender silk handkerchief out of his breast pocket and laid it over his face. He leaned back on the bench and tried to think.

Bart puffed on the foul pipe. Dino watched the seagulls and New Jersey. Bart turned down a shoeshine man's offer silently, shaking his head. Mr. Palladino whipped the handkerchief off his face and sat up straight.

"Fill me in about this president in Haiti," he said huskily.

"Do you know Haiti?"

"Well——"

"You know where Cuba is?"

"Well, yeah. I been there. It's near Havana, right?"

"Cuba is ninety miles away from Florida. Haiti is about six hundred miles east of Havana, sixty miles off the far end of Cuba. The fake reason you will be going to Haiti is to lease the casino. I have a gimmick to bring in tourists. A lot of tourists means a country is stable. When it's stable, that means we can restore foreign aid because then Haiti will be a bulwark against Communism."

"I think I am getting you," Mr. Palladino said. "A little bit. Maybe."

"When you get home, pick up a pencil and figure out how much money there is in the manufacture of uppers, downers and acid, then figure out how much the legitimate pharmaceutical houses are ripping you off when they leave you just the wholesale end. When you get the heroin plants operating smoothly, then you'll set up your own plants in Haiti to make uppers, downers, speed and acid. And mandrax and STP and mescaline and Phencycladine."

"What's that? We never handled that."

"It's going to be very big. It causes frightening hallucinations in humans. It makes them feel extremely tiny, as if they could hide in keyholes or matchboxes. It gives them a sense of already being dead."

"Jesus, that will be a real seller," Mr. Palladino exclaimed.

19

January–February 1971

Mr. Palladino's greed overcame his fear. He sat in motionless fright after Bart left him, thinking about one man walking around with information about the Sesteros and Abramo in his head. Mr. Palladino didn't want to think about anything until he had figured out how to handle this peril. The smartest thing, he knew, would be to have the little prick hit. But he couldn't bring himself to have that done because the man was going to get him so much money. Worse, the man wasn't interested in money. He was really tilted on that one thing: politics. He must be crazy. This man wasn't really interested in nailing J.D. Palladino. He didn't really give a shit about the Sesteros or Abramo. But who could be sure? Who wanted to make a billion dollars with this son-of-a-bitch standing behind the door with a raised pickaxe? All right, maybe he couldn't bring himself to like the situation entirely, but with the kind of money involved like it was involved here, he could get himself to forget it. If he could only figure out how to get a lock on the man, then everything would be all right. If he could get something on him as big as what the man had on him then it would be an Indian stand-off. He could do it. That was his specialty: planning. They were going to meet again that night on the Staten Island ferry and the man was going to fill him in on what to say in Haiti. So he would have him followed when the man got off the ferry and maybe find out something useful.

Mr. Palladino didn't know what he wanted to find out but he knew he would know it when he saw it. And he knew he had to get a lock on this man or go back to living the way he had lived for fourteen months after he had betrayed the Sesteros, while he waited for their people to find out who had done it.

Eight days later Mr. Palladino's Jet Star with its six Pratt & Whitney JT12A-6A turbojet engines and a 2,000-mile range took off for Haiti. When they were airborne, Mr. Palladino dictated letters to Angela. Dom and Dino played gin. Eight days had been enough to find out a little about Hobart Willmott Simms. Palladino was beginning to think he would be able to throw a lock on this man. The Haitian deal was clear, the Indian stand-off was getting clearer.

When they touched down at the President François Duvalier International Airport at Port au Prince, there was a big crowd waiting, so Mr. Palladino sent Dom to find out what it was all about while he continued to dictate to Angela. Dom opened the door and stopped short on the ramp. A black colonel of the Haitian Army in full dress uniform was starting to come up the ramp.

"You," Dom said. "Off."

Had Dom remained there the outraged colonel might have shot him, but Dom went back into the plane and slammed the door.

Dino was helping J.D. into his green silk suit jacket.

"They got about a company of troops outside," Dom said. "And about thirty plainclothesmen. And they all got guns."

"Whatta you expect soldiers to carry, fahcrissake?" Mr. Palladino said amiably, deeply pleased by the military reception. "Come on. Let's go."

Dom went out first, then J.D., then Dino; Angela last. At the foot of the ramp the Haitian colonel saluted smartly, his face stiff with rage. A sergeant bawled out to present arms. Mr. Palladino set his face into an important cast.

Everybody sweated out layered heat. The Secret Police were duplicates of each other; expressionless faces, large shades, Hawaiian shirts, and tiny fedora hats with one-inch brims. No one but the arriving party moved; no one spoke. There was no breeze; only the pounding heat and the weight of the sun. The colonel led the way to a Cadillac limousine. The heat was awful. The heat reminded Mr. Palladino of his trip to Sicily. "You gotta go back someday, Joey," his mother had said.

"How can I go back, Mama? I never been there." But he had gone back. That was the last time he had ever felt heat like this. So the limousine was air conditioned, so instead he'd get pneumonia.

The colonel's staff car led the motorcade, which included two filled personnel carriers bringing up the rear. The motorcade rolled them through the worst slums Mr. Palladino had ever seen including Cortile Cascino in Palermo. "Jesus," he said, "somebody up there is really sore at these people. The people gotta be the enemy here."

"Listen," Dino said, "the guy is probably takin' us t'rough duh heart of the high-rent district."

The procession stopped in front of an elegant guest house with about four acres of grounds at Petionville. As they walked up the path to the house, the colonel explained that it had been built for Haile Selassie, Emperor of Ethiopia, but that the Emperor had decided he could only stay in Haiti for the afternoon so the house had never been used; a relief to Dom.

Mr. Palladino tipped the colonel ten dollars in the front hall and walked on through the house to inspect the furniture. It was the best. It cost plenty. When he got back to the front hall he found the ten-dollar bill on the floor. "What is this?" he asked Dino.

"He t'roo it onna floor and spit on it. I swear to God."

"Fuck him," Mr. Palladino said. "Pick it up by the end and burn it."

There was a large swimming pool in the gardens

beside the house. There was plenty of help. The help wore guns, shades, and little hats. Dom and Dino didn't want them to wear guns. The help didn't want to take the guns off. Dino whacked a couple of them around while Dom covered him. One of the help pulled a gun, so Dom shot him in the arm. Everybody but Dom and Dino took their guns off after that. Mr. Palladino came out after he heard the shot and told the help to get them a platter of roast beef sandwiches on whole wheat toast and a couple of bottles of red wine. It was impossible to believe, considering the amount of help, but the food never came.

"They don't dig English, Mr. Palladino," Angela explained. "They speak French here."

"Well, what the hell, then—that explains it," J.D. said generously.

They sat around the pool. Nice music came from behind the bushes on the other side. At about nine o'clock three sharp-looking black foxes came over in a green Bentley. Dom and Dino took turns fooling around with them upstairs. Mr. Palladino dictated steadily to Angela, sipping a very small rum with a lot of ice and pineapple juice. He was wearing his silver granny glasses, looking like the wolf in the fairy tale with his kingfisher nose and his tiny eyes focusing his concentration.

"Fahcris*sake*, Angela. I am starving here," he said at last. Angela got up and ran toward the house to see what was in the Frigidaire. She found some people in the kitchen and made them bring out a big plate of cold chicken, some bread and butter, and some cold white wine. Everybody ate.

At twelve fifteen, nine large black cars came roaring up the driveway behind a weapons carrier crowded with armed soldiers to meet President Duvalier's seven o'clock appointment with Mr. Palladino. For once Mr. Palladino was grateful that somebody was a little late because he had been able to get rid of all his dictation.

He wasn't exactly unclear anymore about the President of Haiti. He knew they called him Papa Doc, which sounded nice. Bart Simms had told him that Papa Doc wore his high silk hat into the bathtub because it helped him to meditate and that he kept the head of his (former) enemy, Philogenes, in his office, right on his desk and, when possible, preferred to have his opposition stoned to death after reading the auguries for the day in the entrails of slaughtered animals. Mr. Palladino thought Papa Doc sounded very Sicilian.

As Simms had explained it, as long as Papa Doc voted with the United States against Cuba in the United Nations and the OAS, he did all right because they paid cash for the vote. Papa Doc needed a lot of money because one half of the revenue of the country was spent on his personal security.

The four visitors watched the weapons carrier screech to a stop, disgorging troops, which scurried to surround the third Cadillac, which had stopped directly at the footwalk to the swimming pool. From the other eight Cadillacs forty-eight men wearing large shades, Hawaiian shirts and beanie fedoras debouched rapidly and arranged themselves around the soldiers or found positions behind shrubs, or placed empty chairs.

"Jesus, you gotta admire this operation," Mr. Palladino said to Angela. "Get in the house." Angela left quickly.

Two thrillingly bemedaled large, black, gold-aguilleted military figures got out of the key limousine. The second man out wore a circle of five stars on each shoulder. He stood at attention holding the limousine door open. A shortish, white-haired, elderly black man wearing a black Homburg hat, a blank-white shirt with a black four-in-hand tie and a black suit got out of the car and came smiling up the path. Mr. Palladino now got to his feet, turned his head slightly and said, "Okay, Dom. Cool it. This is the deal."

The security men blended into the foliage. Only François Duvalier, President of Haiti, his Chief of Staff, and his aide came forward to greet Haiti's guest. He reminded Mr. Palladino of a Jones distributor in South Chicago named Grunts Patterson. The two leaders shook hands cordially.

"My Chief of Staff, General Guerin-Reynaud," Mr. Duvalier said simply. "My son-in-law, Lieutenant-Colonel Max Drouax, who is also my aide-de-camp." The officers bowed stiffly. The President sat down. Mr. Palladino sat down. The officers seated themselves slightly behind the President. Mr. Duvalier spoke excellent French-accented English. (*And you better believe it,* Mr. Palladino told himself.)

"I apologize for the unpleasant need for the shooting here this evening," the President said, "but you were absolutely right."

"No, no!" Mr. Palladino protested. "It was a mix-up. The help here were all wearing guns and it made my people nervous except they didn't know how to explain it in French."

"Well, bless you, sir—but these were not household staff. They were a part of my security force whom I sent out to protect you."

"Protect me from what?"

President Duvalier smiled sweetly, giving his head a sideways wag. "It will be hard for a freedom-loving man such as you to grasp, sir, but I was born under the military dictatorship of Nord Alexis. I was one year old when General Simon overthrew him, four when the revolution threw out Simon, five when the explosion blew up the old Palais National and President Cincinnatus LeConte. I was six when President Tancred August was poisoned and so on and on. The mulatto population are violent people, Mr. Palladino. But I am teaching all of my people calm and to do this I have chosen only associates I can trust, no matter how ignorant they are."

"Aaaaahh," Mr. Palladino said, "no wonder they wouldn't bring any food."

"No *food?*" the President for Life snarled, turning to stare into General Guerin-Reynaud's impassive face. The General got up and strode into the house.

"Oh! Hey! Wait!" Mr. Palladino called after him. "We straightened it out! We finally got some food ourselves in the kitchen."

"Guests of the Republic don't get their own food," Dr. Duvalier said. "Inevitably, you will want to eat again. It is possible that my Tonton Macoutes have trussed up the household staff."

"Tonton Macoute?"

"Yes," Dr. Duvalier said, smiling at the chance to impart Haitian folklore. "Tonton Macoute means Uncle Knapsack. He was a legendary giant who strode from mountaintop to mountaintop, stuffing bad little boys and girls into his knapsack. With affection, my people have named their security force after him."

"I don't get it."

"But—with all my talk of shooting, trussing and revolution you must not form the impression that we are an uncivilized people."

"Hey! Never."

"Richard Nixon has had glorious times here in our new, luxury marble mountain villa at Turgeau. When he was vice-president. Oh, *yes!*"

General Guerin-Reynaud returned with a basket of apples and two bottles of Seven-Up for President Duvalier.

"Forgive me," the President said, "but I *adore* imported apples. Then, last week, after your present vice-president called me about seeing you, I took the liberty of making inquiries about your work, and I must say the results have stimulated my curiosity."

"Call me Joe," Mr. Palladino said.

"How kind. Joe, I go to a sad mission tonight. Nineteen of my officers have been revealed as traitors to the Republic and I am on my way out to Fort Dimanche to have them shot. So you will understand why we will be unable to have a lot of time together tonight."

"Listen! You can be as quick as you want. I have a very simple proposition. I can lay out all the details."

"Never mind the details. How much money is involved and how do we share it?"

"It's a large piece of money."

"Good."

"You get fifteen percent off the top. Of the gross. From the first dollar."

"No."

"In Cuba we gave only nine point three percent and it threw off so much money it buried them."

The President shrugged delicately with the slightest shiver of disapproval. "Cuba is not Haiti," he said.

"What's your idea, Doc?"

"Equal shares. I supply the country and total protection. You supply the capital, the knowledge and the technicians."

"I supply much more than that, Doc."

"For a gambling casino?"

"The casino is only the flash," Mr. Palladino said slowly. "Also I'm gonna turn this place into a tourist paradise because it already is a tourist paradise. When that happens we can claim total stability here, which means my friends can get you back on foreign aid."

The President's white eyebrows lifted.

"And that's only the beginning," Mr. Palladino said.

"How do you bring in the tourists?"

"Look—Doc—there are maybe four big travel wholesalers. The biggest. They buy up all the hotel rooms, all the hot dogs, the broads, whatever, and when everything is in, they roll it out, piece by piece, to the retail travel agents and they tell them this is the country the retailers are going to buy and feature for the next seven years and everybody wins. If you can't make a little country like France or Greece in seven years it's never gonna get made."

"France?"

"A friend of mine has dug up some information on Charley Graffis, you never heard of him. He is one of the four biggies. Out of Detroit. When we talk to him he will agree your country rates it."

"Fascinating."

"The people walk into a travel agent. They think they're gonna go up to the Catskills and—*voom*—they end up here."

"What do I get fifteen percent *of*, Joe?"

Mr. Palladino ticked the items off his fingers. "Casino action, car rentals, hotel construction, hotel throwoff, roads, organized broads, post cards and native souvenirs which we will design and make for you in Akron, Ohio. You get one hundred percent on airport taxes, gasoline taxes, fishing boat rentals and night club action. You raise the price on post office stamps by three cents and you pick up a half a million dollars. You use dollars here?"

"*I* do. The people use gourdes."

"Jesus. When my partner gets foreign aid back for you—how much were you getting when they cut you off?"

"Twelve and a half million a year."

"My partner will make that twenty and our finder's fee will be the same as your cut on my end—fifteen percent, no more."

The jungle was close by and its night noises became deafening all at once. Then the noise faded down, giving everything to an enormous yellow moon that hung almost within reach like an overripe melon waiting to be cut up as Mr. Palladino told Dr. Duvalier about the loan for Education and Potable Water from the Inter-American Bank. Dr. Duvalier had become very much interested. "Now," Mr. Palladino said, "all that is just the chickenshit part, Doc. That is just the flash."

"I cannot anticipate you," Dr. Duvalier said imperturbably, "excepting that our own investigations indicated that you were mainly in the narcotics business."

"That is correct. And that is the real part. That is the important bread."

"I get fifteen percent of that?"

"You get a thousand a kilo on the raw."

"What do you pay per kilo?"

"It isn't settled yet."

"Let's say five hundred a kilo."

"I don't know. It just isn't settled yet."

"Well, I know. I know because I checked it."

"What are you driving at?"

"At five hundred a kilo you will be making a prodigious, breathtaking profit when you convert it to heroin."

"You can't begin to imagine my expenses. The people in Asia, the transport, my partner, the chemists, the mules, the risks, the greed of the cops and politicians—present company excepted, naturally."

Dr. Duvalier nodded acknowledgment as he said, "I think you can afford to pay me four thousand a kilo for this kind of security."

"Listen, Doc—I can go up to fifteen hundred a kilo. And I'll be dealing in hundreds of tons, here."

"Then you'll have to reduce your finder's fee on the foreign aid to three percent."

"I am showing a lot of good will here. I mean a whole tourist industry, foreign aid, the Inter-American Bank, the souvenir design and manufacture. But I'll tell you what I'll do. I'll accept the three percent finder's fee for the foreign aid and the bank loans if you will pay for the construction of the heroin conversion plants."

"How much is that?"

"Say eighty thousand dollars—a token."

"All right," President Duvalier said decisively, clapping his hands down hard upon the arms of his chair. "I guarantee construction costs up to eighty thousand dollars. Not a penny more, Mr. Palladino. Now you must excuse me. I must go off and shoot my officers."

20

July 1971

The Operation Enigma committee of the Joint Chiefs of Staff was composed entirely of General officers. Lieutenant General Ludlow "Petey" Doncaster chaired the meeting. General Richards "Biff" Marek represented the Special Intelligence Section. Fleet Admiral Harold "Seagull" Matson sat in for the Navy even though the Navy could not have anything to do with this kind of operation. Two Major-Generals, Luther "Bosco" Beemis and Gordon "Kiddo" Manning completed the committee. Every man in the room was a preeminent Intelligence specialist; cold war or hot.

There were no recording stenographers, full clearance or not. General Doncaster didn't want any of the proceedings leaking to the White House.

"I'll set down some rules for procedure. We will refer to our operative as the Agent because it makes no difference whether that agent is a man or a woman. And the Chairman, Joint Chiefs, regards this as such an important mission that we do *not*—I repeat, not—even want to refer to the Agent by the name of the person replaced. Now—not everything has worked out as planned. The first subject de-briefed by Dr. Baum survived only long enough to provide insufficient information to shape up a vitally necessary new profile for the Agent and we had to start over again. General Marek got some lucky breaks when his people worked with prison and probation information records and with personnel at Joliet, Dannemora and

Canon City. We were able to complete the shape of the person's background and psychical profile without difficulty.

"Well, the Agent is now operating. The group must be inside China now. General Marek?"

Marek was an enormous man whose shoulders looked like they had come in pre-fab sections and were going to fall out through the sleeves of his tunic. He was an intent, possessed man with a fanatic's eye.

"More importantly, *the Agent* must have had time to reach the destination, which we assume is China. Now—it is absolutely in-evitable that the instant those persons reach a base inside China, wherever that base may be, and we have the most sensitive Air Force reconnaissance working on that, it is in-evitable that everyone in that party, including our Agent, is going to be debriefed. The question is this: is the seal Dr. Baum locked into the Agent's consciousness and unconsciousness going to be strong enough to withstand a really painstaking Chinese brainwash? I mean, that's it. Right there. Everything stands or falls on that."

General Manning cleared his throat. Manning was a psychiatrist. He did not approve of Dr. Baum or of the Intelligence Services' use of Dr. Baum. "Well, speaking for myself, and this area is *slightly* more my field than anybody else's here today, I don't see how this Agent has any more chance than a snowball in hell to beat an expert Chinese de-briefing. Those guys in*vented* these kinds of tactics. They've been at it *cen*turies longer than Baum or any other German sadist-quack."

"Well, the hell with that, Kiddo," General Doncaster said. "We've got to go along. And I don't give a good goddam what you think of Baum. He hasn't failed us yet, and if he says the Agent is sealed then that Agent is sealed."

"All right then, Petey! But for the record, of which there is none present, I say right now that the Chinese, with their guile and techniques, are going to nail this Agent."

Bosco Beemis spoke delicately, to get them on to a new subject. "Did anybody figure out *any* way for the Agent to get intelligence out of China?"

"'Well, maybe it could be done, General Beemis, if we knew where he was. We could probably pay some Chinese to go in from Hong Kong to contact him, but there are two things wrong with that," Marek said. "First, we can't let go of the identity of the Agent, and certainly not to some makeshift Chinese drop. Secondly, finding where those people have been sent in a country the size of China is really going to be like finding a needle in a haystack. We've got to start with some educated guesses as to where *we* would establish a base camp for people like that, then we've got to begin to overfly it and photograph it systematically and take our chances on the political flack.'"

"Well," Gordon Manning said, "I'll tell you something that is no news to anyone here. This thing purely scares the *shit* out of me."

21

April 1971

The seven American soldiers were flown by daylight from Kunming to Chengtu in the Szechwan Province, about 600 miles, in a battered, gallant DC3. At Chengtu they were transferred to a railway train which took them 480 miles northeast to the big junction at Pao-chi, then by another train northwest for another 390 miles to Hsi-ning, capital of the Tsinghai Province.

"You gotta say one thing about these people," Teel

said to Kranak during the rail journey, "they sure don't worry about comfort."

The Tsinghai Province, in the far west of China, on the Plateau of Tibet, which is the loftiest highland area of the world, had an average elevation of 13,000 feet, sustaining about 12 percent less oxygen than at sea level. The mountains of the Tsinghai Province descended in broad steps from The Roof of the World at Ch'iang-t'ang, down to mountains that ranged at about 6,000 feet, then, at the eastern part of the province, at the Kansu border, down to only 3,000 feet.

The Tsinghai Province had the smallest population of all the states of China; 2,000,000 people in 278,000 square miles; eight people to the square mile. (The Kuang-Tung Province, in south China, had an area of only 87,000 square miles and a population of 42,800,000 people.) Perhaps the Mongols and Tibetans—45 percent of the people of Tsinghai—were responsible for the small population because of their tradition of having one son from every family enter a lamasery. Tsinghai had come under Chinese control in the third century B.C. It was made a province of China in 1928. Summers were intensely hot and dusty here; winters dry, cold, and windy with temperatures averaging 12 degrees below freezing.

The eastern part of the province was a high plateau between the complex Ch'i-lien and Nan-Shan ranges on the north and the Pa-yen-ku-la range in the south. These were broken by a series of ranges with their axes running northwest to southeast. The mountains reached 11,000 feet and enclosed the basin of the 70-mile-long, 45-mile-wide Lake Kokonor.

"Lissen, I'm tellin' ya something," Buckley said. "I gotta get outa here. Who ever saw so many Chinks? It suffocates me."

"So—mail yourself home to Mommy," Kranak said.

"Mail?" Buckley snorted. "Where's the mailbox? Where's the telephone? Where's the *Daily News*?"

"You can't even buy a fuckin' samwitch. On a

fuckin' train platform, you can't buy a samwitch," Fingus keened.

"Aaaa, shaddup!" Kranak said.

"How many days we been traveleen?" Reyes said rhetorically. "What they gonna do—hide us someplace? What kinda job ees thees gung be, hombre? I tell you what I tell them when I see them. Shove you job up you ass. I quit. Get me outa here."

"Listen—fellas—" Dawes said quietly. "Now you might as well take it easy because any operation that is as long and elaborate as getting seven Americans into China, then keeping them traveling for days, sure sounds to me like we're in for a long, long stay."

"How long?" Buckley said harshly.

"How do I know? I mean—well, say, maybe a year —who knows?"

"A *year*?" Fingus sounded really frightened.

"I can't take it in any *kind* of army for like even a month," Anderson whined. "I just cain't take any army. I mean, I wasn't meant to *be* in any army."

"You been in prison?" Teel asked abruptly.

"Course I been in prison. What that got to do wid anything?"

"This is better than bein' in prison, ain't it?" Kranak asked. "I mean, you got travel, you got twenty-five grand to fall back on, you got mystery, excitement and ——"

"Better than *prison*? Man, are you crazy? What's wrong with a good prison? What the hell good is my twenty-five thou out here with a buncha people who talk like they won a free two weeks in a zoo? Travel —this travel is breakin' my *ass*——"

"Lemme tell ya something. No fuckin' around on this thing. Sooner or later we got to get where we're going," Buckley said, "and I'm gonna lay the facts on The Man. These are The Facts: I'm gettin' out of this fuckin' country, if I gotta walk all the way out."

"These goddamn people out that winda all look alike!" Dolly Fingus said wildly.

The seven Americans had no layover in Hsi-ning,

the only large city in the province. They were hustled out of the train and into an ancient but immaculately kept Reo sedan and driven to the local military airport where they were put into a Japanese-built Sikorsky S-62A helicopter, which could be pushed along as fast as a cumulus cloud, about 105 miles per hour.

"Where we going?" Kranak asked the bald, middle-aged Chinese who had been assigned to them. Kranak spoke very slow, probably very broken, P'u-t'ung-hua, the most universal Chinese speech. He seemed to get through. The man answered, 'Ssu-hsin."

"How far?" That was an impossible question because the man didn't understand distances in miles. Only in changs. Kranak couldn't figure changs. It took 154 minutes to get to Ssu-hsin, so Dawes later figured the camp must be 200 miles west of Hsi-ning.

"How did you ever pick up the lingo?" Dawes asked Kranak.

"Hell, it's the basic speech of Southeast Asia as well as China. These people trade everywhere. I been out in Asia a long time, like maybe six years before I went in the army. That's how I made Special Forces. I always had an ear. Well, not an ear, you know. I was never afraid of wadin' right into these languages."

Everything turned back into Armyland when they alighted at the training camp. A spit-and-polish, parade-ground major of Chinese regular infantry was waiting for them at the chopper-pad. He spoke California American, all dipthongs and drawls with R sounds as hard as diamonds and a two-note lilt. He shook their hands like an insurance salesman let loose in a fold of lottery winners. He motioned to three Chinese enlisted men to take the American gear.

"I'll hang on to my rifle if you don't mind," Kranak said nervously.

"In a pig's ass," the major said. He snarled at one of the soldiers who pulled the rifle off Kranak's back. "It'll be a long time before you need a rifle," the major said sweetly.

He led the way toward a gaggle of wooden buildings saying, "This is Camp Cody." It looked like most forward military reservations around the world. It had barracks, offices, classrooms and an officers' club grouped around a central common. Scattered over the electrically fenced 495 acres, some of them wooded, there were weapons ranges, jump towers, a maze of metropolitan city streets complete with sewers and underground conduits just as if this were the old back lot at Metro. Away in a different direction from these central and sprawled facilities were heavily guarded off-limits sites, used for the heavy clandestine work, simulating super-secret projects such as training an important agent from the enemy side, or for torture techniques expansion, or for de-briefing a recent defector. The more painful side of brainwashing was done out in these areas; called "psychological debriefing." Every trainee had to undergo fourteen weeks of this rigorous experience beginning the second day after his arrival.

Classes from each country were shown films of city problems of their own country four times a week. These films directly applied to the courses of study so that the students could relate the abstracted problems to the terrain with which they were familiar, right down to traffic patterns, lighting, uniforms, and the people they would be expected to destroy. Specific films showing interiors of various government buildings in many important cities of the world had been obtained to provide clear lessons in assassination opportunity.

"How many trainees you got here?" Dawes asked.

"About sixty right now," Major Wong said. "Now —hear this! This is the general rule. You fraternize with the other trainees at night—if you can still stand —at the Officers' Club. There is no Enlisted Men's Club because there are no enlisted men. Every trainee here is going out of here to become an important, high-ranking guerrilla leader. But you are going to earn it. All day long, from six ayem forward, we work your ass off and you better believe it."

"We're back in the fuckin' army," Kranak said.

"Right. Now—practice calling me Cal—not Major Wong, repeat, not Major Wong—because psychological studies say the use of a given name makes everything easier for Americans, Australians, and Irish. Each man has his own room. Each man has an orderly. Each man gets four American magazines and comic books a week and a copy of the Albanian edition of *Playboy*, called *Po*, with whom we have a special deal. Each man gets forty minutes with a woman each week, on a staggered schedule, and an option, not compulsory, for another forty minutes on Sunday afternoon between four and six."

"I thought you guys had outlawed prostitution," Dawes said.

"Prostitution? These are female non-coms from our Western Army! They're entitled to a little recreation, too, you know."

They were given the rest of the day to get settled. "Feel free to wander around the compound but no farther," Major Wong said. "Beginning tonight and for the next three years you'll be messing at my table, Little America. Chow at six peeyem. Only me or the doctor can get you out of chow."

"What's the food like?" Jonas Teel asked.

"You'll be so hungry after a day's work, you'll love it."

"But what's it like?"

"It's army chow. Does that answer your question, mister?"

"I got a coupla questions myself," Tom Buckley said. "What the hell is this? Whatta we doon here?"

"Yeah!" Anderson said. "Nobody told us we gone end up wid a buncha fuckin *COMM*nists! What you guys trine do here?"

Major Wong looked at them with elegant distaste. "You have been paid—each one of you—enough money to keep this entire province eating for some time." He walked slowly to stand in front of Anderson. "When you speak to me, you will ask my permission to speak, then you will stand at attention as you speak." Anderson began to mumble. Major Wong struck him across the face so hard that he spun almost entirely around. Every American gasped.

"Attention! All of you!" Wong barked. They came to attention.

"You are here to be trained. Fortunately for you it is going to be easy and pleasant for you and you are going to look forward to each day when you awaken because you are going to be indoctrinated—debriefed—then, if you reach the standards that have been set by your American leader, you will become important military commanders in your own country. If you fail in this matter of adjusting to what we require of you, you will be considered psychologically useless and you will be shot."

"Sir!" Dawes said smartly.

"You may speak, Lieutenant Dawes."

"The basic question that seems to be repeated by the men, sir, is—how long can they expect to be on this duty?"

"Four years." There was a strangled sound from the men. "But, you have your revenge," Major Wong said smiling. "I will be required to be here with you. When you have dismissed the men, Lieutenant Dawes, they will go to their quarters and you will remain here and Private Teel will remain here."

"Yes, sir. Dis-miss!" The five men tumbled out of the area to sit down and talk the catastrophe over.

When they had gone, Major Wong said, "I have all the dossiers. I know you are a West Point graduate, Lieutenant Dawes."

"Yes, sir."

"What is your opinion of these men?"

"They have no morale, Major Wong."

"Don't worry about their morale. Our modern techniques, based on ancient studies, will take care of re-conditioning them. Are they healthy?"

"Yes, sir."

"Are they murderous and deeply violent?"

"Yes, sir."

"Those are the things we cannot instill in them, so that is good news indeed. Private Teel," he smiled. "Mr. Teel, I should say. You will be leaving to spend the next three years away from these great and good friends," he smiled more broadly, "working with our nuclear scientists in the Hupeh Province. Very international there, Teel. You'll be able to use your French."

The five other men gathered in Kranak's room. "Okay, democracy rules," Buckley said. "I move we conk the Chink and hijack that helicopter and then make him fly us out to Hong Kong."

"I'm witchew!" Dolly Fingus said.

"I'm the one who gits to do the conkin'," Anderson said, " 'cause I'm the one who hadda take his shit."

"Well, I theenk you guys is crazy—but—" Reyes shrugged—"eet's the only game in de tonn."

"What you say, Sarge?" Buckley asked Kranak.

He looked at them blankly. "Say? Say what?"

"Say let's conk the Chink and hijack a plane outta here."

"Oh, fahcrissake!"

"Whatsamatta? You chicken."

"That's it. That's right. Exactly right. I am chicken."

"Whut the hell you talkin' 'bout, man?" Anderson said aggressively. "You jes' do whut you told and maybe even then you won't be all raht."

"I'll do what I'm told. Every time that major tells me. Did you happen to notice the Permanent Party here or did yiz find some blow someplace and you are too stoned to see? There are about three *hundred* Chink soldiers inna Permanent Party here an' they run with nice, new Russian automatic weapons. Does that tell you something, Dr. Einstein?" he said to Anderson. "There is a doctor inna balcony, Captain Marvel," he said to Buckley.

"Oh, shit! We stuck," Dolly Fingus moaned.

"You bet you ass we stuck," Reyes said. "But not oney that, hombre."

"What?" Fingus asked, always ready with the straight line.

"We stuck for four years, amigo."

Dawes and Teel came in. "What goes?" Buckley asked.

"Teel goes," Dawes answered, grinning. "He's being sent to nuke school."

"Nuke school? You mean bombs?" Anderson said blankly. "When did we give up the secret of the bomb to foreigners?"

Dawes said, "It's not going to be too bad, fellas. I can tell. This is a good, professional operation."

"It's sure isolated, even for China," Kranak said. "Do they keep it out here just to age it, then send it in to the Middle West? Or do they keep it here so we can't get out?"

"We know there's a town only two hundred miles or so away," Dawes said. "There's got to be a road to it."

"Some town," Buckley said. "Metered yaks."

"At least you guys'll have each other's company and hear American. I'm goin' out there into Babel," Teel told them.

"But, Jesus," Kranak said, "could you screw a Chinese noncom?"

"Jes' make it another famous first, Eddie, you be all right," Teel chuckled.

Major Wong appeared twenty minutes later to take them to meet the Commandant. "You look fine," he said. "Real soldiers. The Commandant will like that. He's new here."

They walked in pairs to the headquarters building. They were shown into the commandant's office.

"Sir!" Major Wong barked, saluting.

The Commandant came out from behind his desk

where, because he was so tiny, it had appeared that he was sitting down. He shook hands with each man. "I am Colonel Ho," he said. "Welcome to Camp St. Patrick and call me Paddy if it puts you more at ease."

"This is the new *American* group, Colonel," Major Wong said.

"Aaaah. So. Our first American group. Well, well, well. Welcome to Camp Cody." He walked to a fireplace, turned abruptly to face them, teetering on his boots, his hands clasped behind his back. "Psychological tests show that each national group enjoys calling this camp by a familiar, nationalistic name," he said. "To our Latin Americans it is Camp Cantinflas. To the French it is Camp Moi. To the English it is simply called The Teabreak. And so on. Tomorrow begins your psychological de-briefing. That de-briefing will last for fourteen weeks. It was designed to indoctrinate trainees into the most unwavering concepts of world revolution as expressed by Chairman Mao. It was also designed to uncover imposters, if any, because the entrenched society beyond China would very much like to place their agents in here. Also, the de-briefing will recover from your minds a knowledge of your attitudes, skills and other factors which will permit us to make the most of you. Some men complete the de-briefing in seven weeks. Some men have taken as long as eighteen weeks to yield anything useful. We have shot two agents. You will be more valuable human beings if you can last through it. In four years you will lead the finest revolutionary program we have ever seen, itself the creation of your leader. You will return to your country highly trained to destroy its counter-revolutionaries by terrorizing and destroying your petit-bourgeoisie to create an international society of safety for your people. Major Wong is your link to me, but you must call him Cal. That is all. Enjoy your dinner, gentlemen."

The food wasn't bad. They couldn't recognize a lot of it, but it was better than just army food. Cal kept up a lively patter throughout the meal. There was a small American flag at the center of the table. At other tables, each with up to ten men and one or two Chinese officers, there were other small identifying flags. A lot of the world was represented: black men from Central Africa being trained to go into Rhodesia and South Africa; Arabs learning how to demolish Israel; Irish learning how to kill the Irish; stolid groups of Japanese, Dutch, Czechs, Italians, French and Pakistanis. One table at the far side of the room was long and rectangular. Its diners seemed to be a cross-section of all nationalities in the room.

Major Wong identified them as Upperclassmen who were about to move out to advanced studies at the Guerrilla War College in the north.

"How come no women?" Reyes said. "Women are always a big part of the people where I come from."

"There is a women's camp. It's just like this one."

"If we gone work with them, I don't see why we don't learn with them," Dolly Fingus said.

"We tried it," Major Wong said, "but it made too much trouble. It creates too many personality mysteries. A very bright Italian guy got killed and two guys had nervous breakdowns from all the screwing. So we had to reorganize."

"Are they near here?" Dawes asked mildly.

"I really have no idea where they are," Major Wong responded. "But you'll meet them in the fourth year at the War College."

"Who do *they* screw on Sunday afternoons between four and six?" Buckley asked. "Male non-coms from your Western Army?"

"Oh, I imagine some of them get the occasional officer," Major Wong said.

On their first morning at Camp Cody they were awakened by batmen at 5 A.M. After a hearty breakfast they were moved out through the Weapons Area into the vast off-limits site, into the Psychological De-Briefing Area. They were separated. Each man was taken into a separate building, each building approxi-

mately ninety yards from the next. The buildings
themselves seemed to be tiny two-room arrangements,
but the rooms were only for interviewing and early
sedation. After that they were dropped sixty feet into
the ground by elevators to a large common hospital
area that had six cubicles on each side and two projection rooms at each end: four in all. By the time the
men reached the lower level they had fallen into an
ambulatory hypnotic state from the chemicals that had
been contained in their breakfasts. The men were put
into separate silent cubicles where two technicians to
each cubicle stripped them down and strapped them
firmly to steel stretchers, which were capable of lying
horizontal, standing vertical, or achieving any angle
in between, with the patient either right side up or
upside down. The stretcher could be whirled centrifu-
gally by an electric motor or could be turned end
over end.

Feeding tubes leading to bottles containing Chinese-
developed preparations (some perfected over centuries,
some in recent years), which opened the doors of
consciousness and led the interrogators to the truth
locked inside the minds of each of the men, shadow-
thin layer upon shadow-thin layer, were inserted into
nostrils, into veins at wrist, thigh, and ankle so that
the saturation of the unlocking mechanisms could begin.

The American recruits seemed to be sleeping. The
technicians checked their body temperatures, breathing rates, blood pressure and REMs constantly on the
monitor dials. The saturation process took forty-one
hours, tended by two twelve-hour teams for each patient. The interrogation began. Each man was taken
through his childhood, his adolescence, into his young
manhood. Routine areas were investigated and pains-
takingly checked off: political background, governmental connections, sabotage experience, espionage
backgrounds; skills, loyalties, resentments, hostilities,
ability to love and accept self; ability to welcome
authority to find solution, teamwork capabilities; sexual

drives, sexual malarrangements, sexual relationships with Areas 1 and 2 and 3 (life background; group background; emotional responses).

The processes of interrogation required ten weeks of twenty-hour days with chemical stimulation and sedation. The interrogators were, in every case, women.

The terminal process was the re-educative process. This took four weeks, was enormously painful, both physically and emotionally—continuously, unendingly painful because it required that negative lessons be laid down which, if the subject deliberately chose to transgress the necessities of those lessons, caused extraordinary, instant electrical pain to be induced into the central nervous system. Some men took longer than others. Those totally anti-authoritarian must have felt, before the end, that they had been fractured everywhere by sledgehammer and taken the burns of corrosive acids into hundreds of knife wounds throughout their body. A man like Dawes, however, accustomed to discipline, went through the negative lesson period with minimum intensity of suffering. Lurky Anderson remained in that twilight zone of agony for three days longer than the others.

When the negative lessons had been mastered and each man was ready to welcome authority as he would welcome love and attention, the positive lessons, to be a fixed part of their characters forever, were firmly addressed. These fixed characteristics were largely identical: The men existed to serve their Leader, an unknown face and form somewhere in the United States, whom they would never meet but would always obey. They were in China to be taught how they could develop as soldiers of the revolution, as great and model leaders themselves who would accept the responsibility for taking hundreds of thousands of Americans into battle. They had ascended to the highest level. They adored Authority, Discipline, Service and The Team. They were as one intricate, self-involved body, which helped itself to triumph over social and political wrongs. They would willingly labor to learn how best to kill millions of the enemy so that the revolution would overcome the status quo and American glory would once again rise up to the heavens like a great and shining light, even if it were necessary for all of them to die to bring it there—if their Leader wanted it there.

When it was over, when they came out the other side of the mysteries and found themselves seated in the small reception room of the little building of the Psychological De-briefing area where they had first entered, none of them remembered anything that had happened, what they had suffered, or how much time had passed. They all looked worn and thin and each man had deep restraint marks on his arms and legs. When the entire group had reassembled, they met in a small, wooden building known as the American University. It was a classroom with blackboards all around and swivel seats at small desks for thirty.

Major Wong arrived eleven minutes after they had seated themselves. They had been sitting quietly waiting for him.

"Good morning," he said. They did not answer.

"You must answer—Good morning, Cal," he said gently.

"Good morning, Cal," they said in unison.

"I am happy to see you all together again and pleased to read your outstanding reports from the debriefing. We begin. You are at Camp Cody because you are revolutionary specialists at war who will become supremely skilled at guerrilla war. As Chairman Mao wrote in December 1936 in the uncompleted study called *Problems of Strategy in China's Revolutionary War:* 'War, this monster of mutual slaughter among men, will be finally eliminated by the progress of human society and in the not-too-distant future, too. But there is only one way to eliminate it and that is to oppose war with war, to oppose counter-revolutionary war with revolutionary war, and to oppose counter-revolutionary class war with revolutionary class war. History knows only two kinds of war—just and unjust.

We support just wars and oppose unjust wars. All counter-revolutionary wars are unjust, all revolutionary wars are just. Mankind's era of wars will be brought to an end by our own efforts and, beyond doubt, the war we wage is part of the final battle.'

"But also beyond doubt," Major Wong continued earnestly, "the war we face will be part of the biggest and most ruthless of wars. The biggest and most ruthless of unjust counter-revolutionary wars is hanging over us, and the vast majority of mankind will be ravaged unless we raise the banner of a just war. When human society advances to the point where classes and states can be eliminated and private possessions are abandoned, there will be no more wars, counter-revolutionary or revolutionary, just or unjust; that will be the era of perpetual peace for mankind. Each country, especially a large country, has its own characteristics; therefore the laws of war for each country also have their own characteristics. Those applying to one cannot be mechanically transferred to another.

"In the great Chinese revolutionary struggle, because of the nature of our country, Chairman Mao chose not to drive to seize the big cities. You come from the American industrial society. In the coming revolutionary struggle which you will wage, the immediate goals will be changed. You will fight *inside the cities,* ignoring the vast countryside. By bringing ruin in their name to the people of the cities you will cause them to overthrow the counter-revolutionary forces, demanding to be allowed to live their lives—which will of course never be the same again.

"In the next three years at Camp Cody we will experience together how this will be accomplished— this chain of limited urban wars—within all vital parts of the American nation. But allow me to tell you how Chairman Mao expressed protracted, limited war: 'Enemy advances, we retreat; enemy halts, we harass; enemy tires, we attack; enemy retreats, we pursue. It is all waiting for us to study—for whether guerrilla warfare is fought in the mountains, in a pasture land, or in the mazes of a great modern city—it still uses the same strategy: Guerrilla war is the finest possible way to fight this kind of war.

"We will carry with us one golden rule: 'The guerrilla wins if he does not lose. The conventional army loses if it does not win.' "

The men, now six, minus Teel, who had left for the nuke school, were taught the basic applications, in actual practice and in theory, of what Agatha Teel was then, at home, working to provide for them: The Plan, *the* great weapon they would use when the Thirty Cities' War began with a *trained* army of 700,-000 men and women, white and black, students, preachers, junkies and dropouts, loosely 25,000 in each of the cities (depending on its size), drilled, organized, equipped guerrilla troops to fight a conventional opponent, the government forces, trapped in a maze. Their army would be equipped with modern weapons, from nuclear devices to light automatic rifles and small arms and including artillery, bombs, grenades, dynamite, gelignite, bacterial weapons, fire extermination systems, propaganda and poison gas. Munitions, weapons, food, and medical supply dumps and depots would be dispersed and concealed as caches; secured hideouts, hospitals, money cut-outs, plus a habitually bribed opposition within the government would be available to every commander on Army Corps, Divisional, Brigade, Regimental and Company levels. Battle plans for each individual city were currently being developed by seasoned professionals of international guerrilla war which would, during the first seven months, give an 8 to 1 advantage of surprise. No quarter would be asked or given and, for the first time in any revolutionary struggle, fitting to the nature of big city warfare, better-than-adequate financing over an indefinite period would be available, more than enough financing to exhaust establishment forces, to reduce the American population by ten to twenty million people, until a new world could be entered and all lives (remaining) fulfilled.

Each night the Americans at Camp Cody fell into an exhausted sleep from the exertions of their studies, which highlighted:

Mountain climbing (for later translation into ascent of the exteriors of high buildings and chimneys);

Metropolitan fire equipment operation and instant disablement;

Advanced Karate and aikido (Tomiko);

Familiarization with layout and superficial techniques of television and radio station operation and their semi-permanent/ permanent destruction;

Speaking, reading, and writing knowledge of the second languages of the regions of their country: Spanish, Yiddish, German and the New York dialects;

Certified qualification in Gr-1, the favored assassination technique;

Proficiency in the major studies of American city street universities: astrology, pot cultivation, I-Ching, the Druid religion, palmistry; Ouija, group sex, women's liberation, etc.;

Water main destruction, river bridge demolition, underground transportation paralysis, stadium, theater and church firing during performance for maximum loss of audience; efficient mass child murder; the uses of throwing acids by power hoses, etc.;

Proficiency with small arms, grenades, own-made bombs and devices, flame-throwers, ropes, clubs/ sticks, and knives;

Techniques of bribery, coercion and corruption; spread of venereal disease, spoliation of children;

Memorization of dry and wet sewerage systems for cross-city passage of troops, couriers and assassination teams:

Wreckage of elevator systems, electrical generators, water supply systems, food distribution, garbage disposal;

Forgery: counterfeiting money, ID cards, automobile licenses, passports, evidence, military credentials, credit cards, general evidence;

Advanced arson;

Destruction of crowds: the American leader was determined that no crowds should be allowed to form whether civilians or government troops, and to discourage this at its source all congregations of people whether shopping, walking, marching, rioting, or worshipping at church carried DESTRUCT signals;

Inducing dependency on the occult; promotion of auguries, omens, and reliance on their infallibility;

Education in the basic requirement: execution, out-of-hand and on-the-spot, of *anyone* in uniform: Boy Scouts, nurses, policemen, priests, park employees, soldiers, nuns, athletes, etc., so that people could not judge to whom they could turn for assistance;

Random Death Planning: people must return home to find pets slaughtered; baby carriages shoved into street traffic; high floor falls for crowded elevators especially in the first three weeks of warfare; car bombings in crowded areas; heavy accent on random slaughter with greatest display of blood and dismemberment;

Emphasis on follow-up action in all conquered and unconquered suburbs;

Detailed attention to principles of propaganda; improvement in rumor spreading, causing rumors during first three years of warfare of a profoundly optimistic nature, constantly giving "inside information" of early future dates when the war would be over to cause hope to vanish systematically as those dates retreated;

Overall objective: inability of 85 percent of the citizenry to dare to leave their homes.

"Even though you have been expertly indoctrinated at your de-briefings," Major Wong said, "I have noted from some of your expressions that you find these tactics difficult to accept even though all of you have lived lives of crime and violence. However, that is how you feel now. You will accept these tactics in time as you gain calm understanding, just as the American people watched death on television each night at dinnertime throughout much of the Vietnam war, accepting it, finally, as they became so bored with the war it had to be taken off the air for lack of a sponsor.

"Let me ask you this: is it a wholly different thing to you, when a formal war is declared by old men in a capital city, a war which implements instant nuclear strikes and megadeaths, laying cities or villages—because sizes in terms of human death don't really matter—to waste without any offer to capitulate?"

The female non-coms turned out to be a sensational bunch of kids. Everyone had a marvelous time except Kranak. Kranak would not fuck a Chink.

22

February 1971

Mr. Palladino completed the arrangements with President Duvalier in two more meetings. Each was satisfied that he had made an extraordinary deal. When Mr. Palladino returned to New York, he passed the word to Senator Karp to set a meeting with Bart Simms on the Staten Island ferry because Mr. Palladino had given his people the problem of how to bug the Staten Island ferry and they had solved it. But Bart refused to meet on the ferry. They met at the shallow end of the swimming pool at the St. George Hotel in Brooklyn Heights.

"I can't even swim!" Mr. Palladino protested to Senator Karp.

"No swimming, J.D.," Karp said. "You just stand in the shallow water and talk."

"I don't spend on four-hundred-dollar English hand-tailored suits so I can stand around in a pair of trunks and look like a slob," Mr. Palladino argued. But the biggest money of his life was involved so he agreed to the meeting.

They settled several matters: first, Mr. Palladino was to put a down payment of two million dollars into escrow with Herbert Ryan Willmott as fiscal agent for Delmarva Popular, a trust account; that Bart was to leave "within ten days" for Asia to make the arrangements for the purchase and transport of ten tons of raw opium for delivery to Fort Axelrod, a former establishment on the south coast of Haiti; and that the actual deal for the price of the opium would be made by Mr. Palladino personally, with the Kuomintang representative, at Mr. Palladino's office in New York while Bart waited in Hong Kong for the deal to be closed.

Those were the essential matters. Bart had already applied for medical leave from his work as Assistant Curator at Spider and had given the agency to understand that he was about to resign because of the pain in his leg. The news was accepted with a great deal of regret and considerable sympathy, and a collection was taken up to present him with a quartz clock.

A significant part of the arrangements, quite invisible to Bart, lay in Mr. Palladino's intention of putting a lock on Bart during this first trip. He had finally figured out how to equalize Bart's knowledge of the Sesteros and Abramo. Bart was going to forget he had ever heard about the Sesteros or Abramo.

"My God, you are certainly a lot fatter in trunks than you look when you are dressed. I'd like to get the name of your tailor," Bart said as Mr. Palladino came up the ladder out of the swimming pool.

"Oh, yeah?" Mr. Palladino said. "Yeah? Well, you're a lot dopier-looking, so whatta you think of that?"

"It must be the rented trunks," Bart said.

23

April 1971

Bart and Enid had a very nice time on the ship to Hong Kong. They took the ship in case there was going to be any routine surveillance by the agency. A sea voyage looked a lot more like a recuperative necessity than a plane trip. There was a good crowd aboard and Enid won an alarm clock for filling out the most correct answers to a zoology quiz that the steward had slipped under their door. They had perfect weather and the chance to play a blissful amount of bridge and to really catch up on movies.

After four days of shopping in Hong Kong, an island that is really the world's biggest cut-rate department store, Bart left Enid for a few days to visit his old friend, Lieutenant General Franklin M. Heller on Taiwan. The agency's de-briefings in recent years had cured her psychotic loneliness. He booked into the Park & Green House Hotel in Taipeh where a telephone message from General Heller was waiting for him. On the first night he went out to the Heller villa, happy to eat so well again.

In Bart's honor, as a Maryland man, the General had flown in a signal Maryland meal of black bean soup cooked with veal and seasoned with sherry. They had diamond-back terrapin from Crisfield, which was almost as rare as hummingbird steak and with a wonderful flavor.

They ate oyster pie and crab cakes made with just the right amount of hard-boiled eggs and parsley, and ham slices that were striped red and green from having been stuffed with a mixture of chopped watercress, kale, cabbage sprouts and green garlic leaves wilted in ham liquor and then boiled in a cloth bag. General Heller said proudly that the whole meal had arrived from Andrews Air Force base that morning.

After dinner they settled down with some good Cuban cigars and a bottle of Pelisson cognac. Bart said, "I'm leaving the agency, Frank. I just can't hack it."

Heller belched. "The knee?"

Bart nodded. "I've decided to go into politics. I'm going after the Senate seat in Maryland next year. Uncle Herbert is talking to the State Committee right now."

"You'll be a fine senator, Bart."

"Thank you."

"But it takes a lot of money."

"Yes, it does. For openers we're going to have to spread about a million six around the state among the boys. Old man Murray was offering nine hundred thousand so Uncle Herbert said, what the hell, we'll just double that."

"He knows."

"He knows how to make things stick. But the fact is that was just for openers. I'll still have the cost of the campaign and some sweeteners for the National Committee before I ever get up to Election Day. And that's why I'm here."

"I see."

"I've made an arrangement with a New York organization, and with the Haitian government to find them a supply of raw opium. It will be processed into Number Four in Haiti and the New Yorkers will market it throughout the fifty states. So the fact is, I am

here to ask you to ask the family here if they will sell
me the opium I'll need."

"Of course they will, Bart. I think I can tell you that
right now. How much do you want?"

"Ten tons to start. F.O.B. here or in Hong Kong for
delivery to Haiti by Southern Air Transport."

The General made a note in a black loose-leaf
book. "You want to talk price?" he asked.

"New York wants to handle that."

The General seemed to study Bart then, his eyes
far back in the dark pouches that surrounded them
like catcher's mitts. "I see," he said.

"But ten tons is just the opening order," Bart said
quickly, "so all this could run into a lot of money so
we can't fault him for that."

"Perfectly all right."

"Can you have someone contact him in New
York?"

"I'm due for some Stateside time myself."

"Well—great!" Bart gave the General Mr. Palladino's address and telephone number. "When can
you see him? He wants me to stay in Hong Kong until it's settled."

"Actually, I can head out of here tomorrow."

"I'll be at the Hotel Peninsula with Enid."

Mr. Palladino and General Heller haggled for some
time over price but it stayed at $6,000 a kilo. They
agreed that a 50 percent deposit of $27,272,727 was
just and necessary and that the rest of the money
would be paid on delivery to Haiti. Mr. Palladino
wrote the deposit check on the Surrey & Berkshire
National Bank, in Zurich, which was owned by the
Mucelli Family. While General Heller put the check
in his wallet, Mr. Palladino began to apply the lock
on Bart. "You know Simms long?" he asked.

"God, yes," General Heller said, adjusting his corset
so that it didn't cut so much into his waist. "Bart is
one of my dearest friends. I've known him since about

the day he arrived in Asia. That must be three years ago; about the spring of sixty-eight."

"Then he is a pal of yours?"

"How do you mean?"

"Look—you and me are in a tricky business. Simms isn't really in this business if you know what I mean. You know what we're up against. It's a tricky thing, this business. I mean—I certainly hope and trust you and me will be doing business for a long time. I mean —you are the source and I am the merchandiser. We have to depend on each other to make the good times roll, if you know what I mean. But, in a certain way, I mean where does that leave him—you know?"

"I see," General Heller said.

"I think, like we have the right to have a handle on him. He is free and clear. We are involved. We are the producers. What is he? Just that he is free and clear. I can't even get a tape on him."

"What did you have in mind?"

"Well—I think in terms of an obligation. I'm a Sicilian, you might have guessed. He has a sister. This sister is out there with him now. Maybe you know her. I can see where we would have a lock on him if maybe the sister was kidnapped or something out there and he had to come to us for help to get her back, you see what I mean?"

"I see." General Heller's eyes, deep within their sooty bags, were like the shiny backs of beetles and equally filled with expression.

"The first thing he does when he gets news like that is he goes straight to you because you are the man on the spot with the connections. When he goes to you, you tell him the whole thing could be my idea because I had talked like that. When he comes to me I'll tell him the whole thing was your idea because you said your people wanted to have some kind of a lock on him. Then I go out there and we all have a meet. Then we tell him we think we can get the sister back if he signs this paper."

"What paper?"

"A paper which tells how he originated the entire deal, how he is the sole source and operator of this dope combine. And we will tape him."

"Are you taping me now?"

"Of course."

"I want the tape."

"You got it."

"Except you are probably making two tapes."

"Why not? Who knows except me? Maybe four. What's the difference? I don't have you in writing. You are the source. I need you. How could you be safer?"

"Keep the tape."

"But the thing is—Simms will know we were willing to pick up his sister just as a warning, therefore he will behave himself because he knows if he doesn't we will really pick her up and maybe hurt her. Therefore, we will have a lock on him."

There was a knock at the door. Mr. Palladino gave permission to enter. Angela came in. "Mr. Simms is calling from Hong Kong, Mr. Palladino. He is very upset."

"I'll take it." He grabbed the phone behind his desk.

"On two," Angela said.

He punched a button. "Hello, kid?"

Bart's voice sounded pushed across his sanity into a far corner like a loose piano lurching across the ballroom of a ship during a storm at sea. What came through was a kind of hoarse scream. "Palladino! My sister! I—Jesus—they kidnapped my sister!"

Mr. Palladino looked across the desk blankly at General Heller.

"They kidnapped your *sister?*" he said incredulously into the phone. "Who kidnapped your sister?"

"Palladino—I have to talk to Heller. Where is he? Do you know where he is staying?"

"He's right here! He's in my office right now. Just a minute." Mr. Palladino put his hand over the phone and spoke with awe. "Did you have his sister snatched in Hong Kong?" he asked, his eyes popping.

General Heller got up and took the telephone. "No," he said. "This is very bad."

"Whatta you mean—bad?" Mr. Palladino was shattered by the idea that the fucking kidnapped sister might have the power to ruin the whole deal. General Heller spoke into the phone.

"This is terrible, *terrible* news, Bart," he said.

"Frank! I have a letter. It was here on the bed when I got back. I haven't called the police. I want to do the right thing. I need your help. I need advice."

"I'll turn Asia upside down, Bart. You know you can count on that. And I am going to get out to Hong Kong by some time tomorrow and direct this little operation myself."

"Oh, Jesus, Jesus, Jesus."

"Bart! Bart, get a grip on yourself. You've got to do a lot of thinking. What did the letter say?"

Bart was sobbing. He made himself speak. "It said —WE HAVE KIDNAPPED YOUR SISTER WAIT WHERE YOU ARE."

"I think you must inform the police immediately," the General said. "I'll be at my desk in Taipeh in two days and in the meantime my people there who are THE people there will be on the other end of this phone in ten minutes and they'll really stir up a storm."

Bart had hung up. Heller turned his moleskin-wrapped eyes on Palladino. He said, "My people have been at this kind of thing longer than you people have but I am almost certain that they didn't do it. But—if I were a realistic man I would think, from the way you talked before his call, that you did it."

"I wish I did it but I didn't know how to organize it out there," Mr. Palladino said. "But you're gonna have a very tough job convincing me and him that you didn't do it."

The two men sat silent for some time. Then Heller said, "An American woman is kidnapped in Hong Kong. There could be two reasons. The obvious one

MIGNON G. EBERHART
Family Fortune. Eberhart's newest best-seller. A border-state family is divided by the Civil War and an inheritance that leads to murder. (Publ. Ed. $7.95)

JOHN D. MACDONALD
The Dreadful Lemon Sky. (Publ. Ed. $7.50)

JOHN CREASEY (as Gordon Ashe)
A Shadow of Death. (Publ. Ed. $6.95)

LEN DEIGHTON
Catch a Falling Spy. (Publ. Ed. $7.95)

LILLIAN O'DONNELL
Leisure Dying. (Publ. Ed. $6.95)

BRIAN GARFIELD
Death Sentence. (Publ. Ed. $6.95)

J.J. MARRIC
Gideon's Fog. (Publ. Ed. $5.95)

GEORGES SIMENON
Maigret and the Apparition. (Publ. Ed. $7.95)

MAJ SJÖWALL AND PER WAHLÖÖ
The Terrorists. (Publ. Ed. $7.95)

ROBERT B. PARKER
Mortal Stakes. (Publ. Ed. $6.95)

AGATHA CHRISTIE
Nemesis. (Publ. Ed. $5.95)

ERLE STANLEY GARDNER
The Case of the Postponed Murder. (Publ. Ed. $5.95)

ELLERY QUEEN
_____ Ed. $5.95)

OUR BEST OFFER EVER: 15 MYSTERIES, WORTH $104.80 IN PUBLISHERS' EDITIONS, ALL FOR $1.

These fifteen thrillers, including *Family Fortune*, the very latest by Mignon Eberhart, cost $104.80 in the publishers' original editions. But you get all fifteen full-length novels in five handsome hard-bound volumes for only $1. We would like to send you these fifteen great mysteries to prove to you that The Detective Book Club gives you more and asks less than any other club.

You pay no membership fee. There is no minimum number of books you must buy. You may reject any volume before or after receiving it. You...

SAVINGS OF $4 OR MORE ON EVERY MYSTERY YOU READ

When you accept a club selection, you get three complete, unabridged detective novels in one hard-cover triple-volume for only $3.89. That's $2, $3, or even $4 less than one mystery costs in the publisher's original edition. The club's editors select the best from some 400 mystery books each year...

would be that she was taken for ransom. But if the reason had to do with opium, then some entirely new organization has sprung up which I don't know about. And, if so, then the new people took Bart's sister to tell him not to do business with us. But neither reason is likely. The Simmses haven't got the money to make a ransom interesting and I am the source. No one else has a source. The others are all wholesalers and dealers working out of Hong Kong and they don't want any boats rocked."

Bart flew from Hong Kong to San Francisco to Washington, then took a taxi directly to Langley where he asked to see the Director of Special Operations, Brom Keifetz. He pleaded for the agency's help.

Keifetz seemed shocked by the news. The agency would do everything in its power to get Enid back but he urged that Bart seek the help of General Heller and the Kuomintang families because their influence with the Asian criminal cartel was total.

"I know that," Bart said. "But if Heller and the Taiwan people took her, then the agency's influence with *them* is total. The agency is the source of everything they have."

"I am going to put the entire thing to our analysts and see what they come up with. You look terrible, Bart. Are you going to be able to get back to Hong Kong?"

"Yes. I'll be at the Peninsula."

Bart felt as if he had died. He had taken four downers since finding the letter but they changed nothing. The fear was on him that someone might hurt Enid. Keifetz gave him a government first-class travel voucher to save him a little money on the trip back to Hong Kong and called for a car to take him to the airport. He and Bart shook hands and Keifetz was able to smile at him sincerely.

24

March–April 1971

Senator Karp had that inner vision of gifted politicians. He was able to smell who was going to have the power. He never questioned what he sensed, he just moved toward it and did his best to surround it with service and friendship. When he met Agatha Teel on the Presidential Commission to Stabilize Taxation Security Through Added Fixed Charges for the District of Columbia, he sensed the overwhelming attraction of power and moved in to cement a friendship. Teel had uses for all senators, so she welcomed him aboard.

For four years she had been building up the values of her soul food salon at her expanded brownstone in New York. Every Thursday night she entertained, by invitation, a small, widening list of people whose places in the national and metropolitan order had grown more and more glittering. The Thursday night invitation to Teel's had come to have the highest social value because one never knew who one might meet there but one knew that whoever one did meet there would be able to do one some considerable good. Every Thursday night Teel just "cooked for the folks," in her emeralds or saphs: people from the arts, very oral, always eating or talking. The arts were Hollywood if one could say Visconti was Hollywood; or Russian, if Nureyev ever was *really* Russian. One Thursday evening a (filled) belly dancer arrived from Iran because the Shah could not or would not make it. The arts were the bait at the beginning but, as time went on, Teel's regulars were mainly White House staff, Pentagon high brass, key committee chairmen from The Hill, most of the best of the Senate who were still able to walk, FBI executives, New York police inspectors, National Guard colonels and generals and the over-communications industry.

Karp became a regular. He was impressed deeply by the small and large pools of money and power that bubbled all around Teel. Why, the woman was a wonder! She didn't fool around with getting you things wholesale, he told his (elderly) secretary, "she goes out and gets it for you free." Senator Karp had no idea that the new Lincoln he was driving had been stolen for Teel from a depot in Terre Haute, Indiana. He tried to repay her, here and there and now and then, with fresh information which he thought she might like to know.

"A CIA man is going to file for the Senate in Maryland shortly," he said one night after he had outstayed the others at a Thursday cook-out.

"No kidding? How come?"

"His uncle is Herbert Ryan Willmott."

"I didn't think Herbert had that kind of money for a nephew. Say, that's quite a connection—the CIA and politics. Was he CIA a long time ago?"

"Hell, no. Right now. He ran Air Opium for them in the Golden Triangle." Teel was sharp. She didn't miss much. Her reading on Karp now was that Simms had him scared shitless and that he was really trying to back into some way to do Simms in. Some day it would be useful to know why, she thought.

"Well, fascinating," she said. "I'd like to help him all I can."

"Help him?"

"Maryland is a border state. There's lots of black layers between the white layers on that cake. Maybe I can get the brothers to give him a hand. When the time comes."

"Well—frankly—Simms won't need it. He's spread

more than a million and a half around with the boys all over the state so he's got the nomination in his pocket. Since he has more of that kind of money, that will settle the election, too."

"Where does the money come from?" Teel asked playfully. "I'd say that's a whole lot for a government employee to be spending."

"You could be right," Karp said. "But he's no government employee anymore. He quit the job and took off with his twin sister for Hong Kong. Maybe that's where he keeps the money. It's his old stamping ground, you know. That kind of money has to come from somewhere off-limits."

Teel eased Karp out of the house and settled down on the fur rug in the bathroom with her feet propped up on the tub to have a good think. She liked the opportunity of the combination of a CIA man who would be a senator because of big, new money. If he was going into the Senate the CIA would see the opportunity too. What was good for them was good for Teel, if not the reverse. Then too, there had to be somebody else standing far, far back of Simms, somebody who knew they could get something back if they put that kind of money up. It made Simms all that much more valuable to Teel. This Simms cat could be a great big power station if she could get a lock on him. She settled down to thinking quietly about what kind of lock.

The People's Republic of China allowed Hong Kong to be called a British Crown Colony, but China controlled the unloading of every ounce of food Hong Kong ate and, until China had given permission to build the reservoir, China had controlled every drop of water inported into Hong Kong because the territory had no water of its own. The managers and the labor force, rich and poor, knew that they were living by the sufferance of the giant next door. Therefore, the real—if unofficial—resident governor of the People's Republic Crown Colony was a Mr. T'ai-shan, the Chinese government's security forces representative.

He was based in the Bank of China, an arsenal of small arms and grenades, which had a four-month supply of rice on hand in case of siege. This building stood on the near corner of Statue Square across Jackson Road from the Hong Kong Cricket Club ground. The Bank of China, which was in charge of all Communist financial affairs and exchange control in Hong Kong, symbolized China's chief source of foreign exchange, 50 percent of the total obtained from the world, amounting to $800 million a year, and explained why the People's Republic allowed Hong Kong to exist as a British Crown Colony.

The bank guards wore carbines across their shoulders and had disciplined military bearing. Somewhere in the building were the anonymous offices of the Democratic Republic of North Vietnam. The Bank of China was China's party and diplomatic headquarters in Hong Kong as well as its financial and espionage center. On behalf of Peking, Mr. T'ai-shan also controlled the movements of Hong Kong operations (for informational, and even financial, reasons) such as gold smuggling, opium and heroin traffic, organized crime like the Five Passports operation, and gambling. Despite dozens of daily preoccupations, Mr. T'ai-shan was a wholly amiable man who enjoyed the violence of power.

When Teel asked her friends in Peking to watch Bart Simms and his sister in Hong Kong, the assignment was passed to Mr. T'ai-shan. When the report came back that Simms was negotiating with the MACV bagman, General Heller, in Taipeh, Teel was able to put the Kuomintang dope together with the million and a half Simms had spent on the boys in Maryland and the million and half more he was probably going to have to spend on the campaign and salt-water taffy. That meant he was her competitor in the dope business, among other things. Appreciating the opportunity of throwing such a golden lock on a

U.S. Senator as unique as Bart Simms, she arranged the kidnapping of the unique near-senator's sister and had her held where this unique man's sister could do Teel the most good.

Although Mr. T'ai-shan reported it in full to Teel's friends in Peking, they did not reveal to Teel that the Kuomintang clients, through General Heller, had also paid well to have Mr. T'ai-shan arrange Miss Simms's kidnapping. Nor did they mention that the Corsican *caids* with whom the Chinese had once worked closely (at the time when *they* needed money to finance their movement when the French had occupied Indochina, and the Corsicans and the newly vested Chinese had exchanged many a golden handshake) had also paid well, on behalf of a certain client, to have Miss Simms abducted. Mr. Palladino had told General Heller the strict truth when he said he would not know how to help himself in Asia; he had had to ask the Corsicans. They had all wanted a lock on Simms, through Enid, but of the three kidnappers, Teel alone had Miss Simms's slender body. And it hadn't cost her a cent.

It was a tenuous chain. Teel was only the final accidental link designed to deposit Enid inside China, a messenger who had made the delivery of Enid into China possible. But the CIA, in forging the long, long chain that had begun with the indoctrination of Bart and Enid upon university graduation, turning Bart into an assassin and then the most active narcotics transport executive in the world, had not had the power to foresee the opportunity they had created for themselves as spy masters and power brokers when they had plotted across all those years to put an agent in place inside China. For twenty-seven years the CIA had been the mockery of the Communist world, the African world, the Asian world because they had never contrived to plant an agent successfully within the largest country on earth. All they knew was that confirmed reports showed that "somewhere" inside China foreign guerrillas were being trained. That had been corroborated by interrogations of Arab and Japanese terrorists. They were willing to risk a lot of planning on the gamble that, if she were taken into China by the narcotics industry's Chinese connections, since she was young, had languages, was sensitive and cooperative, Enid would be sent to one of these training camps and "indoctrinated" until she was a guerrilla soldier of international revolution. The genius of the CIA planning gamble was the building-in of Enid's "counter-brainwashing" before her Chinese indoctrinations took place, so that she could be split precisely into two halves and loyally serve both masters without conflict.

In view also of the political future they had planned for him, the CIA wanted to have a further lock on Bart. They arranged all their pieces on the board in a total fail-safe fashion toward the funnel wherein General Heller would, by professional inclination, have Enid kidnapped and taken into China, merely to hold and maintain the lock on Bart, his business partner. As the back-up apparatus they knew they had Mr. Palladino, the Corsicans and the Laotians standing by to move from Vientiane to take Enid, should General Heller not respond to the opportunity (which the CIA knew would then instantly occur to the Sicilian Palladino as a matter of business ethics: Get a lock on your opponent).

The irony that it was their own unknown enemy, Teel, who moved before anyone else and pulled Enid into China, remained a mystery to the CIA, who assumed it had been either General Heller or Mr. Palladino since they had planned it that way. Nor did Teel know, at the time she ordered the kidnapping, that she was serving and abetting the causes of the CIA against her own revolution but, unlike the CIA, she would find out.

25

April 1971

Enid wanted to get out and get shopping again among the ten thousand bargains of Hong Kong, but she hadn't started her novel for the day. She went to the writing desk in the living room of their two-bedroom suite at the Peninsula. She began to write almost immediately because she had been composing in her head since she awoke.

THE SABLE SOUTANE
by
CARLOTTA YOU

There was the requisite purple plain where the people wandered, picking each other's pockets or sauntering into the salt mines where they raced rats. Far in the dim distance, unreachable on foot or by chartered jet, were the great blue mountains of morals. "Look here, Your Honor," Buster said to the exigent priest who was shaking an aspergillum at him, "our Gangrad worked like the very devil to get the oil together. It is our oil and we are not going to give it away for any 97¢ a gallon."

Just as Enid finished her work for the day the doorbell buzzed. She crossed the room and opened the door. A tall, good-looking man wearing an absolutely beautiful honey, black, and amethyst striped tie and, oddly enough, wearing gloves, entered the room, smiling pleasantly, by crowding her backward. He closed the door with his foot then struck her across the side of her head with something hard. She fell unconscious. The man opened the hall door just wide enough to put his head out. "All right," he said.

Two Chinese attendants in white rolled a stretcher down the hall and into the room. The tall man went into the bedroom at the left. (Bart always insisted on separate bedrooms even though they weren't always both used.) He tossed a letter on the bed. While he did that, one of the Chinese attendants slipped the long needle of a hypodermic into the vein of Enid's left forearm. They lifted her limp body upon the wheeled stretcher and covered it carefully. Before they finished the tall man had left the suite. The attendants rolled the stretcher along the corridor to the service elevator. When the lift arrived, they put the stretcher into it and directed the operator, in P'u-t'ung-hua, to go to the basement level. The operator looked in the general direction of Enid's covered face and said, in Cantonese, "Anyone I know?"

"She'll be all right," the smaller Chinese said.

The ambulance was waiting. One attendant got into the rear area with the patient. The second man started the engine without haste and drove up the concrete ramp out of the rear of the hotel into Middle Road, then into Nathan Road and headed north away from the Tsimshatsui District moving briskly along past the shuttered girlie bars toward Shatin.

At the second checkpoint at the near side of the Lo Wu bridge, the driver showed the papers bearing Mr. T'ai-shan's chopmark with the seal of the Bank of China. The ambulance moved across the bridge into the People's Republic and kept going northeast for seventeen miles to the military airport of Hui-chou where Enid and the stretcher were off-loaded into an ancient, four-motor Handley-Page Hastings C.2, a transport plane with a 4,200-mile range.

"How long will she be out like that?" one of the pilots asked.

"About five hours," Shorty said. "How long is the ride?"

"Three hours fifty-seven."

"Then let's go.

The big old plane put down on schedule at Hsining. The stretcher was taken fifty-five yards across the tarmac to a Chinook helicopter. They were off the pad in seven minutes, flying west by southwest across Lake Kokonor to the Women's Guerrilla Training Camp base at Hei-ma-ho, forty-one miles from the men's camp at Ssu-hsin.

In terms of real effectiveness, Enid did not regain consciousness/awareness for one hundred and sixty-one days. She was kept in median sedation, her mind open and plastic to the program of impressions and requests that the technicians had ready. She arrived at the camp on a chilly April afternoon. She returned to full, if changed, awareness well into September. She had been given the fullest de-briefing Chinese technology could achieve. The de-briefers had expected a routine yield. But Enid was a warehouse of interesting knowledge because the agency had designed Enid's long ago basic brainwashing specifically with such a possible de-briefing in mind. Enid's subconscious mind could defend itself against self-betrayal by triggering her to pour out facts and half-facts within her immediate recall about her twin brother, not herself.

She told them the details of Bart's recruitment by the CIA (but not her own). She told them about his work as an assassin in Europe, giving the names of those he had murdered and where. She was explicit, and often truthful, about CIA installations, personnel, policy (as she knew it), methods, operations. They ate it up. Sixty-one copies of 4,216 pages of typescript were circulated throughout China. Case officers and residents were called in from many parts of the world to study Enid's de-briefing. They knew everything she had to say about Air Opium was true because they had participated in its services. Their people who had worked with Bart were able to confirm all data. She revealed the intention of making Bart the President of the United States after he had become a senator and how this was to be done with capital from uppers, heroin, speed and downers; about Bart's alliance with Mr. Palladino and the Haitian government. She was as resounding as a drum. Every time they tapped her she gave out the sounds they wanted to hear. They were very much pleased.

When they had completed the de-briefing they began the painful work of nailing new beliefs and purposes upon Enid's frail personality. This new briefing assured her dedication as a revolutionary who was eager to bring maximum terror to her country. Enid had been put through so much pain to earn points for two opposing systems, the only blessing to her was that she was induced to forget the pain had ever happened.

Everything cohered. Enid was wholly transformed once again as if she were changing costumes in a school play.

She was now a carrier pigeon who could home in either direction. She was so deeply locked in acting out what she had been told she was that she could no longer quite remember who she had ever been, excepting underneath all the detritus piled on her psyche by some of the greatest minds of their generation, there lived on and on in fright and shame the small girl home from school who had entered a room to find Daddy.

26

September 1971

The record of Enid's account of Bart Simms's overall arrangement with J.D. Palladino was coded in Peking and sent out to Agatha Teel by courier. The courier, chosen for her intelligence and because her parents were still in the tiny Albanian village of Yn, was Miss Norma Engelson. She had been called in from Zambia to make the drop. On arrival in New York, Miss Engelson checked into her apartment on West 24th Street, washed her hair, drank two slow glasses of cold Wente white wine and then, at quarter to seven, called Teel at her apartment in Murray Hill.

"Teel?"

"This is she."

"Remember Engelson from the porch in Locarno?"

"Yeah!"

"When can I see you? Business."

"Name it."

"Tonight?"

"Well, late. I got people coming for dinner. Hell, come for dinner."

"No. I already got a lot on my plate. I'm due in Belfast tomorrow."

"Then come on by at eleven thirty."

"Now is the best time."

"Okay. Sure. Fine."

Engelson handed over the envelope, gave Teel the Women's Liberation handshake grip, backed into the elevator and was off toward the Irish Riviera.

The first dinner guest, a Pentagon assistant secretary, arrived within four minutes after that, so Teel didn't get around to decoding and reading the Peking message until after midnight. She read it twice, very slowly, memorizing everything, then she burned it and flushed the ashes away. At one twenty she called William Buffalo. They made a meeting for two fifteen at an all-night cafeteria on Fordham Road in the Bronx.

"You surprise me every time," Buffalo said. "I never seen you in a rush before."

"It's just a trick, William," Teel said easily. "I'm always in a hurry. Now, I got bad news and I got good news. Which you want first?"

"I take the bad for the hurt and the good to make it better," he grinned. He looked more frightening when he smiled; a trick of light.

"I am going to give you two head bookkeepers, William. My own fellows."

"Hey! Anything you say is okay, but I got my own bookkeeper, y'know, Dawes, Binchy Dawes. I *trust* him. Y' don't trust me?"

"You're a good man."

"But—how come? You think you not gettin' a count?"

"Oh, I know the count is for true. You been solid. Nothing like that."

"Then—what?"

"The what is that the good news is so good that the takings are going to get so much bigger and fatter and sweeter that, just as insurance, because we all only human after all, I want my own two head bookkeepers counting it as it come in and go out. Why, the good news is so *good,* my bookkeepers may want to put their own bookkeepers to check on *them.*"

Buffalo chuckled as if he were doing an imitation of a man he had just strangled. "I never thought things could get better'n they is right now. Hey, how are my boys and girls doin' out there somewheres?"

"Who?"

"You know—them ones who done time for armed robbery."

"They're fine. Okay?"

"Sure. What else is good news?"

"The competition—Palladino, the Sicilian big one— is selling for thirty-one thousand a keye shoreside what he got for six thousand.'

"*Six* thousand? No way."

"Oh, yes. Palladino has a clean connection out of Formosa backed by high brass out of the old MACV and the CIA is muling it for them."

"You lost me. I mean—that's good news?"

"It could work out. Find me the best shit chemist there is, like a Corsican. I don't care what you pay him. Send him to the Sicilian. I want an inside man when we take over. Taking over, William B., is the good news."

Teel's Rolls was parked around the corner from the cafeteria. Her chauffeur, Marty, who packed heat, held the door open.

"Take it easy, Marty," Teel said. "No rush. I got to think."

"You want to loop the island once, Miss Teel?" Teel liked to make the drive around the edges of Manhattan.

"That's it. Let's loop it." She got in and Marty closed the door. She didn't talk to the driver. As the car started she settled back in the darkness to think about how she wanted to handle Hobart Willmott Simms.

27

October 1971

When she was ready to be released from de-briefing for guerrilla training, Enid was billeted with the American cadre in the buildings called Camp Barbara Fritchie. There were five American women installed in the dormitory who had been released from de-briefing two days before Enid arrived. They were less well oriented than Enid because so much more work had gone into putting her together by the Chinese neuro-psychiatrists. Enid's psyche had been re-arranged nicely. She felt deeply at home at Fritchie, eager to learn how to kill.

The other women were: two blacks, Janie Bossle Weems and Sally Winn, thirty and twenty-six; a Rhode Island-born Filipina named Chelito Gurma, twenty-four; a kinetic New York radical named Zelda Gussow, twenty-five; a New Orleans woman called Fantome Duloissier, thirty-one. They all had records for armed robbery and assault. Weems and Winn had been lady Marines. Gussow and Duloissier had been WACs. Gurma was a special case.

"Fantome?" Enid said, "Are you kidding me?"

"So what the hell is your name, sister?"

"Sister?" Enid said, greatly amused. "Are you playing the Wallace Beery part?"

"Listen, whatta you want here? You want trouble here?"

"Where?"

"Whatta you mean where?"

Winn said, "If you gotta mix it get it over. We got work."

"You ast me if I'm kiddin' about my name?" Duloissier said shrilly. She wheeled to glare at the other girls. "She's makin' fun of my name! What else have I got since I lost my looks?" She pulled a switchblade knife out of the pocket of the work suit. Enid didn't wait for any further explanation. She stepped out of her shoes and struck Duloissier at the bridge of the nose with a double flying side-kick known to Enid's trainers at Langley as *yoko-tobi-geri*. After the fast double kick, Enid withdrew her leg instantly to maintain her balance when she landed beside her shoes into which she immediately slipped her feet again.

"Say, you real good at that," Winn said.

"I hate knives," Enid explained.

"I think you broke her nose," Chelito said. "Wow —what a mess."

"I'll get her over to the infirmary," Enid said. "All she needed was a broken nose. She looked too much like Khrushchev as it was."

"Jane Bossle and me gone witchew," Winn said. "In case they make any fuss."

They dragged Duloissier outside to the hand truck that had carried Enid's gear to the dormitory and threw her into it. They rolled the cart across the compound.

"Where'd you learn to fight with the feet?" Winn asked.

"My brother showed it to me."

"Well, you gotta show me."

"Me, too," Weems said. "That is one fuckin' great stunt."

"Oh, they'll be teaching it here," Enid said. "There's no getting around that."

Duloissier was brought around by the corpsman and taped up. Nobody asked any questions. Duloissier held no grudge. "It's the twelfth time I broke it," she said. "I'd sell the fuckin' thing if I could get anything for it, for all the good it ever did me. Jesus, when I think of some of the things I hadda smell wit' it, I don't know why I ever kept it."

"No kidding," Enid said earnestly, "did your parents really name you Fantome?"

"I got it out of a paperback," Duloissier said. "My real name is Jenny. For Janine."

"But—Janine is a *beautiful* name," Enid exclaimed.

"You really think so? Well, great. So yizzle all call me Jenny."

Everybody got along fine after that. In fact, Weems and Gussow got along so fine they became lovers and passed by the Sunday afternoon sessions with the Chinese officers for the first couple of weeks. Nobody else passed the officers by. Winn had been scragging a little Japanese girl at Camp Tempura a little bit but when they got the news about the Sundays she switched back.

A Major Cal Wong was the greatest among a standout team of all-time greats, every girl agreed. He belonged to some far-out Taoist sect which was so keen on sex that it had, since the second century, accumulated a six-foot shelf of sex manuals such as: *The Manual of Lady Mystery, The Secret Codes of the Jade Room, The Art of the Bedchamber* and *Important Guidelines of the Jade Room,* and Major Wong had memorized them all. Wong was a practical poet of sex. He showed them all of the dozens of variations from "The Dragon Turns," which was the old-fashioned missionary position with which several of the American girls were familiar; "The White Tiger Leaps," which was the woman taken from behind, which Weems worked on with her traveling dildo, making Gussow gasp and whinny with pleasure; "The Fish Interlock Their Scales," the woman on top, which was how Winn thought everybody did it; "Approaching the Fragrant Bamboo," both standing; "The Jade Girl Plays the Flute," in which Wong was able to instruct them with incredible variations and which made Enid so homesick for Bart; "The Butterflies Somersault," "The Seagull Hovers," "The Rabbit Nibbles the Hair" and other popular favorites. Each girl took a turn rotating with Major Wong at the two screwing sessions set aside each week. "That Wong," Winn said. "Like he's gone turn me off little chicks forever. He gone make me hate to leave this camp." Oddly not one of them got jealous or possessive.

The food was just as good as the sex, Chelito said. It was a long way from Mandarin cooking; as indigenous as the western Chinese dialect. Most of the food, the mess sergeant said, came up from the moist and mild Chengtu plain where everybody eats hot, red peppers to keep out the damp. Fish were scarce, but everything else was in long supply. The hot pepper stimulated the palate and the digestive juices, opening a spectrum of flavors. After the hot taste passed, in came the mellowness of the many-tastes: all flavors at once: sweet, salty, sour, bitter, fragrant and hot; each one tasted separately yet all of them tasted at once. Though basically army food, it was largely made with seasonings and relishes: hot, cold, and piquant sauces, prepared so artfully that the food was delivered into the mouth as a single, manifold flavor. It was dry, chewy food. Even the flavors had to be chewed. The Peking food, which Enid remembered, was soft and gliding. Their food, because it was now definitely their food and would stay with them for the rest of their lives, was food for the strong; food for chewers.

28

May 1971–November 1972

Bart haunted the Far East for twenty-five days before he could understand that he wasn't going to find Enid. General Heller had worked like a demon for him, living on the telephone, commandeering planes, lending weapons, and disclosing a network of his intimate connections with the underworlds from Hong Kong and Vientiane to Jakarta. He had Bart taken to meet the co-leaders of the Five Passport organization, who permitted him to cross-examine them. These men put out a dragnet in the eight most active crime cities in the Far East to shake out the kidnappers. Bart flew to Vientiane, the capital of Laos, which was called the heroin capital of Asia and, through his own connections from the old days, talked desperately to Corsican, French, American and Thai criminals. The MACV checked the CIA who checked the British Constabulary who checked every exit from the colony, by air, by sea, and across the Lo Wu bridge connecting Hong Kong with mainland China. They were looking for one woman among 4,200,000 people on 398 square miles. General Heller even got Bart an appointment with a Mr. T'ai-shan, a Chinese banker of influence who amiably agreed to notify all authorities concerned with such matters in the People's Republic, although he took pains to explain to Bart that the concealment of a Caucasian woman inside China would be impossible.

Bart's body enclosed his memory; all else was gone.

173

If Enid was not with him he lost contact with his feelings: he did not exist. Uncle Herbert was urging him to come home to prepare for his campaign for election to the senate. Uncle Herbert was blunt: Bart must come home and face the great responsibility on which he had already spent so much to win his party's loyalty. When Bart demurred, he was reminded by his uncle that there was no going back. Zombie though he had become, Bart loyally responded to the quaint threat. So, on the twenty-fifth day of his despair, Bart flew to Washington. He kept going on three downers a day; they numbed him nicely and interfered with his memory rather than his mind.

When he had made his plans, he asked Marvin Karp to notify Mr. Palladino to meet him in New York at ten o'clock the following morning, rain or shine, on the sixth bench north of the marina at the river's edge of the park on West 79th Street.

"I want you to know I am sorry for your troubles," Mr. Palladino said, all kindliness.

"These are my Haitian projections for the first year," Bart said, unable to talk about Enid. "It looks like a million one net on the casino action, six million three on our share of the Haitian foreign aid payments, about a million six on construction projects, nearly seven hundred thousand from prostitution and souvenirs and about seventy-four million six hundred thousand on the heroin you'll turn out. Considering that there are no taxes on these items, it represents a good operation."

"It's marvelous," Mr. Palladino said. "I never saw a moneymaker like it. And watch those figures climb as soon as I can get the pharmaceutical line organized. My father used to think we were running the U.S. Mint when we had Prohibition, but that was nothing."

"I want to be very precise about the way you make the contributions to my campaigns, Mr. Palladino," Bart said. "It is vital that my seven million three seep into my campaign coffers in an extremely careful, absolutely legal, grass-roots manner—so much so that I am going to supervise the whole thing myself. Therefore, in three days' time please have all the money ready in one-hundred, five-hundred, and thousand-dollar bills, favoring the hundreds."

"Certainly. Of course. Sure."

"My people will break it down into envelopes and mail it in, first from different parts of Maryland, later from different states around the country, right after my first two television speeches."

"A real grass-roots reaction, hey? You want the cash in suitcases, a trunk, or how?"

"Well, suitcases, I think."

Bart, Uncle Herbert, and Uncle Herbert's two loyal secretaries who had been with him for twenty-seven years spent eleven days stuffing envelopes with letters wrapped around hundred-dollar, five-hundred-dollar and one-thousand-dollar bills. The letters were produced by two rented IBM MC82 typewriters and were sixteen different forms of grateful tributes from people whose names and addresses were listed in telephone directories who, presumably, would have wanted to contribute to Bart's campaign if they had heard his two speeches from Annapolis. Sixty-four percent of the stuffed envelopes were mailed within Maryland boundaries but 36 percent were postmarked from outside the state, mailed by Family organizations whose cooperation Mr. Palladino was able to arrange. After a solid story in *Human Events* convinced Bart that people even farther away from the Delmarva area would have been able to respond to his appeals, Palladino's funds were mailed to him by willing workers who saw no more than sealed envelopes (and who had had a lifetime of training at questioning nothing) from the Oranges in New Jersey, St. Petersburg, Florida, from the Sun Cities of Arizona, and from Anaheim and Pasadena, California. The press covered the great ocean of contributions as they poured in. Television covered The Candidate as, bemused and awed, he opened envelope after envelope to pull out thousand-dollar bills. He read letters at random as he plucked them out. The clip appeared on the *A.M. America* show and inspired a lot of legitimate contributors to mail in a total of $327.80 from all over the nation. The newsmagazines pronounced that Bart had great charisma to account for the uncanny voter appeal "while not yet really saying anything." Bart's limp, his background as "a CIA planner-statistician" and his neat, dark dress worked for him. The grass-roots money promotion was so successful that Bart never did have to say much of anything in the campaign itself. Big industry in the state got behind him with Uncle Herbert's help. Labor unions on all levels announced their support. Uncle Herbert herded the banks, the insurance companies, the church, the public utilities and the dairy industry into the fold. Bart announced a "realistic stance" on energy problems and won a large contribution from the oil companies. After a quiet campaign of mostly waving and limping, Bart was elected to the U.S. Senate with 67 percent of the vote, which proved that no one can screw all of the people all of the time. Nor would he want to. It would look bad.

29

February 1972

Major General Luther "Bosco" Beemis was the CIA's plant for Pentagon operations. He reported regularly to his masters at Langley the progress of the Army's penetration of China: i.e., that they had succeeded in planting an agent there, that they were conducting a full-scale secret investigation of all members of the American cadre whom the Chinese had taken inside, to try to uncover the American instigators and managers of the movement within the United States, and that they were waiting—and sweating—for their agent to get out of China so the agent could be debriefed and the plot totally uncovered without any help whatever from any other governmental investigative agency.

The Director of the CIA instructed his White House undercover agent to leak the information of the Army discovery upward through the White House. The CIA White House plant told an assistant legal counsel that he had heard on the cocktail circuit the night before that the Army had planted a man inside China. The legal counsel told his boss, Special Counsel to the President, who ran it straight in to the President's Chief of Staff.

"Im-possible!" the Chief of Staff said, waving the man out of the room. When the door had closed, he got the President on the telephone.

"I have a crazy rumor on my desk that the Army has planted a man inside China. What do you want done about it?"

"Check it out."

The Chief of Staff called the Director of the National Security Council. "The President wants us to check out a story that the Army have planted an agent inside China."

"Oh, my God! A *news*paper story?"

"No. Call it a rumor right now."

"This is terrible. Just when everything is going smoothly some crafty cluck has to pull a thing like this."

"Maybe it never happened, but he wants it checked out."

The Director of the National Security Council called the Chairman of the Joint Chiefs of Staff, a fleet admiral, and put the question to him.

"How the hell would I know a crappy little thing like that? If the Army has agents they must move them around, right?"

"Admiral?"

"What?"

"You have a choice—either spend the rest of the goddam week"—the Director's voice rose in anger —"checking this story out—or if you prefer it that way, I'll have the President call you and ask you."

The Admiral hung up on him, but he wasted no time in calling the head of Army Intelligence. "Do you have a plant inside China, Petey?" he asked.

"Butch—if we did—and I did not say we do—that is the kind of operation I can't talk about."

"You know how come I asked?"

"How?"

"The President told NSC to check it out."

"Why is he always inter*fer*ing?" General Doncaster said wildly. "Why don't these goddam civilians stay behind their desks and take their little goddam bows and let us run this country the way it should be run?"

"Call the Chaplain-General, for Christ's sake!" Admiral Melvin barked. "Do you have a plant in there or don't you?"

"Yas—*YAS!* We have a plant in there. The first American agent ever successfully sited in that country in twenty-seven years! The first! I mean the CIA with their billions couldn't do it but we did it! The United States Army Intelligence Corps planted their agent inside a Chinese secret operation and now these civilian fuck-ups want to muddy the water before we can even begin to fish!"

"I'm sorry, Petey," Melvin said. "But we need these people. They provide the money we have to have to win."

"This is very, *very* delicate stuff. I say this—it better be between you and the President—for his ears only. Will you do that, Butch?"

"I'll try it on," Admiral Melvin said.

The agenda of the National Security Council meeting held in the Cabinet Room three months later at the White House was routine. The first twenty-eight minutes were devoted to Vietnam. All statutory members of the NSC were present except the President. The meeting was chaired by the NSC Director, the President's Assistant for National Security Affairs.

The Director said he had something he wanted to read into the record. He said, "I have a lulu today. Wait till I tell you what took ninety days to turn up because it was put in a ninety-day file. The world isn't crazy enough. Army Intelligence has succeeded in planting an agent inside China." There was an instant rhubarb. Everybody tried to speak at once. The Director waited for quiet. "You have anything on that, Sam?" he asked the Defense Secretary.

"Jesus, no."

"You, Butch?" the Director asked the Chairman of the Joint Chiefs of Staff.

"I'm knocked out. I never heard of it. A ninety-day file? Why, for Christ's sake, this is a historic event."

"When the memo crossed my desk," Director told them, "we sent out a query to all friendlies for any knowledge they might have picked up about camps inside China, and interrogations of captured PLO thugs, Japanese Red Army members and Tupamaros made clear that facilities do exist, as we have suspected, where Chinese are training not only people of many other countries, but also our own, including, ah, American women . . ."

"Women! My God, Al! American women?"

"We thought we should send Dr. Baum out to debrief the captured PLOs and the rest"—everyone at the table looked uncomfortable—"and his transcript is unequivocal. The women appear to have reached the Far East by ship from South America. That's all we know about them.

"On the basis of the de-briefees' information I asked for an overfly and we got photos of two identical camps about forty miles apart on Lake Kokonor. Army Intelligence knows only that their agent went in with six other Americans, some of whom were ex-convicts."

"Odd, you didn't know anything about a thing as big as this, Al," the Director, CIA, said.

"It gets more interesting, gentlemen," the NSC director said. "Before the de-briefees—ah—before they died, they testified that they were graduates of a guerrilla training camp facility at Ssu-hsin, in Tsinghai, where urban—repeat *urban*—guerrilla warfare is taught. They told Dr. Baum that there is only one exception to these courses of study as laid down by the Chinese. Our American group is being trained under the plans of their own leaders in a *four*-year course, not an eighteen-month course as are all the others."

"Well, Jesus Christ, Henry! Who the hell would want to fight a war like that?"

"The question is, what are we going to do about all this? And the first and most important thing to remember, gentlemen," the Director said, "is that the President does not want the Chinese disturbed whatsoever. I can tell you that he was very, very, touchy about the Army putting their agent inside China at all, this year. But, of course, he understands the need. I mean—that goes without saying."

"You mean our people can't go and even *talk* to the Chinese about it?" the Vice President demanded.

"I have an idea of what we can do," the Director said.

"What?"

"We will give the Army Intelligence agent a nice present on graduation day."

As the meeting broke up, the NSC Director asked the Director of the Central Intelligence Agency to meet him in his basement office in fifteen minutes. When the two men were locked in, facing each other, the NSC Director said, "In consideration of the enormous favor Army Intelligence was willing to do for the President in sharing with him the information that they had succeeded—a first in twenty-seven years for any of our agencies—in planting an agent inside China, I took the liberty of checking with the President before coming down here to see you, and he has instructed me to order you to tell me, so that I may tell him, whether or not the CIA has been able to plant an agent somewhere in that same grouping in China."

"Yes," the Director of the CIA said. "I'm glad you asked me that. As a matter of fact, we have."

30

1971–1976

The United States Army's agent inside China had had nightmares on the trip north, thinking about the merciless de-briefings to come. But fear was mastered because Dr. Baum had planted a slow, slow gain in the agent's imagination that gradually brought total confidence that no Chinese de-briefing system could overcome the locks and balances of Dr. Baum's system. And Dr. Baum was right.

The agent watched and memorized. A new realization, much more encompassing than fear, took possession of the agent's imagination. Dr. Baum's design had been total. (Dr. Baum was a genius to whom the United States Army would owe far more than even the defeated German armies owed him.) What Dr. Baum had done with the agent was to plant a delayed realization, surfacing sixty days after the Chinese de-briefings: *the agent was not to be governed by any orders planted by the Chinese briefings intended to make the agent into a revolutionary filled with murderous violence against the United States.* This delayed realization worked to an extent, but *pari passu* with the Chinese brainwashing objectives. The agent was in a sense changed into a true schizophrenic; one part an agent of the United States Army, not only assigned to the task of saving the future of the United States of America but *locked* into that concept by Dr. Baum with neither voluntary nor involuntary means of evasion; the other part a convinced, cold-blooded, violently murderous revolutionary re-educated to help direct the execution of the Teel Plan against the United States. By the most advanced technological procedures of military psychology, the agent had been rendered insane.

The agent was sane of course while remaining within only one area of imagination. Sensing this, the agent tried to become the total revolutionary while in China —because that was demanded. But the other half kept insinuating itself, crying out its rights and the agent's duties.

So the agent solved it all, made peace out of what could have been an unsolvable conflict, by retreating deep into schizophrenia. Watching the other Americans, the agent listened and studied harder than anyone there, pounding every scrap of the information of every day into memory so that when the agent returned from China, America could be saved. By being forewarned, it would be forearmed against the revolutionary scourge.

Yet—at the very same time—the agent resolved to bring havoc to America, to kill more men, women, and children than anyone had ever killed in history. The agent would destroy more property, and lay waste larger areas of more cities than had been done by all the conquerors of all the cities of the world in history before.

The new insanity really helped: the agent became thereby the most modern of the new people, exquisitely capable of serving two masters.

part
two

1

April 1971

General Marek's unit at the Pentagon had temporarily been separated from any Army Intelligence activity other than Operation Enigma. He had assembled an Intelligence strike force of ninety-four people; they were officers, men, women, blacks and whites. He had settled them into the most intensive investigation of the backgrounds and motivations of the soldier Dr. Baum had had to kill to get them started, and the others Marek assumed were now in China. He assigned nine professional investigators to each of the names. He briefed each team exhaustively although mainly on the considerations that would lead to the single objective they *had to* achieve.

"Somewhere in the United States there is a power grouping that organized these people—all from different cities and states—all entirely separate from each other—insofar as we know—until the time when they came together in Three Platoon. Most of these people seem the furthest possible distance in any society from being political types. It's a pretty sure thing they had to be bribed to agree to what must be to them—these anti-authoritarian criminals and resenters—probably profound hardship. Bribing people to join the Army and desert to some unknown destination takes a lot of money. And how can they make it stick? Therefore, our job is to weave every recurring clue that pops up in the backgrounds of those people into a pattern that will lead us to the political power unit—inside the

185

United States beyond a question of a doubt—the command unit of what may be a revolutionary force. We've got to find the people *here* who sent those people *there*. We've got to smash this thing, whatever it is, before it can get started."

In the second week of the investigation, Captain Maas, recalled from Saigon, was assigned to follow up the nuclear devices possibilities when it was determined that Albert Cassebeer, an experimental physicist, was missing from the laboratories at Las Cruces, New Mexico, and that his name matched that of one of the people who had disappeared from Three Platoon. After three months of intensive investigation Maas could find no trace of Cassebeer: He was a freak; an orphan, friendless, a bachelor who had spent all of his life at his work.

Captain Maas told General Marek he wanted to go up to New York to run down a lead. "It could be a little tricky politically," he said.

"How?"

"Well, this Cassebeer is gone and he didn't leave a trace. Now that don' mean he'd be the same Cassebeer that went into China, does it? Don't answer. I'll answer. No. It doesn't. But it could be the same, couldn't it?"

"What could be a little tricky politically?" Marek asked.

"Well, Cassebeer ain't the only one who disappeared out at Las Cruces. Another experimental physicist name of Jonas Teel is gone. Teel is easier to run down an' that's why I was goin' to New York. Jonas Teel's sister is Agatha Teel, the big lady lawyer. The black lawyer who goes in and out of the White House."

"Be sure you check out all the angles before you talk to her at all, but don't waste too much time. You know how to walk softly," Marek said. "Wear your soft walking shoes."

In the fifth month of the investigation Captain Maas telephoned Agatha Teel at her office to ask if he could see her the following day. Teel invited him to dinner. Maas was on-the-dot prompt, in civilian clothes. He was a prematurely white-haired man with a wooly pate and the expression of a fat lady's knee-cap. Teel had prepared an all-out Mexican dinner. Captain Maas groaned with pleasure. "Oh, mercy! That is *somethin'*!" He had been about to begin his careful questioning, but now that he knew the kind of chuck she was coming up with he decided to eat first and talk later.

After dinner they settled down in the library with a Montecristo in the Captain's face and a glass of Laber-dolive '09 in his hand. It had been one of those perfect evenings, just him and this purty little nigger woman, one of the nicest celebrities he had met since Chill Wills.

He had to prod himself to get talking. "Miz Teel? We wanted to ask you what you might be able to tell us about an Albert Cassebeer?"

She felt a hot steel rod go right through her head at the temples, but she sipped at the Armagnac before she answered, good and cool, "Albert Cassebeer?"

"The experimental physicist?"

"Do I know him? No, I never heard that name."

"Well, your brother is an experimental physicist. And they ain't too many of them. We thought your brother mighta mentioned him?"

"Not that I can remember."

"When did you see your brother last?" He spoke very carefully. He had put his soft-walking shoes on.

"About three months ago."

"Recent letters?"

"Has something happened to my brother?"

"The fact is, Miz Teel——"

"Jonas can't be at Los Alamos or you'd be questioning him directly. Now, you just explain all this to me or I'm going to get on that telephone and call the President to find out."

"No need for that, Miz Teel," Captain Maas said hurriedly. "This is jes' a routine check jes' like we allus got to do when these kind of people don't show up for work."

"Then Jonas is not at Los Alamos?" She made her eyes fill with tears of relief that they knew much less than the shocking amount they had told her.

"No, ma'am."

"Then where is he? Goddammit, where is he?"

"We don't know.'

"You know more than you're telling me and if I have to do it, I'm going to turn this administration upside down until you tell me everything you know about my brother."

"He could be at a guerrilla training camp inside China. We know that's where either your brother or Albert Cassebeer is right now."

"*China?*" She felt glacial. A great distance now separated her from Captain Maas and the rest of the world.

She collected her genius like an armful of spears. It was open-and-shut that they knew the who, what, when, and where. They had to be kept from finding the why, and the who behind the who. Tough, committed genius pushed her forward into the arena, as she thought about beginning her own investigations from the White House downward, to find out how much they did know, and simultaneously about how to mollify and neutralize Captain Maas to get him out of her life. She put up a bleak front. "There is no steadier or more loyal man than my brother in the United States of America," she said. "If he is in China then I say flatly that he was kidnapped to China because of his knowledge of nuclear devices. My brother is incapable of disloyalty to his country."

As soon as Captain Maas left at 11:20, Teel telephoned William Buffalo. She had to call four numbers before she reached him. "Mr. B.," she said amiably, "they is a very big package coming in tonight and nobody but me can take it from them because that's the only way they'll do it. They said I could bring one man with me, and I'd feel best if that man was you."

"You got the deal," William Buffalo said. "Where we gone blend?"

"Can you make it the corner of Park and Thirty-seventh, like in front of the Matson Foundation?"

"Locked in. When?"

"Twelve fifteen?"

"See you there," he said.

They got out of the car at an empty stretch on the Belt Parkway. Teel apologized, then shot William Buffalo to death. She drove back to town feeling blue. He was a good man, but with the whole American government after just one name, that name, William Buffalo, had to keep turning up as they rolled those histories over and over and over. When every one of, say, 150 sources on the backgrounds of those twelve people had been put through the sieve, it had to come out—sooner or later—that the one thing they had in common was William Buffalo.

If they had gotten to Buffie, she had to believe Buffie had told them what he knew—how he had recruited the people now inside China, and who had told him to recruit them—because Buffie would have made his deal to give information and names in return for guarantees that they keep their hands off the business. She had to proceed with that belief. Buffie was a good old boy, and so was everybody else. If they hadn't reached him, then maybe she had wasted a good man. If they had already reached him, she still had Senator Hobart Simms's sister under a lock in China. She would be able to trade her way out with that.

2

1971–1974

Jonas Teel spent three years at the nuclear energy station at Hupeh among cultivated Harvard-trained Chinese—and French, German and English scientists of considerable note. The distinguished foreigners came and went, never staying longer than six months. The characteristic view they all shared, however, was that the effects of nuclear bomb damage had been distorted and exaggerated; that the largest nuclear device ever exploded as a bomb was sixty megatons, merely one thousandth the force of an earthquake, one thousandth the force of a hurricane; that mankind had lived with earthquakes and hurricanes for a long, long time; and that fear of nuclear devices was merely a collective ego trip by which insect-sized man was able to believe he could actually blow up the earth and end the world. But they agreed that "dirty" bombs with millions of times the explosive force, in terms of *human* killing power, were, by and large, nasty things. Mostly, Jonas noticed, the distinguished theoretical physicists tended to keep classical music playing all day, while the experimental physicists always preferred that any music be turned off; they would much rather relax with billiards. Jonas learned a lot about billiards in the Hupeh province, playing on a five-by-ten-foot antique table that had been imported from Australia at a cost of 100,000 Australian dollars, to keep the experimental physicists happy. It had been hand carved out of Tasmanian blackwood by the Scottish craftsman, A.W. Thomson, featuring, in magnificent carvings, the British and Australian flora and fauna of the late nineteenth century.

Jonas was there to learn how to design and build bombs; to reduce their bulk with technology and imagination so that they could be easily transportable in suitcases by guerrilla bomb squads much in the way that *plastiques* had been used in Paris during the Algerian war; the way gelignite was used by the IRA to blow up automobiles and children. When he arrived at the facility, the bomb's delivery package was about the size of a youth's sled. When he left the Hupeh Province to attend the War College, the bulk of the essential bomb with its sixty kilograms of uranium-235 was about the size of a baseball, a design greatly to Jonas Teel's own credit.

He had faced these problems as a bomb designer: sixty kilograms of U-235, in metallic form, weigh 132 pounds. The metal is compact, almost twice as dense as lead. As a cube, the sixty kilograms would measure about half a foot to a side. A nuclear explosion is a chain reaction which moves so fast that pressures build up in the material and blow it apart.

Jonas sweated over methods of delivering less of the critical mass of U-235 than had been delivered at Hiroshima—say, twenty kilograms (smaller than a grapefruit), because such a mass can yield an explosion equivalent to anything from a few tons of TNT up to hundreds of thousands of tons of TNT. It all depended on efficient design.

Jonas was, other than the Chinese establishment at the facility, the only full-time experimental resident. As blocks developed, as imponderables appeared, he had the full collaboration for two to six months at a time of the outstanding nuclear scientists of the western world whose countries maintained diplomatic relationships with the Chinese government and who affected to be in China to assist in the organization of nuclear energy for Chinese industry.

He succeeded, at the end of his second year in

Hupeh, in designing a packaged nuclear device containing nine pounds of fissionable U-235 in a space slightly larger than one of the old-time, "turnip" pocket watches. It would achieve the detonated equivalent of 420,000 tons of TNT, a force more mercilessly destructive inside a great American city than any hurricane or earthquake.

3

1971–1974

"I mean, I tell you," Jane Bossle Weems said at the Women's Camp, "this here place is like the Garden of Eden. Man, you jest try tasting the food in them American prisons. And the broads! Ech!"

They followed the same curricula as the Men's Camp. Everybody was exhausted and, at first, pretty frightened by what they were being trained to do. "Shit, I like tough, man," Winn said. "But this is somepin else, I'm tellin' you. This Gr-1 thing. What kinda way is that to kill somebody? Push 'em outa windows to look like they commit suicide!"

"It'll get easier," Duloissier said. "You keep doin' it and it gets easier. That goes for everything lousy, you know what I mean?"

"What they are telling us," Chelito told them, "is that we got to do this and all the people who fight with us got to do this because we do it straight to the people and for once, for once in their whole lives, the American people knows what war is and maybe, now, when this happen to them—they hate war."

"I think Chelito is right," Enid said. "We can make

life very, very precious for them, I think. I never cared much for life—except when I was with my brother. But now, I don't know, everything we are learning to do is so far beyond pity or forgiveness, so completely vicious and inhuman, that it is what we were never meant to be. I can believe that now. I really can."

"Well, I don't think about it," Jane Bossle Weems said. "You fucked ever' time if you starts thinkin', I'm tellin' you. The food is good and the sex is right. The clothes is warm and the people act fine. Well, comes the payoff. We owe them. What do they want? They want us to blow up a few thousand li'l babies. I ask you—what's so bad about that?" She began to cry. Winn and Enid led her off to the infirmary. They gave her some pills and she said she felt better. She told them she was crying because she was having a hard time with a pretty little Arab girl over at Camp Saud, a sweet little girl who just played around and played around until Janie Bossle didn't know where she was at. "And I'll tell you something else," she said to them fiercely on the way back to the dormitory. "I ain't gone blow up no babies, no matter who."

But the re-indoctrination changed all that, just as motion pictures, television, a responsive press, comic books, novels, advertising, gadgets and gimmicks—and the sense of a loss of God—had bent the American mind too into eager acceptance of any kind of murder, loss of passion or hope of innocence. It took longer that way. In order to create hollow men, an American child had to be led to the tube at twenty months and left there until the football season was over and he was sixty-three. But, at Camps Fritchie and Cody, the best minds of their generations had devised ways to achieve that terrible loss by a crash course. Within two years there wasn't a woman at Fritchie who would flinch at blowing up a few thousand babies.

The first winter was bitterly cold, but there was no let-up on the outdoor training—they all just ate twice as much. As time went by, as they moved up, each year, in knowledge and, above all, understanding of what it was they were being trained to do, they became quieter and more deliberate; steadier and deadlier. Life was operating by stealth, leaving the world to bleed to death behind them in silence as they darted away in shadows. Everything they could lift seemed made to maim or to kill. Mastering the arts of massive terror, they became themselves calm, mobile and icy. As they moved up, class by class, new arrivals came to the camp from Germany, Paraguay, Egypt, Holland, Zaïre, Italy and Japan. In the final days of the third year the six senior women at Fritchie were moved out of the lakeside camp at Hei-ma-ho to the guerrilla War College at Karlik Tagh, also called K'a-erh-li-k'o Shan, 4,925 feet high in the eastern Sinkiang Province, 80 miles from the Mongolian Frontier.

All the American women made tearful farewells with Major Wong. They knew thay would never see him again. "You have been a *wonder*ful class, a really moving class," he said brokenly (for him) in his Pomona, California, accent.

"You the greatest piece of poontang I ever had, man or woman," Sally Winn said, her lip bobbling. "You a little guy and you pecker don't look like much but, man, do you know how to use it!"

Enid told him softly, "I can honestly say, Cal, that the off-duty afternoon hours I spent with you will always remain among the high points of my life. You are an artist."

The Americans, men and women, had finished three years of intensive field training on every conceivable guerrilla problem. They were ready now for more abstract studies: the problems of commanders of large units of guerrilla troops and the efficient uses of staff and line officers. They reported to the War College separately, twenty-three women of mixed nationalities and a selection of thirty-eight men. For the third year running Kranak had led all others as an achiever. He was voted by faculty and student body

to be the best officer material the camps had ever produced. He was certain to make the uppermost available American command.

There was much joy, much lust, and a great deal of
instant fucking beginning with the first night. Kranak
saw Gussow in the half light and dragged her and
Fantome Duloissier into the room assigned to them
and performed prodigies upon them for at least
twenty-five minutes, after which he collapsed and they
ran out of the room looking for some real action.
There was nothing faulty about either Kranak's inten-
tions or his equipment. He was just so out of practice
since he had refused sex with anyone for three years,
that his gun went off at the touch of Gussow's horny
hand, and how long could anybody, even a top
achiever, be expected to keep that up? At least they
were honed by Kranak, so when the women ran into
Buckley in the corridor everybody was ready and
waiting. They dragged him into the laundry room and
raped him on a pile of denim sheets. Then he raped
them. Then they raped him again. Before they finished, they had worked up a wonderful appetite for
dinner.

Throughout the campus, men and women from the
same countries tended to seek out the same love-
making tastes and styles. As Sally Winn said, Major
Wong was the greatest, but he was so far-out that she
suddenly knew how much she had missed that real
American home cooking. In the first two months or
so they worked it out by having all the people from
all the countries screw all the people from the other
countries, but after that they began to settle down
slowly until half the women were permanently paired
off with twelve of the men, leaving eleven women for
twenty-six men, or, depending on the viewpoint,
twenty-six men for eleven of the women.

A few paired off as "permanent" couples. Out of
all those sixty-one people, only one of them "fell in
love." Enid fell in love with Kranak from the first mo-

ment she saw him. She didn't analyze why, she just loved him as the schoolgirl loves the French professor; because he was there, like Everest; perhaps because there were attitudes, expressions and postures he assumed which were so much like Daddy. Kranak simply did not see Enid. He would have been drawn to Enid had he *seen* her; he had a strong distaste for these coarse, criminal, disgustingly liberated women. There were too many goddam niggers, and Jews, and guineas and greasers and gooks.

If he had seen Enid he would have appreciated her. She could fuck in French or German, which would have impressed him. She could have played the guitar or piano to him. Her soft, cultivated, helpless voice knew poetry and that was surely a gentling thing in a woman. She *washed* several times daily. She showered each evening. She cared for her hair, her fingernails and the men she was with and did not cry "Shit!" with every fourth word. Enid was a lady.

But—he didn't see her, so she moved in with Jonas Teel, who was back with the class for his final year at the War College. Enid grabbed Jonas because he was strong, he was new, and he was American. She wanted to be with just one man. She was confused from the rapid-fire, free-lance fucking she had been enjoying during the first few weeks on the campus. Jonas was the gentlest man of all of them. He was her *gentleman*. It would have been better if he had come from Maryland instead of way up north. But none of that mattered because she didn't love him.

Sally Winn and Orin Dawes were the most successful alliance during the year at the War College because they were opposite numbers of the same kind. They had both always believed in the destruction of authority but they had each mastered separate ways to achieve this. They fascinated each other. She was a master street fighter. He was a West Pointer. That unbelievable proximity stunned, almost muted, Winn. Dawes had the feeling that, at last, he was going to get away from classroom theory on guerrilla warfare and hear it from someone who had looted and killed in the streets.

Winn had seen two recent West Point movies on television before she left the States, one starring William Haines and the other with a new young actor named Dick Powell who sang all the fucking time. So she knew about West Point. In between the eating and the hard studying and the fucking, she and Dawes talked about West Point all the time. "How come they don't let women go there?" Winn asked.

"I can't understand that," Dawes said. "I mean—look at us. I mean we could be at West Point right now."

They talked about Blücher, Grant, Caesar, Bradley, Napoleon and Von Paulus; Winn at the level of West Point, Dawes trying to put it all into the context of street fighting.

After two weeks of living with Jonas Teel (and making him very happy) Enid was finally discovered by Kranak. Winn told Dawes how Enid was feeling about Kranak. "That man don' deserve a woman like Simms," Winn told him. "But she want him, so we gotta get him for her."

"Get him? How?"

"There's somethin' wrong with him. You told me yourself he didn't touch a woman for three years, an' I know why."

"Why?"

"Because they was all Chinese women. He ain't touched one black woman here. So you just pass the word on Enid to him for me and tell him she's a real lady. Tell him she's the niece of Herbert Ryan Willmott. Then stand back, man."

Kranak dropped everything and everyone to get at Enid. He sat with her in the mess hall for two days talking earnestly in a low voice. She said she couldn't just walk out on Jonas. He said she had to walk out. She walked out. She told Jonas, "I don't mean to hurt your feelings, Jonas. This is something else. I mean, I don't have any control over this."

"It's all *right*, baby. I dig. I do. I swear, I understand."

Kranak and Enid were right for each other for nearly six months. Enid picked up quickly that he wanted her to play the Victorian lady. She knew how to do that. He sensed she wanted some special private consideration which he could identify with something the song writers called "tenderness," some element of inner courtesy she had always had in her life with Bart. Kranak knew how to fake that. Enid went deeper and deeper like a gambler with her last inheritance because Kranak was infallible in all things, as her father had been when she was a little girl. And he môved like Daddy. And he talked in the same commanding, slow, self-important way while he handled his pipe as if it were the sword of Arthur. He was so strong. He could keep going at the same set pace whether they were in a blizzard or without water in the desert. He was so narrow-minded and jealous, it brought Enid security. If, basically, it was possible that he was a very cruel man, he taught her the golden values of snobbism all over again.

Then it all got smashed. He and Sally Winn had been working out mustard gas problems for the public school systems. It was a matter of pre-placement in school ventilators, then a remote control trigger. Kranak had gotten himself into a temper because he was working alone in a room with a black woman and he had called Sally a nigger slut. Sally asked him, all sweetness, if the term had been meant to be affectionate or vicious. He had hawked phlegm and spit it into her face. Sally wiped it off carefully, staying very, very calm. She said—even and cool—that she thought everybody at the War College adored niggers—because his own special shack-up certainly did.

"Watch your filthy tongue," Kranak said.

"I was only saying that Miss Enid was fucking and sucking Jonas Teel for ten hours a night before she moved in to do the same for you, so she must adore us niggers like the rest of the folks here."

"That's a goddam lie!" Kranak's voice shook so much he could hardly get the words out.

"Well, say, I'm sorry—you hear? Because if you shaky about niggers—how you feel about Chinee men? Miss Enid love Chinee men. She gone down on Major Wong so many times he call her his li'l Yo-Yo."

Kranak knocked Winn over four desks and left her unconscious in a corner of the lab, then he raced out to look for Enid. He found her crocheting little white gloves, the kind he felt a lady should wear, at their small apartment.

"What's the matter, Ed? You look terrible. Gizza-kiss."

"You listen to me, then you tell me the truth—you hear?"

"Which truth?" she said naïvely.

"Did you live with Jonas Teel before you moved in with me?"

"Well—yes." Enid thought everybody knew that.

"You screwed that big, sweaty nigger?"

"Sweaty? *Nigger?* What kind of a word is that? *Sweaty?* You're a lot sweatier than Jonas Teel will ever be. Jonas is a gentleman who believes in showers, Eddie."

"Shad*dop!*" Kranak was working himself into a frantic state. "Did you screw the Chinese on off-time?"

"Of *course.* Didn't you?"

"What I did is different! I am a man, you are a woman! Man dominates the woman and he throws her away when he's through with her the way I am through with you now!"

"Ed, what is this? What is happening? Don't say things like that."

"A woman is just a part of man's hard-on," Kranak yelled, "not a part of his life. Everything is opposite for women!" He threw a lamp at the wall and it crashed into splinters. "A woman mews for the attention of the man. She lives for the man and she would die for him if she had to do without him. But she cannot do without him so what you have done with a stinking, rotten nigger and a pile of Chinese bodies is just dis*gus*ting! It is cheap and perverted and pukingly low and dis-*GUSS*-ting." He began to beat her; a hard left hook to the side of the head. She staggered backward; a viciously hard right cross into the other side of her head. "Get out of here!" he screamed. "Out! Get out!" He kicked her in the stomach. "You little whore! You slimy, nigger-loving, chink-loving whore—*get out of here!*" He dragged her to the door by her right wrist and flung her out into the stairhall and a quarter of the way down the stairs. He ran back into the room, piled up her gear into his arms, her foot locker, cakes of soap and hair curlers and flung them down on top of her, yelling hysterically. Two men came out into the hall and shoved him back into his room. Three women helped Enid down the stairs and out of the wooden house.

Enid stumbled out of the common yard and along the company street to Jonas's building. She knocked at his door. He let her in without a word. He made her a cup of tea.

"He beat you up?"

She nodded and sipped the tea dumbly.

"You want me to really take him apart?"

She looked at him in fright and shook her head. "He couldn't help it, Jonas. He suddenly lost his mind the way my father could just lose his mind." He washed her face. They put talcum powder on her bruises.

Three hours later on the way to the mess hall, Enid and Jonas were walking along silently in a dispersed group of people all going in to chow, when they heard heavy running behind them and turned around. It was Kranak, coming up fast, wild-eyed. Kranak was yelling, "Nigger! You, nigger!" Jonas grinned at Kranak's despair, and when Kranak came flying in at his throat, Jonas picked him up and threw him contemptuously into the winter river making its way down the slope from the mountains. They all moved along into the mess hall, ignoring Kranak trying to get a foothold on the river bottom.

Kranak came into the mess hall late, wearing dry clothes. He ate silently. As the mess detail was clearing the tables, Sally Winn got up and walked across the big room to where Kranak was seated. She opened one of the long, clean, straight razors in her hand and dropped it on the table in front of him.

"Pick it up, good-lookin'," she said, "then come on outside. There's good light out there and we won't make a mess. Come on. You and me gone fight."

He stared at her coldly. "I don't fight with women or with razors," he said loftily.

"You gone fight this woman with that razor or there won't be anything left of you but about three yards of ribbons." Winn moved the razor in her hand very fast. Her razor opened a deep, slanting wound in his right cheek. He held his hand under the dripping blood with amazement. He looked at her, hardly comprehending what had happened, then, grabbing the razor with a great and terrifying scream, he was on his feet overturning the table. He moved so fast Sally never had a chance. He had her by the hair, snapping her head back, exposing her throat to the razor and would have taken her head off at the shoulders with it, if Enid hadn't hit him with two tremendously hard double kicks, knocking him sideways to the floor, sprawling him out on his back. Winn darted in and using all her wiry strength delivered a mighty backswing kick into his balls. Kranak's scream before he passed out made his screams at Winn and Enid seem like little theatrics.

A whistle was blown. The hall emptied, leaving Kranak writhing there.

A formal investigation was held by the Chinese authorities while Kranak recovered slowly in the hospital. Wise men in Peking decided it was not their problem and sent the file to Teel in New York, via

Bogotá. Teel weighed all of it and replied. She said that a man could not help his prejudices, that he had very little to do with them. She wrote that Kranak was a great officer who was potentially a great commander. "What the hell are we running," she asked, "a revolution or a popularity contest?"

After graduation all American assignments were made. Ed Kranak was given the Eastern Action Area. Sally Winn drew the Western Action Area. Orin Dawes got the Army Corps command for the dense midwestern urban region; the units under his command were divisional, brigade, regimental and battalion. He reported only to Kranak. Jane Bossle Weems became Army Corps Commander in the cities of the American northeast; Lurky Anderson got an ACC for the deep South and middle-Atlantic cities. Buckley took the heavy Cuban and Latin-American sector in the southeast; Reyes commanded the southwest across all the Mexican border states. Jenny Duloissier got the Northwest; Gussow got the far west. Dolly Fingus got blown up while making a bomb.

Jonas Teel was named Central Commander and seconded Colonel Pikow. At the command officer level Jonas was the only guerrilla who knew of Colonel Pikow's existence as Chief of Staff. Only Teel, Pikow, Jonas, and Enid were aware of the existence of the fourteen-man General Staff. The chain of command was always invisible. It went from Agatha Teel to Pikow to the General Staff to Jonas Teel to Kranak and Winn to Action Area Army Corps Commanders, then downward into combat levels. No commander knew of the siting or rank of command of any other. Kranak and Sally Winn knew more than any other operational officer and they only knew how to reach their Army Corps Commanders, no one else. It was a fail-safe system.

Enid Simms, who had acquired Spanish and Chinese to add to French and German, and graduated number three in the class (men and women) was given Inter-City/Intra-City Guerrilla Intelligence, a function which would not really begin until the war started.

For greatest security only on the day before Kranak's departure for New York (first out because he was highest ranking commander) was he given his false passport and his new name—in the same way as these would be given to every graduate just before departure. They had come into China as convicted men and women; the men had disappeared from a U.S. Army combat zone and were therefore deserters, so new, permanent identities were necessary with new American passports. Teel had chosen the new names so she could keep permanent track of her commanders. She had also chosen his name to take skin off Kranak.

He came bursting into Headquarters office brandishing the new passport. "Cal, what the hell is this? What kind of a practical joke do you think you're playing here?"

"What?"

"This fucking *pass*port! What are you *doing* to me?"

"I am very busy, Kranak. Either speak up and state it or get the hell out."

"This—name. Chandler Shapiro. Do I look like a Jew?"

The major stared at him. "Yes. A little. Why? What's wrong with that? I happen to look like a Taoist."

"I am a Lipan Apache! This has to be changed. I demand that this passport be changed or I am not leaving."

"Kranak, llissenamee—that passport came from Peking. You dig? It came from the Foreign Office in Peking and it came from a security department in the Foreign Office which is so high up, you or I

couldn't breathe there. You are telling me that I am
going to tell those kind of people in Peking that they
don't know how to forge a passport—right? *Get the
hell out of here, Kranak!*"

4

January 1976

They moved out of China singly in January 1976.
Through Hong Kong.

Teel, then Enid Simms followed Kranak, everyone
traveling three days apart. No one knew the destina-
tions of the others. Western Action Area Commander
Winn went out next, followed by Dawes, Reyes,
Buckley then Lurky Anderson. The last to leave was
Chelito Gurma, after Weems, Gussow and Duloissier.
The CIA plant sent a cable to Winsted, Connecticut,
which said simply FLYING HOME TODAY MOM AND
DAD. SEE YOU SOON.

Teel had made all the assignments. She had chosen
Chelito, the strangest of all the commander-trainees,
to be her bodyguard in New York. Before recruitment by William Buffalo, through friends, Chelito
had been a monastic for twelve years from the age
of seventeen. She said to Winn who had also been a
monastic, in solitary in state prisons around the country, "You know, it was a wonderful life for me. I gave
myself to Jesus and I did as I was bade. On this earth
my abbess was the symbol of Jesus so that, whenever
I was confused about my life or my mission, I spoke to
her, I put everything into her hands, and she decided
for me. It was a life of pure prayer; very beautiful.

Prayer is not like communication in a letter or by a telephone. It is speaking directly to Jesus. It brings you peace. I was so happy."

"So?" the lanky black girl said. "What the fuck did you get out for?"

"Well," Chelito shrugged. "I had a complete physical and mental breakdown. That is no good, you know? I was the Cistercian order. I hadn't spoken for twelve years except to answer to my abbess for the essential needs of the monastery. But I didn't need to speak. My abbess loved me. Jesus loved me. But I began to decompose and I don't know why."

"Did they know how to handle it? I mean—that must happen all the time in a place like that."

"They tried. My spiritual adviser worked with me. They brought a woman psychiatrist. Then they brought a man psychiatrist. They tried. Then my abbess said I must be sent out into the world again to find out if that was what Jesus meant for me. They sent me out and I got well. I went to prison but I got well."

"But what you doin' *here*, baby?"

"My abbess said to me—Chelito, find the truth. So I looked. I said, if the truth is not in peace perhaps the truth lives in the violence men do. Because violence is so much more the mark of all of us than peace I wondered if Jesus meant us to be violent. I look for the truth."

"Okay. When you find it, what you gone do with it?"

"I am going to take it back to my abbess and to my cell in Rhode Island and offer it up to Jesus in my daily prayers. She will let me stay there forever when I have found the truth."

"The abbess?"

"Jesus."

"Oh. You said she."

"Jesus is a woman, Sally. Perhaps a black woman."

Of all the women of any country at the camp at Hei-ma-ho, Chelito was the most accomplished at violence. She could throw a knife with greater accuracy than most people could use a flashlight beam. She could kill with her hands in eleven different ways. She was accomplished with all small arms, all explosives. She feared nothing but loss of the love of Jesus. All she required in order to excel, with total devotion and no questions, was to be led by a purposeful woman. After Teel had gone over her records a few times, she ordered that Chelito be sent to her.

5

January 1976

The Army Intelligence agent who had just come out of China fifty-six hours before had posted a short letter to a name and address in St. Louis, Missouri. It said, as arranged four years before, *Dear Jack: Just got back from the Laundry Convention. Will wait for your call at the Hilton, New York, beginning tomorrow.* From San Francisco the agent also called someone named T. Garfunkel in New York.

"I'm part of the Hong Kong shipment," the agent said. "I just got into San Francisco."

"We want you in New York."

"Can I take three days here? I got bad jet lag."

"Take until Monday morning. Call me from New York Monday morning."

The agent flew into New York on the next available plane and checked into the Hilton Hotel.

They couldn't wait. When the door opened into a large suite on the twenty-sixth floor, Dr. Baum and the three colonels were waiting there.

When the CIA plant who had spent four years in the Chinese guerrilla training camp had landed in San Francisco from Hong Kong, the agent had followed instructions that the air stewardess had handed over twenty minutes before touchdown. The note said the CIA plant was to sit at a table in the airport's pancake joint.

There were plenty of empty tables. Almost as soon as the plant sat down, a short, trendily dressed man wearing gray pork chop whiskers, thirtyish with a high, bald head, sat down across the table. "Call me Langley," he said. "We want you to take these pills." He handed over a labeled vial of brown glass. The waitress arrived. The trendy man ordered trendy lindenberry pancakes for both of them without looking at the card, while the plant read the vial label. It said: *Three Pills at 1 p.m. (Yellow). Two Pills At 4 p.m. (Green). Call at 5 p.m. When There Will be Abdominal Pains: Dr. Abraham Weiler, 2459 Pacific —Walnut 2–4282.*

While they ate the pancakes, the man said that a room had been reserved at the St. Francis Hotel for the pill-taking.

The plant called a New York number from the St. Francis, asking for T. Garfunkel, reporting arrival in San Francisco. The Garfunkel voice told the plant to call again on Monday morning at 8:30.

When the pains began, the plant telephoned Dr. Weiler who said he would be right over. He arrived within twelve minutes, a neatly kept man with a russet moustache that looked dyed. He diagnosed acute appendicitis without any examination and telephoned for a hospital ambulance.

The agent was isolated in a three-room suite at the King de los Reyes Hospital in O'Farrell Street. The de-briefing began at 5:55 P.M. When no call reached T. Garfunkel in New York on Monday morning, Colonel Pikow traced his revolutionary commander through the hotel to the hospital. By saying he was the agent's brother he got a full report on medical progress. On the fourth day when the de-briefing was concluded, the lower abdomen was incised and sewn. On the fifth day the agent flew to New York.

6

January 1976

Admiral Melvin looked down the long table of commanding officers of the Army, Navy and Marine Corps with their aides.

"Everyone here has read the China de-briefing. I don't know about you but when I finished that report I just felt like resigning and running to Costa Rica." He smiled grimly. "But the feeling left me. We all know what we've got to do—we've got to get ready to stop something we never imagined could ever exist. We have staff plans, of course. Every contingency is what staff planning is. But nobody—nobody, nobody —ever foresaw the nature and size of this contingency.

"The fact is—I just don't know how to break it to the civilians. The White House people and the NSC are bound to think, at first anyway, that this is just a rabble to be broken up before they can get started. Maybe so. But it doesn't look that way.

"Our agent gives us minuscule details as far as their system has allowed. I mean the agent knows what is going to happen but not where the other leaders are. The agent knows they have a force of 750,000 *trained* guerrilla troops and you've read right there how they were trained, where and by whom. But the agent doesn't know where any of the leaders are, has no idea who is *the* leader of all this.

"Well, the agent knows the projected operations. On those operations rest the whole nub of this nation's survival in the form in which it has existed since 1776. How can we fight a full-scale war inside thirty American cities containing seventy-eight percent of the population of this country, against a hit-and-run, worse-than-terroristic, fully armed, fully trained guerrilla force whose only military objective is to murder the population? Here is the one-quintillion-dollar question: Can we or can we not fight that kind of war?"

7

1971–1976

From the mid-sixties forward Teel had been working on her plans for recruit training, which she put into operation in early 1971. She did it mostly with ready, steady money. She began by having the smack pushers recruit from 53 street gangs in northern Brooklyn; 41 gangs in the south Bronx; in all from 219 youth gangs in the greater metropolitan area, including Newark and Jersey City. They were all adepts at urban guerrilla warfare, having been at it since childhood and having (effectively) kept the police from operating on their turf since the late sixties. She pulled in some recruits from all of them: the Dirty Ones, the Spanish Kings, to the B'nai Zaken and the Open Fly League. Males and females were welcome. She gave them something they had never seen before: real equipment, real weapons, real purpose and real discipline.

Teel had reasoned purely about their training. To turn slum kids into riflemen at lowest to no cost/risk, she took advantage of the zeal of the National Rifle Association. Already many shooting ranges had been set up in cellars and armories in all Teel's thirty cities to teach housewives how to protect themselves. Teel established others. Some were even self-liquidating because they were part of restaurants which Teel advertised as "Gun Clubs." She turned a profit on meals and fees and weapons rental, she was assigned National Rifle Association instructors, and before and after the housewives had their training sessions, the boys and girls from the Filthy Fifty or the Mayaguez Monsters took their lessons in the same ranges from the same qualified teachers.

When they knew how to handle weapons, Teel moved them along to the second training area. She paid them (with money or shit) to join the Army and Air National Guard, that reserve force available for wars and civil emergencies; a full-time partner in the air-defense network; the operating force for 43 percent of the missile sites around the key cities of continental United States. The Air National Guard flew 52 percent of the fighter-interceptor planes on a round-the-clock runway alert.

Enlistees had to be between seventeen and twenty-six. The hitch was for six years on a part-time basis. On enlistment they served from four to six months on active duty, having the choice (Teel's choice) of training with the Army or Air Force. The remainder of the six years' service was spent in part-time training with the guard unit in which they had chosen to enlist. A Guardsman received a full day's pay of his military rank for each day of his Annual Field Training plus any other days on active duty for training at military schools or special assignments. Guardsmen were not subject to Selective Service. Over 73 percent of the personnel Teel had caused to enlist were able to qualify for special guerrilla training by the government. Deserters or malingerers were killed by Teel's people. But she paid the others well.

In the five years between 1971 and 1976, Teel arranged for the enlistment of a rounded-out average of 4,000 of the very best marksmen from her Gun Club-NRA training to enlist in the National Guard in each of the Thirty Cities, giving her an elite armed force of almost 125,000 street fighters.

When the governors of the states had to call out the National Guard units to fight Teel's urban guerrillas beginning in July 1976, four thousand of the best-trained Guardsmen in each city would be able to kill a preponderant number of their fellow Guardsmen before they switched over to the urban guerrilla forces with their weapons, after having dismantled Air National Guard planes and all protecting missile sites on city perimeters.

Effectively, Teel's Guardsmen would reduce the total complement of the National Guard from 500,-000 fighting men to (probably) 70,000. But Teel's true coup, overall, was that the explicit training of 125,000 guerrilla troops had been done at no cost to the Freedom Fighters movement, except for a few dozen killings to enforce discipline; it had all been done at taxpayers' expense. Teel was fond of the name Freedom Fighters. It was the essence of the sublime bullshit that the people liked to pretend they understood or cared about. Teel's guerrillas would be fighting for free tecana, not for abstract freedom. They had too fucking much abstract freedom as it was. They would be fighting for rich ass in the midtown and suburban areas because rape was a weapon that terrorized the square men if not (in the long run) the women. They'd be fighting for the freedom to burn and kill and loot until they got more than their share of all the gold the squares had taken two hundred years to corner.

Backing up the trained and disciplined guerrillas, the 125,000 Guardsmen, were the real foot soldiers of the Teel intention: the entire population of the narcotics industry with their relatives and families; illegal aliens; all the disaffected and disenfranchised who wanted deadly action for the sake of action, to bring death cheaply either to escape boredom or to get revenge for not having been born privileged. Teel had the working criminal classes: the whores, the hoods, the muggers, the armed robbery people, the thieves— everyone who worked in crime with their hands; she had only a very few who worked in crime with their heads. There were no patriots. Teel didn't want to have anything to do with patriots, idealists, scene-savers, brotherhood-of-man hustlers or anybody else like that. They found out too quickly that they had too much to lose in this new kind of war where there was only one objective: to destroy *everything* that stood for the immediate or ultimate benefit of anyone.

When the trained cadres of field commanders came home from China in January 1976, Teel had everything ready for them. She gave them marksmen, tested troops, a rabble disciplined by their need for heroin, large arms caches at multiple sites in the Thirty Cities, medical support, and a nuclear strike force—all of it scientifically dispersed; all lost to the eye deep within every part of the cities. The ten combat commanders moved in with the mercenary foreign guerrilla Army Corps commanders who had been organizing for Teel since 1968. When the Chinese-trained Americans convinced the others (and Pikow and Teel) that they were ready to take over, they were in full command.

Four of the mercenaries stayed on as a seconded General Staff Plans Unit for a shot at the most organized action urban guerrillas would ever see. The first eleven nuclear bombs would be detonated, the first two water supply systems would be poisoned, the first twenty-eight hospitals and schools would be burned down beginning at dawn on July 4, 1976, two-hundredth anniversary of the Republic.

8

1971–1976

For four years Bart had lived through the days and had tried to sleep through a thousand despairing nights, his mind full of the crowding images and memories of Enid. He taught himself that she was alive until he *knew* she was alive. He tried to accomplish everything she had wanted him to do so that, when she returned, she would be proud of him.

He won the election to the Senate with a plurality of 29,812 votes. The national press consensus had him on the end of a rope and was pulling him toward some future White House. The state chairmen, county leaders, ward captains and block stewards had known in advance how much the plurality would be but they were bewildered by the extent of the unprecedented national ground swell, in terms of hard money, which the candidate kept generating. Of course, they revealed this phenomenon to all other professional politicians in the party. The press only knew what the professional politicians told them. When the Maryland people told the California state organization that Simms had pulled in $67,000 in cash from their western state while running for office 2,800 miles east; told the New York pols that their voters had sent him $209,000; Illinois, $174,000; Pennsylvania, $136,000; Massachusetts, $91,412, none of the professionals could explain how it had happened. But they knew that an awful lot of usually indifferent people had put their money where their mouth was.

Simms never said anything much himself. In the Senate, he didn't do anything much either. Yet, in the first year after his election, his campaign managers, all full-time professionals who did not kid each other, admitted to the national fraternity that the party head-quarters in seventeen states had received *over $4 million in unsolicited campaign contributions from individual voters* urging that he run for the presidency in 1976. The professional politicians were very, very much impressed. All of them cross-checked all of the seventeen states for confirmation. They knew in 1973 that he was a sure winner for 1976, but they were baffled by how to help the press interpret why he had this effect on the voters. They decided it must be something in his looks that they were not yet able to see. They decided he had something somebody had called charisma when they had to find a similar label for the also-mystifyingly popular John F. Kennedy.

None of them linked the $1,900,000 that Bart had paid over to state county and ward level organizations in Maryland with the rest of the money that had poured in from outside the state for this totally un-known candidate. If a man didn't have that kind of money to spread around, he wouldn't be allowed to run for the Senate anyway. They didn't make this connection because they were told that Simms had a limited amount of "inherited" money and they sup-posed his uncle, a power broker, was helping out for his own reasons. They believed the rest of the money was genuinely from the people because it was so prof-itable to believe it.

Smelling big money, the professional politicians of seventeen of the most populous states of the Union began to instruct the captive political press about Senator Simms's destiny, his charisma and his man-of-the-future profile. The grand message was repeated in print, on the air and in front of TV cameras hun-dreds of times as early as 1974. Senator Simms re-mained aloof from the constant insistence that he was the next president. But he would be, every man and woman who made a direct living out of it knew that. As these party sachems bayed and tipped, Senator Simms went out after them to nail them down on their home bases.

He began with Pennsylvania because Senator Marvin Karp was already prospering so very well in the national heroin industry due to Bart's own invitation. Senator Karp took Senator Simms to Harrisburg to "meet the boys" five weeks after Bart's induction into the Senate. Bart hired national committeemen to do "research" for his candidacy. The fees were deposited in a Nigerian bank or in Switzerland—as they chose. By the end of Bart's first year in office, while remaining respectfully silent, thereby earning the respect of his fellow senators, Bart was able to retain the "research services" of national committeemen and state chairmen from seventeen of the stronger key states.

In the ninth week after his induction, Senator Karp took Bart along with him to one of the Agatha Teel Thursday "cook-outs" that had become so important. There Bart met eight of the members of the Council on Foreign Relations (the lay body which was called "the real State Department" until Mr. Kissinger became Secretary). Bart felt himself persuaded that it would be smart if he were to attend Teel dinners every Thursday and used what charm he had on Teel to have himself invited again. As weeks went on he appreciated Teel's tact and wisdom. He liked to think that they had become friends.

In the summer of 1975, Senator Simms accompanied Teel to open a clinic in Harlem. Three weeks later he accepted an invitation to attend the presentation, at the New York *Daily News,* in the presence of a cross-section of leaders of the eastern Negro community, of a Golden Disc for Teel's latest recording, "Dance on Me, Baby," which had sold 1,200,000 copies, from which Miss Teel donated all proceeds to the Black Easter Bunny Fund. They were photographed. In the picture, which ran in the *Daily News,* were Miss Teel and the Senator; Binchy Dawes, a community leader; and, somewhat in the background —to Senator Simms's dismay—Joseph Palladino. The next day Bart telephoned Teel. "How did that man get in the picture?" he asked abruptly.

"What man, baby?"

"Next to the punch bowl. His name is J.D. Palladino."

"Oh. Yeah. Well, he's been a big donator to the Black Easter Bunny. He heads up the whole Italian-American Convention for a Cleaner Manhattan."

Senator Karp stopped him in the corridor of the Senate Office Building the following day to ask him if he were out of his mind to allow his picture to be taken with J.D. Palladino and Benjamin Disraeli Dawes.

"Who is Benjamin Disraeli Dawes?"

"You were standing beside him in the picture."

"Who is he?"

"He's the most important black wholesaler of heroin in the United States."

"I'm shocked!"

"You've got to do something about that, Bart."

"What? What should I do?'

"I think you should ask for Agatha Teel's help to get that negative out of the newspaper files."

Bart got on the telephone in his office and insisted that Teel set an earliest meeting, then and there. He felt he had every right to be indignant. He was running eleven points ahead of the nearest party rival for the nomination, and two point four points ahead of the president. He was about to announce his candidacy and on the fifteenth of January he would begin real campaigning around the country, barnstorming and bribing his way into the hearts of the people. So he was truly irritated that Teel had put him on this spot. He had to go up to New York for the appearance on Meet the Heat and to talk to the Southern

District people. He pressed Teel for a meeting after that.

"Why don't just the two of us have a real nice little supper right here?" Teel said.

The wine was a *very* good Taittinger '59 bubbly, and he enjoyed hearing the cork pop and watching the smoke curl out of the bottle and seeing the golden champagne pour into big, paper-thin crystal glasses because Teel had handed him the negative of the annoying picture in a *Daily News* envelope as he had stepped out of the elevator into her living room.

They clinked glasses and smiled happily at each other.

"How did those two men ever get anywhere near that picture?" Bart asked amusedly.

"Well—they are big contributors."

"To the Black Easter Bunny?"

"Well, yes. To the Black Bunny, too."

"And to what else?"

"I am a criminal lawyer. And Mr. Dawes and Mr. Palladino are my clients."

"Ah. Yes, of course."

"I'd like you to become one of my clients, too."

"Me?"

"Why not?"

"What for?"

"I think I can get your sister back, for example."

He dropped the glass of champagne and did not know he had dropped it. He stared into Teel's eyes, unable to speak. His face drained. His mouth moved convulsively. He put his hand tightly across it.

"Four years is a long time," Teel said sympathetically.

"How did you know that?" He was able to whisper.

"I guess interest is the key of life," she said.

"Where is Enid?"

"Safe."

"Oh, *God!*" He stood up and walked away from Teel. After a while he got control of himself. He stood facing the window as if he were watching the street. "How long have you known this?" he said.

"About four years."

He turned to her. "Why are you telling me now?"

"I thought—about now—you'd want her back."

"How much do you want?"

"Senator—please! I am not the agent for the kidnappers."

"What do you *want*?"

"There are two separate transactions here," Teel said. "One is getting you your sister back. The other is having you sign a paper which I need signed—and that's all there is to it."

"What paper?"

"Have a glass of this good, old champagne," Teel said. She got another glass, then filled it and hers too. "Sit down, Senator," she said pleasantly, smiling at him sympathetically. He returned to a chair near her, lifted the glass and took three sips from it.

"You'll want to read the papers I've drawn, but we'll talk about them first," Teel said. "They are a statement from you which tells the world at large that you made all arrangements to supply J.D. Palladino with raw opium, that you used your influence with members of the Senate to secure the cooperation of the Inter-American Bank and restored foreign aid for Haiti, in payments to the President of Haiti, so that the opium could be processed into heroin in Haiti for sale throughout the United States and that you used your share of the profits from this to secure your nomination and election to the Senate as you have been doing to get the Presidency. That's all."

He wanted to have the single-shot Liberator pistol in his hand. He wanted to kill her. He covered his face with his hands and leaned forward on his knees for a few moments, then he looked at her and said, "Miss Teel—I am more than halfway there. I have over twenty million dollars committed to key state organizations. I—I am almost certain of the nomination. If you—"

"Senator Simms!" she said in a troubled voice. "You have this all *wrong!* I want to *help* you. I think our country *needs* you in the White House." She filled their glasses again to the brims. "Hear me out," she said. "I intend to give these papers back to you and so that you will know that they could not have been copied we will put them in the nearest bank, under an escrow agreement. When your sister arrives here we will make an exchange. I give you your sister. You sign the papers, then together we take the papers to the bank."

"Why?"

"I may need help and if I need it I may need it fast."

"What help?"

"I don't need it yet. And if I don't need it by inauguration day, on the second of January 1977, you get the papers back to burn."

Bart closed his eyes and leaned back, breathing irregularly. Teel sipped champagne as she flipped through the pages of *The New Yorker*. More than five minutes went by.

"When can you have my sister brought to New York?"

"You can meet her in this room on January fourteenth."

"Must it be here?"

"Yes. I give her to you. You sign the papers for me."

9

1969–1976

In her first full year in the narcotics enterprise, 1969–70, Teel grossed $91,983,426. By the end of 1969 she had finished the reorganization of the makeshift sales and distribution apparatus which William Buffalo had improvised. Her effectiveness for his organization was so dramatically profitable that other wholesalers and dealers were happy to cooperate with her in setting down procedures that greatly increased their mutual profits while not requiring that the increase be shared with the pay-off side of operations. She kept bringing in more and more territories, more and more users. By 1973 she was sharing total profits with the entire black narcotics-merchandising national community, but always invisibly.

In 1972, Teel's own share of the national turnover was $423,441,829. In order to distribute the money into normal bank accounts across the country so that her Army Corps commanders, returning in '76, would have instant access to it for operational needs, she had established her network of hundreds of business enterprises, service organizations and drops. This meant steady and heavy expenditure for personnel, equipment, stock and overhead. By 1973, Teel was the owner-manager of commercial assets and accounts receivable whose value exceeded $780 million.

When she had had William Buffalo require all black distributors and dealers to cut away from the Sicilians as their source of heroin and blow, the giant stirred uneasily. Expected gang warfare began but Teel provided such strong protection and such emphatic counter-attack that the Sicilians, glutted with the fat of their enormous profits for so many decades, decided to play it the straight way: they owned the law (they thought), they owned the streets (they thought) and they (certainly) owned the people who used their heroin.

Teel made sure Buffalo (and later Dawes) kept the black operations strictly inside the black ghettos. The Sicilians had the police and the Bureau lean very hard on the blacks but Teel increased her pay-offs and, rather than get themselves into an auction for police and Narcotics Bureau services, the Sicilians decided to cool it.

When the Chinese de-briefed Enid Simms and passed the word to Teel of the heroin connection between Senator Simms and J.D. Palladino, grandest of all Sicilian operators, Teel developed her plan to control the *entire* national heroin market. There could be no possible anxiety now about whether the revolution would be securely financed.

She decided either to merge with the Sicilians or to eliminate them as competitors. In any event, she would control the importation, distribution, sales and collections on all heroin sold in continental United States—a euphemism which included eleven Canadian cities—in a way that booze and beer had never been controlled by any one unit during Prohibition.

In November 1974 Teel called J.D. Palladino to ask for an appointment for herself on behalf of her client, Binchy Dawes. Mr. Palladino said he would be glad to see her. It was an amiable meeting and after some light talk about the Black Bunny and Mr. Palladino's current favorite charity, Italian Boys in Leavenworth, Teel got down to business by saying, "Mr. Dawes has taken a good look at his computer print-outs and everything tells him that there is a very, very big five years ahead."

"Dawes uses a computer?"

"Why not?"

"Of course, why not?"

"The print-outs show the way for Mr. Dawes and you to make a lot more money than he—or you—have ever made before."

"How come?"

"The computer indicates that price wars are out. Why have a lot of trouble? Most of all—why have double overhead?"

"*Double* overhead?"

"What he is saying is: why not combine all strengths and eliminate all weaknesses that are costing both of you money?"

"I don't get this."

"Who has the best connections with the law? The Sicilians. Who has the best street operation and potentially the biggest market? The blacks. Both sides seem to have about the same supply of Number Four and Mr. Dawes feels, if his costs are less than yours, then he wants to pass those savings along to you, he wants to combine all the shit there is on one big five-billion-dollar bag and—according to the computer print-out—increase his take and yours by eighteen percent, none of it claimable by the pay-off."

"Are you talking about a *merge?*"

"That's it. Exactly."

"*Merge?* Merge with *niggers?* Excuse me, Miss Teel."

"That's all right."

"Even if I wanted to do it, which I don't, there isn't another family in this country which would okay a thing like that."

"Why not?"

"Because it's ours, that's why. We found the whole business. We made the whole thing in this country. We set up the cops and the Feds and the politicians and everything else like France and Turkey and you think a black guy is gonna come in here and take half of it away with our permission?'

"The black part of the industry already has over

thirty-eight percent, Mr. Palladino. Mr. Dawes isn't asking for any half. Like every merger he would take out what he puts in. But both sides could win eighteen percent."

"No, Miss Teel. Absolutely never. Tell Dawes for me that I would get out of the business altogether and so would every other Eyetalian or Sicilian family before they would do business with a buncha niggers. I apologize to you in advance, Miss Teel, but I want Dawes to understand."

"Well—we tried, Mr. Palladino."

"Listen, if you don't ask, you don't get."

He stood up. The audience was over. They shook hands ritualistically. He walked her to the door. Dino was waiting in the French room. "Show Miss Teel to the elevators, Dino," Mr. Palladino said. "Can we drive you anywhere, Miss Teel?"

"No thanks, Mr. Palladino," Teel said softly. "My Rolls is waiting."

On February 16, 1976, Teel called Colonel Pikow into a meeting. Their meetings were rare. They met in Teel's uptown bunker, which was thirty-nine feet below street level, under a used car lot and junk yard at 157th Street and Seventh Avenue. Each entered the bunker through different tenement buildings. In the bunker Chelito sat behind a screen next to the principal door with an Armalite rifle propped against the wall beside her. Pikow drank plain tea. Teel sipped chilled wine.

"How's everything?" Teel said, all relaxed.

"You know better than I do," he smiled at her.

"You're looking great."

"Not as good as you."

"We don't meet much, do we? But I have a story to tell you. On September 11, 1931—instead of saying once upon a time—about two years before I was born —a nice, tight operation took place on one day right across the United States. That was the day Luciano Americanized the Mafia by murdering sixty-one of the old-timers—the Founding Fathers whom the new generation mocked as The Moustache Petes. The old guys weren't all that old and they were powerful men. They had done a great job—for their time—but they had to go because crime had to be nationalized and industrialized and the Moustache Petes didn't understand where the real buck was anymore. Prohibition was less than a year from being over and Luciano decreed that the whole game was going to have to be played under new rules. I mean, like Maranzano was still smuggling aliens for nickels and dimes when gambling, skag, and big industrial extortion were waiting right up ahead." She stopped herself short. "Hey, Peek! Don't tell me you know all about this stuff?"

"We mentioned it at the War College. But, the fact is, Teel, we've done it ourselves sixty or seventy times in the past three thousand years." He smiled benignly. "Power grabs aren't new."

"So what happened for Luciano?" Teel tested Pikow.

"He killed all the old Sicilians and scooped up the billions."

"That's right!" Teel said with excitement. "And that's what we gone do. The Sicilians are through in the dope rackets. Their time is over. The black man moves in."

"When will the transfer of power happen, Teel?" Pikow asked mildly.

"I'll have a list for you in about five days. If you think three weeks is enough time to plan the operation, then we can set the date right now."

"Three weeks will be fine."

"I want an all-black executive on this. Bring in Winn, Anderson, Weems and Dawes. No mix-up about who is taking over. Everybody on the operation got to be black so all the Sicilians know who done it —did it, I mean."

"About how many executions?"

"Roughly about six hundred and nineteen in the Thirty Cities. That is their entire executive. When they are gone, we inherit. I'll have Dawes's whole organization standing by to make sure everybody understands that."

"One thing we know," Pikow said. "The user doesn't care who sells it."

"Make a big note. J.D. Palladino won't be on the list. He's gone run the Haitian end for me. They ain't nobody know the shit business better than J.D. Palladino."

It averaged out to about twenty hits per city, more or less. Men were shot in bowling alleys and in Turkish baths. One hundred and nine were thrown out of high windows in the Gr-1 exercises. Sometimes their women and children had to go with them. It was a precisely executed military operation. Only three Sicilians escaped and one of those was Palladino. The work was done by squads handled by Freedom Fighter sergeants. Officers were forbidden to get into any operation personally, but Winn had a couple of grudges in Chicago; old scores from prison, nothing to do with Sicilians or the Jones industry. She cut the throat of one of them, settled behind a fan magazine in a beauty parlor. She Gr-2'd the other one, a variation on Gr-1: threw the woman under a subway train. Chelito personally killed sixteen.

The Sicilians went as they had lived, like anyone else; in pool halls and taxi cabs; while they were counting money and while they were getting laid. Sixty-one people who were not on the list went too, the innocent by-standers of song and story: cab drivers, kids, pushers, waiters and shoeshine men. The most waste was in the dope houses but a witness was a witness.

At the close of the Sicilian business day on March 3, 1976, Teel controlled the narcotics industry of the United States and Canada and everyone involved preferred it that way: one pay-off system for graded politicians and police; one simple share-out with customs and immigration people and the Narcotics Bureau, and one high, insured standard of shit. Teel believed in moving the very best because it addicted quicker, made for worse withdrawal reactions and therefore was better business in the long run.

With a single merchandising and marketing organization Teel was able to upgrade the efficiency of the distribution of shit in the prisons by a 37 percent factor. She accepted IOUs that were collectable on the street ten days after the customer left state care. Very few tried to evade payment. She tripled sales among the college crowd and high school kids because the invidious situation no longer existed in which the Sicilian opposition would use its press and police contacts to start up a school-boy junkie scare, making it bad for the other side. Teel had schools where the teachers were pushers.

Everything went smoothly now from maker to wearer, straight into the veins and brains of the kids, with no public whining. Teel was able to increase her own profits by 134 percent by eliminating middle-man breaks along the line. She processed in Asia and in Haiti. But she by-passed the wholesalers and except in rural cases, the dealers, and went straight to dope houses and pushers who sold directly to the market. She had it cut by her own people, then her own people sold it to the bottom so that the bulk of the benefit went to Teel. She was able to increase the payoff to the political people and the police, the judges and the prison system, the armed forces commanders and the educational system, because it paid her best to pay them the most. By the time she had her new-style organization laced up tight she had increased the basics of profit to 3,112 percent, the Freedom Fighter financing was assured, underwritten by the very people the Freedom Fighters would kill. A lot of junkies would be swept away; the Nathan Hales of the new revolution. A lot of establishment "leaders," paid to allow this financing by drugs whose indelible records of corruption were in Teel's sure hands, singing their betrayal, would find this used against them in People's

Courts. The people would turn on them, Teel knew, and rend them.

The day chosen for the Sicilian Massacres was a Saturday. J.D. Palladino had agreed to spend that weekend with Teel at the Teel place in Quogue (the first of the great Negro showplaces at Quogue, in fact). He, Dino, Dom, and Angela were flown out by chopper on a sunny Friday afternoon.

Binchy Dawes arrived in time for lunch on Saturday with two very, *very* beautiful movie stars who were also very large on television and who Mr. Palladino was knocked out to meet. He demanded and got autographs "for my little boy" who was thirty-five years old. The world-famous players flew back to New York after lunch and, as a gesture of appreciation for the way they had livened up the party, Binchy Dawes shyly slipped each one three ounces of the purest.

Mr. Palladino said he had never eaten such stupendous food; some kind of Chinese stuff he had never heard of but strictly sensational, like Sparrows and Pine Nuts and Deer Heart Garnished with Plums, Deep-Fried Lobster Balls. "What do they do with the rest of the lobster?" he asked Teel sincerely. Dom and Dino were careful about their manners; no comments about niggers.

After lunch there was a phone call for Mr. Palladino. It was Mary, his head secretary. He took the call in a private room.

"Hello?"

"This is Mary, Mr. Palladino."

"Hello, Mary."

Mary began to cry.

"What the hell is the matter here? I hate a lot of crying."

Mary kept crying.

"Fahcrissake, put somebody on who can talk!" Mr. Palladino yelled into the phone excitedly.

Gozzi, the accountant, came on. "Terrible trouble, boss," he said. "The thing is, are you all right?"

"I'm okay. I'm all right. What trouble?"

"We been gettin' calls since eleven o'clock. Twenty-six of our people been blown away in the five boroughs. Dealers, salesmen, and in the houses."

"Blown *away?*"

Gozzi had to repeat the basic information a few times except that he added how many people had been thrown out of windows and how it wasn't only New York. He said where there was shooting, the piece men had all been black.

Mr. Palladino held very steady. He was already figuring out who had done it, but he didn't panic. He told Gozzi to call him back in one hour with any news, then he settled down on the phone and began to call the Fratellanza people city by city. He talked to wives, mothers, newspaperpeople, cops—but to no one in the Fratellanza. They were all dead. Then he went into the toilet off the telephone room and stayed there until Gozzi called. He couldn't understand why they hadn't killed him; he couldn't figure it out. They had killed practically everyone else in the industry, but him they entertained. So, it came to him slowly, they must want a deal. He pored over it until he got it. They wanted Haiti and only he had all the keys to the government in Haiti. He began to feel less depressed, and he was sorry he had told Gozzi to call him back.

The phone rang. It was Mary. She began to cry. "Put Gozzi on!" Mr. Palladino yelled.

"It's no good, Mr. Palladino," Gozzi said. "All our people are dead. My brother, my two cousins—whatta business." He hung up.

Mr. Palladino's legs turned to lasagna. He sat down heavily on the bed and waited for Dawes to come for him.

In ten minutes, maybe a half hour, Agatha Teel and Binchy Dawes came in and shut the door. He stared at them blankly. "I just don't get it, maybe," he said. "But maybe I get it."

"Perhaps you'll let me explain as Mr. Dawes's attorney," Teel said.

"You are also my attorney on plenty of things," Mr. Palladino said.

"Then let me explain as your attorney."

"That's better."

"Well, Mr. Dawes was disappointed when you said you felt a merger was impossible. But, on the other hand, he was convinced that it was very important to have only one organization. However, he has always had the greatest respect for you and your Haitian experience. He would like you to run the Haitian operation for him."

"From New York?"

"From wherever you have always run it."

"That's all?"

"No. One more thing. He wants you to sign these papers. They merely say that Senator Hobart Simms originated your most successful heroin operation by finding the raw opium and conceiving the Haitian concessionary plans."

"He wants a lock on me or on Senator Simms?"

Teel laughed deliciously. "Why, I would say it's a lock on both of you."

10

January 1976

When Jonas got back from China, Teel was so glad to see him that she wept while she laughed and held him.

"Hey!" Jonas said with mock reproach, "I didn't know you were the cryin' kind."

"Just cryin' for you for when you were a little boy,"

Teel answered. "You sure filled out in China." She wiped her eyes, grinning. "Come on in the kitchen. Man, have I got some food for you."

"I'd sure like a glass of real wine."

"You got it."

"And maybe some kind of fish. Haven't had anything even like fish for four years."

He ate Montauk capoles: very small, very sweet bay scallops cooked with butter, garlic, parsley, lemon —lightly flavored. She gave him three small lobsters cooked in court-bouillon, allowed to steep in it for hours, then drenched in drawn butter. Then she laid down before him *La Toque du President Adolph Clerc,* one of the three greatest patés of the great cuisine, made of hare, woodcock, partridge, thrush, black truffles, and the livers of ducks, which Jonas ate very slowly while he sipped Clos de Vougeot '59. When he moved on to the cheeses, Teel sat down with him.

"Hey! Lemme give a real party for your friends."

"What friends, Sis?"

"The people. From China. Kranak. The Simms girl. The ones based in New York."

"How about a few more? You're a rich lady. Let's fly 'em all in."

"No good."

"Why not?"

"The day they left China, each one to a different region, they gotta stay separate. If one of them gets hit and they take him in and they talk to him, there is one thing safe. Except for you, and Simms and Kranak, nobody knows where anybody else is, so the rest of them will be safe to keep going."

"Okay. I see. That's clear. But how about Orin Dawes?"

"What about him?"

"He's a solid man. He's a double-trained man, having West Point. His Daddy is Binchy Dawes so you know him and they haven't seen each other for a long time. They're real close, Ag."

"You want Dawes at the party?"

"I sure do." He grinned.

"I'll put it down to compassionate leave and bring him on in." She kissed him and he hugged her.

"Now that everything's okay, have a little Armagnac." She poured for him.

"Just the one thing."

"What?"

"I don't think maybe it's such a good idea to have Simms and Kranak at the same party."

"How come?"

"Well, they were messin' 'round out there till he went a little fruit when he found out she hadn't only been doin' it with the yellow devils but she had even had it off with li'l ole coal-black me. Kranak is one of those racist pigs you read about."

"But never meet," Teel said.

"But never meet."

"Never mind Kranak," she said softly.

"I got to mind him, Sis. He's a pig. What we been doin' is getting together a revolution. And I believe in that."

"He's good at his work. Being just a pig and a little bit racist isn't everything."

"Yes, it is, baby." Jonas said quietly.

"I want you to put the part about Kranak being a racist pig out of your head. Maybe Dawes had twice the training, but Kranak is twice the leader. He's got the craziness it's gonna take when the shooting starts."

"What about when the shooting is over?"

"What about it?"

"We won't want any racist pigs left—will we? And we sure won't want to look back and remember how we were led by the most low-down, no-good, racist pig there is, will we?"

"Why?"

"Why?" His voice rose. "Because that is why we are fighting this whole murderous, ruinous, catastrophic revolution!"

"No it isn't, child. I told you why, a long time ago. We are going to fight it to punish them—all of them. We're going to punish them for being racist pigs and the brothers for holding still to be racist victims. I don't care what kind of salvation they find if they can find any after it's all over—there'll be ten thousand Moseses to lead them to their next pie-in-the-sky promised land. But they got to be punished first! And Kranak is the strongest arm I have to punish them!"

They stared at each other until Jonas's eyes dropped.

"I forgot you told me that, Sis," he said sadly. "Well, anyway," he sighed, staring at the floor, "I got to say two things so you and I can stay with each other and help each other."

"Say them straight out, baby."

He spoke reluctantly. "First, I'm not to judge. I know that. I'm a cold-ass scientist, not a philosopher. And I love you, always will. And I accept your leadership over everything else."

Her eyes filled with tears. She patted his hand across the table. "What else, baby?"

"Well—it's just that this revolution has forfeited all possible good, hasn't it, Sis?"

"Ever'thing in this world depends on how you look at it," she answered. "Since *I* started this thing, then we're all stuck to have to look at it the way *I* see it."

She got up from the table and brought back a large praline pie and a change of subject. "Tell me how you rate the people, baby," she said. "We covered Kranak, I figure. And Dawes. What about Simms?"

"She's a cheerful, brilliant and fairly unstable girl. You placed her exactly right to handle Intelligence. She can go anywhere and speak to anybody and nobody's got the revolution fever like Simms."

"Winn."

"A natural killer. A great, great killer."

"Better than Chelito?"

"There's a whole world of difference," Jonas said. "Chelito kills like a delicate woman working at her favorite hobby; Winn is a butcher. She is a mass killer and she kills with enormous hatred. As a soldier, Winn is to be preferred but—on the other hand," he added diplomatically, "Chelito is a better bodyguard."

"What about the men?"

"Anderson is best after Kranak and Dawes. Very steady. Full of hate. The indoctrinations never extracted the hate from Anderson or Winn. Weems just sheds it like drops of water. Buckley is a good plumber; a steady plodder—wholly reliable. Reyes is the one I would put to diplomatic work when the time comes. He is shrewd and he is crooked and hard. I was only with them a year, but I tell you this, Ag, from the time I left them until I got back to them three years later everybody had changed except Winn and Anderson. They got stronger and better. Everybody else just got quieter and better."

"You know what? Army Intelligence knows everyone who was in China."

"*What?*" It was such a strong reaction that it seemed too great a protest.

"They came to see me during that same year you all went into China."

"You? How could they ever find the way to you?"

"They wanted to know about an Albert Cassebeer."

"Me?"

She shook her head. "Albert Cassebeer. Remember how you argued when I decided you would go in with another name? Suppose you had gone in as Teel? Then what?"

He didn't answer.

"Albert Cassebeer is a dead experimental physicist. He had to be dead so he died."

He couldn't look at her.

"Nobody knew Albert Cassebeer was dead, so how could they know he had enlisted in the Army?" Teel continued. "There had to be a plant."

"No!"

"Yes!" Her voice went off like a gun.

"There isn't a way for that to be," he said hoarsely.

"It has to be! All right. Let's just analyze. Let's just think out loud. Who might it be? Who *could* it be? Not the yard birds. They weren't going anywhere when Buffalo found them but back to prison after some broken bank job. They wouldn't give the Army *sweat*. The Army is just more cops in a different uniform to them. Who does that leave?"

"Well," he said thickly. "It leaves Dawes—and Simms."

"And you," Teel said quickly.

"Me?"

"You gave up a lot, baby. You had a lot to lose and a lot to gain—right? Wait, wait," she said, leaning downward on his huge shoulder. "I am not accusing. I am eliminating."

He swallowed hard. "Then that leaves the same two. Dawes and Simms."

"It's not Simms, baby."

"Why not?"

"Because I put Simms in China. Myself. Separate from all the others."

"Dawes?" he whispered with heavy amazement.

"Maybe. Not for sure. Just maybe." She lost her cool. She shouted. "I got to know!" She pounded one fist steadily on the table. "I don't know how they got a plant in there. I go over it again and again. I been over it a thousand times. I mean, that man was on top of me in this house with those questions about Albert Cassebeer right after you boys went in. Buffalo wouldn't tell *anybody* nothing. Well, I say—them convicts they got wives, they got girls, they talk. But what they have to talk about? Okay. They could talk about how somebody paid them twenty-five thousand dollahs to jine up. Who would believe any girl, any wife, who would tell anybody a story like that? The robbers didn't have nothin' else to tell anybody. I been over it. All over it. Ever' inch of it. How did they get hip? How? Then why did they go all quiet?"

"Maybe they found the real Albert Cassebeer. His

body. Maybe it was a routine check on the Casebeer body."

Her face was grim. "Nobody ever find that body. Anyway since when Army people take on for the Homicide Detail? Something just went wrong. I just gotta wait an' see."

She took a deep breath, held it a long time, then exhaled slowly. She got up and walked to the refrigerator, took out a closed jug, removed the top and poured herself a glass of cold water. She got it all together again and smiled at him with all of the charm of a children's ballet company.

"We will overcome," she said drily. "It will be my pleasure to cut down on Kranak as a racist pig, so let's give a glorious party but invite the Simms girl and her glamorous brother even if she and the pig don't make it anymore."

Jonas was still shaken by their conversation. His mind raced to change the entire subject away from people living to people dead. "Say, Sis—" he said. "Did you ever figure how to get the plutonium for me?"

"All done. All set. Four hundred and twenty kilograms of the purest ploo there is, bro. All stashed and waiting for you."

"Four hundred and *twenty*? But—I mean—Holy jezuzz, how'd you ever do that?"

"I take it four twenty keyes is enough ploo?"

"Enough? It only takes me about three kilos to make one fat fission bomb."

"Well—great."

Pure Number Four heroin began to arrive from the Yunnan Province and from Burma in February 1969. It came in at the rate of 960 kilos for each succeeding month. By September 1969, in her all-cash business, Teel had accumulated a war chest of $53,000,000 while she had her people working out the kinks in the widening distribution system. Excess heroin was warehoused as commercial sugar in Long Island City. Of the 960 keyes each month, 85 were seized by prearrangement with the Bureau of Narcotics or the U.S. Customs; 115 were "lost" to any/all official agencies to be sold by them in their "Free Zones" such as the District of Columbia, Puerto Rico, the U.S. Virgin Islands, and at naval bases offshore.

With the first large amounts of money Teel accumulated, she acquired all shares in the Belvedere River Power & Light Company through eleven dummy corporations. Belvedere provided electricity for a small rural region between Shady and Masters, Vermont, in the far northern part of the state. O'Connell, Carnaghi, Levin, Zendt & Sweeney got everything cleared with the Atomic Energy Commission and with the State House at Montpelier. In 1970, the Federal government changed its policy about the production of plutonium 239, the fissionable material used to produce nuclear bombs, and Teel, through her Thursday cook-ins, and more directly through Senator Karp, had had ample advance notice of this official intention. Private contracts were let by the Federal government in separate parts of the country for the operation of plants built to isolate plutonium from used nuclear fuel for sale to power and light companies who were to stockpile it against the day when commercial, civilian use of nuclear energy would come. That is, after the last drop of fuel oil extant in the country had been sold.

As time went on the power and light companies were stockpiling more plutonium than was stored inside all the bombs in NATO, England, France and China. By 1974, the power and light companies had stockpiled more than 75,000 kilograms of plutonium, enough to manufacture 21,428 fission bombs.

By the spring of 1976, the Belvedere River Power & Light Company had acquired 420 kilograms of plutonium, valued at ten dollars a gram, to an accumulated value of $4,200,000. From this stockpile Jonas Teel estimated that he could make 130 nuclear devices for storage, as required. His sister wanted as many as possible to be accessible and ready to be detonated

before July 1. After July 4, she reasoned, all plutonium stocks would be seized by the government.

The Belvedere Power & Light Company stored its
plutonium in a warehouse, in a woodland, two and a
half miles outside Masters, Vermont. The building was
made of gray steel panels to dimensions of 50 by 110
feet. The building had no windows; one door. It
was surrounded by a nine-foot-high chain-link fence;
guarded by two men working only two shifts.

The plutonium was brought from Vermont to the
huge triple basement of Agatha Teel's house in New
York in Jonas Teel's station wagon, in slender,
stainless-steel flasks, each holding two and a half kilograms. The flasks were held securely in locked wooden
cages.

Nuclear bombs aside, plutonium is one of the dead-
liest substances ever known. Breathing it causes certain death. A small amount of it dropped into the
air-conditioning systems of the Pentagon, the White
House, or the houses of Congress would eliminate
American government. Teel placed highest value on
her Vermont and New York plutonium stores.

11

January 1976

Teel reached Bart Simms at the Senate office building.
There was no delay. He came right on the line.

"Your sister is coming over to visit me tomorrow
and I know how much you want to see her, so why
not try to get to my place at about ten fifteen in the
morning?"

The twins clung to each other and wept at the center of Teel's enormous drawing room. After a while Teel brought Bart some legal papers to sign—she was Bart's lawyer he explained to Enid—then they all took the papers to a bank at 34 East 34th Street. When the ritual of a safe deposit box was over, Enid and Bart said good-bye to Teel. Teel watched Enid with narrowed eyes as Bart handed his sister into a taxi.

Bart took Enid to his hotel apartment on Fifth Avenue in the Sixties. They took a shower together, then they got into bed and made love until the late afternoon. After that he dressed her in his pajamas and sent down for some food.

"You have changed," Enid said, touching his face. "You have changed so much."

"Everything happened the way we planned. I am a senator now. I don't know where it went wrong. It got confused. I got lost somewhere. The reason I say such ridiculous things is that not much has been real since you vanished."

"Before China, when I was here, that is the way it was for me. But everything is too real now. I get frightened. I wish I could go back to how it was then."

"We can't go back." Bart shuddered. "It is a river. We are downstream. Soon we'll find the sea."

"But real isn't *good,* Bart. Everything is too clear and too ugly."

"You have changed, too," he said. "I can hear it."

"If only we could have stayed together." Tears came into her eyes. "We can never be like that again. Not really like that."

"Who took you away from me?" he demanded. "Who took you into China?"

"I can't tell you that now," she said. "I'll tell you some day, I promise. But I can't tell you now."

12

February 1976

The triple drawing room, each part having been a single vast drawing room in each of three houses before Teel bought them and knocked them together, was ablaze with jewels, military decorations, white shirt fronts, and the shine of silver wine coolers. Teel had beefed up her Thursday night list. She had brought the Vice President up from Washington on a flying carpet of blandishments with the new Inspector-General of the CIA. There were Californian, Italian, and French movie queens—all three female. She had lured in the world's most stultifyingly famous celebrity, the American Secretary of State. There was a *prima assoluta* and the chief executives of two oil companies. The Russian ambassador, the Spanish ambassador and a chief of state of a central African nation embellished the room. The Chairman of the Joint Chiefs of Staff, decorated like a bulky Christmas tree, dominated the center of the room near the Chairman of the Atomic Energy Commission. Senators moved like pickpockets through a stadium crowd. One of them was Hobart Willmott Simms, "our next President," accompanied by his lovely sister, newly arrived from Bimini, Rimini or Oz.

Jonas, Dawes, and Kranak came out of the silk-lined elevator that opened directly into the enormous, crowded third floor at a moment when the room seemed most dazzling. Twelve feet away they were faced by Teel's spectacular beauty as she chatted with

239

the Vice-President and the Joint Chiefs chairman. Teel was wearing a heavy silk dress of luminous amethyst and $237,000 worth of stolen but reset diamonds and sapphires, which created an unforgettable display of deeply burnt pink against satin-black, all of it set afire by the cold, shining aureoled gemstones.

Jonas got their rented topcoats into the arms of a Victorian tweeny, uniformed with a white, starched cap, who hovered at the elevator door. Dawes looked sinister in a batwing black tie. Kranak looked like a cruel banker behind a black butterfly. Jonas wore a figured black four-in-hand by Cardin. All the men wore their new post-China names: Jonas was Anthony Jones; occupation, decorator. Kranak was, of course, Chandler Shapiro, importer.

"Who is the colored girl with the giant brass?" Kranak whispered to Jonas.

"Colored girl? Oh. *Her!* That's my sister."

"Introduce us to her."

"Later. Not while she's with the Veep. There's plenty of people here you have to meet." Jonas began to move them around the room, passing them like fire buckets from face to face and group to group. No matter where Kranak stood in the room he always seemed to be gaping at Teel and all those rocks. Jonas left Kranak standing alone. Jonas went across the rooms to join Enid and Enid's brother. Dawes got something going with the Italian movie queen.

Kranak saw Enid across the crowd. Three times their eyes locked, but he did not acknowledge seeing her. She stood this brutality as long as she could, then she took Bart by the wrist, excused them for just a moment, and led her brother through the crowd to where Kranak gaped at everything.

"Oh, hello," Kranak said.

"Bart, this is Kranak. You know all about Kranak. Kranak? This is my brother, Senator Simms."

Kranak was horrified that she could endanger them this way. "There is some mistake," he said. "My name is Chandler Shapiro."

She grinned like a malicious little bitch. This was the brother. *Wait a minute!* Was it possible? Had he just stumbled on discovering the leader of the whole fucking American guerrilla movement? A senator! A senator who was going to run for President! *You know all about Kranak!* She said it. She wouldn't have had the balls to say a thing like that if he hadn't given his okay. *You know all about Kranak!!*

Bart was not able to speak. He held his hands clenched in his jacket pockets as if they were grasping single-shot Liberators. He radiated loathing from fish-like, gelid eyes. Kranak held out his hand to be taken. Bart ignored it.

"I'm not feeling very well, Enid," Bart said. "Will you stand out on the back terrace in the air with me?" He drew Enid away through the crowd. She looked back at Kranak in dismay, frightened that she would never see him again.

Teel watched them as she moved from group to group. She watched Dawes talking to a rather drab woman whom she had never seen before. Dawes was talking intently; the woman concentrating as if she were making mental notes to be repeated. Jonas was at the far end of the room talking easily with the Chairman of the House Armed Services Committee. The Chairman looked uneasy, even worried.

Kranak was shaken. This man was the leader; there wasn't a shadow of a doubt about that. He had no evidence but he didn't need any more evidence. He *knew*. Out of the entire movement, he was the only one who knew and he was going to make that pay off, to get him some big edges. But the leader was a white man. Kranak couldn't understand why there were so many niggers at this party. The hostess was blacker than anyone here but she seemed very, very different, which shows what a couple of hundred thousand dollars' worth of jewels can do, he thought. She was no *nigger*. She was a gorgeous, rich, and famous woman and suddenly he wanted to fuck her. At that moment, she appeared at his elbow.

"Enjoying yourself, Shapiro?" she asked absent-mindedly.

"Oh. Yeah. Great."

"There is something I have wanted to ask you all evening. But it is so personal."

"That's all right. Go ahead."

"I don't know why I—of all people—should flinch at asking such a question. There's certainly nothing wrong with it. Episcopalians do ask Presbyterians if they are Methodists."

"It's all right. I assure you."

"All right then. I will. Are you one of us?"

"Pardon?"

"Are you black, Mr. Shapiro?"

He didn't think he had understood. But he could hear the question over again quite clearly. He stared at her, appalled.

"Oh, Mr. Shapiro! I *am* sorry!"

He held himself stiffly. "I am a full-blooded Lipan Apache."

"You are? Well! There you are!"

"Pardon?"

"I am so relieved," Teel said. "I thought I had made an awful gaffe. But even though you aren't black you aren't white either, are you? Shapiro is a *wild* name for an Amerind." She pressed his upper arm lightly and moved away to a group near the door. Jonas and Dawes came up behind Kranak and said the time had come to be moving along.

When they got out on the street, the enormity of what she had said to him began to suffocate him. He shook Jonas off and hailed a cab. He leaped into it alone, slammed the door, and snarled at the driver to move it.

It had been a terrible night for Kranak. A woman for whom he had been willing to overlook certain things he had never tolerated in his life before, for whom he was beginning to get a terrific feeling, had asked him, very matter of fact, if *he* happened to be a nigger. *Jesus!* That was as bad as he would have thought anything could ever get. Then he had happened to discover who was the absolute leader of the entire FF/AFF movement—a United States Senator, a Presidential candidate! He couldn't believe that what had been so absolutely fail-safe had opened right before his eyes, and then—just when he had the biggest edge of anybody in the entire Western Hemisphere, just when he had real information for once in his fucking life which could really move him to the very top—he suddenly remembered that this man—this leader—was the brother of the girl he had beaten up and thrown out on her ass. He had cut his own throat. He had cut his own throat, fahcrissake. The brother—the leader of the entire FF/AFF movement—wouldn't even shake hands with him! He could have him thrown out some fucking window. If he wasn't careful his life wouldn't be worth a dime.

13

April 1976

On the morning of April 1, 1976, Teel held her monthly dividend meeting with Binchy Dawes and Colonel Pikow aboard a chartered round-Manhattan bus, which Colonel Pikow had hired from 10 A.M. until noon. Three armed men sat in seats in the forward area of the big bus. Two armed men sat in the middle area. The driver mouthed words into a microphone but no sound came out. Teel sat in the center aisle position of the long cross seat. Dawes and Colonel Pikow sat turned to face her in the row in front of her.

It was necessary to hold monthly declarations of

dividends because, like American oil companies, their profits were so inordinate it would have unhinged observers were they known publicly.

The projected income for 1975 had come to $409 billion in gross receipts. Of this, mules, pushers, processers, dope houses, dealers, distributors and wholesalers had taken an override of $295 billion. Of the remaining $114 billion, after operational, sales and overhead expenses, it had been necessary for Teel to pay out $107 billion to political leaders and functionaries on international, federal, state and local levels; to international, federal, state and local police; to heads and cabinets of governments in several countries; to armed forces for their requirements; to customs, immigration and narcotics officials; to educational authorities, and to the piece men Dawes had to maintain in every neighborhood to protect the organization from all of the above when the various narcotics "scares" made openly advertised "enforcement" necessary. There were large fees to the overcommunications industry and to the judicial system as well as to a huge camarilla of separate law firms all over the country, whose fees and expenses had to be channeled through O'Connell, Carnaghi, Levin, Zendt & Sweeney (necessitating their own share), plus deductions for bonding, fines and for the serene cooperation of prison authorities.

Remaining for Binchy Dawes and the enormous organization he had inherited was the fair share of gross profits of four billion dollars for a year's hard work. Teel and her revolution won the remaining three billion dollars. The monthly dividend to Teel, thanks to heroin's ever-growing popularity in the United States, for the month of March, just passed, was $250 million. The annual total would exceed the needs of even an urban guerrilla war—by about two and a half billion dollars. That excess belonged to Teel. Try that on, Rocky, Mr. Getty, Shah-baby, Mr. Mellon, Howard Hughes, Mr. Ludwig, Mr. Hunt, and Henry Ford, she thought with intense satisfaction.

14

June 1976

By June 2, 1976, the government efforts to turn up the leaders of the guerrilla movement had grown desperate, and then frantic. Each Thursday for twelve weeks the Army agent had reported to the clandestine unit of Army Intelligence and FBI agents, analysts and technicians in New York at alternating addresses. Each week the agent reported the growing waves of extraordinary preparation that the guerrilla organization was undertaking in terms of personnel, materiel, strike plans and intelligence for the first three weeks of war in the Thirty Cities. Army staffs whose two hundred years of experience had taken them into every kind of terrain on the planet with the exception of the streets, sewers, roofs, tunnels and alleys of their own cities sat mutely into long nights staring at their secret agent's reports, projecting nuclear strikes in New York, Chicago, Cleveland, Detroit, San Francisco and Los Angeles to give the urban guerrilla war an impetus that would take it past any possibility of adequate defense by government forces, and in the course of so doing account for the deaths of at least a million and a half Americans. The population of cities that had never faced a war of any consequence were certain to react with generated panic and irrationality, the psychological analyses reported, which would send them out into the streets to be in the vicinity of troops for the illusion of protection. His reports responded to this estimate with the guerrilla outline of plans that included gasoline cannon and bacterial gas to be poured into any civilian assembly of more than thirty people. In New York, where the greatest problem of staying alive and healthy had always been one of a continuity of supplies because each of the five densely populated boroughs, except the Bronx, was an island, the guerrillas planned to destroy bridges and tunnels and to mine the rivers and harbors, then to do a little light poisoning of the water supply system, mostly for the propaganda value. There would be no food except accumulated canned goods, and they wouldn't last long. The Army would have to divert men and materiel to land the food on outer Long Island with heaviest protection along mined parkways and roads while under constant attack.

Every week the Army agent met an interrogation squad at a different, and entirely natural place, such as a dentist's office, an upstairs barbershop, a tailor's or a doctor's office. Every second meeting the agent faced a frosty-eyed frightening admiral named Adler.

The agent kept adding minutiae of almost useful details of overall guerrilla intention. But the agent, under the guerrilla system, had been denied (because of the "need to know" rule) the actual times, places, methods and personnel to be used in each form of attack, and the agent's knowledge did not go beyond the first three weeks of the war nor did it apply to the six cities in the far western action area. When Army staffs multiplied all of this vague information by the dread number of thirty intensely populated cities, all of the action to happen simultaneously, they were overwhelmed by hopelessness and by a driving despair that caused a loss of eleven officers to mental breakdown and suicide.

That was not, however, the reaction of Admiral Adler. Adler was a fattish man with a black claw for a right hand who had commanded destroyer flotillas.

He had been called out of retirement especially to tear the agent apart.

"You say the first day targets will all be hospitals.

Why? How does such a strike plan originate and how is it executed?"

"I don't know," the agent said dully. They had been over this four times. It was a quarter to two in the morning.

"You know!" Adler yelled. "Who tells you that the hospitals are the first day target?"

"I meet with four men on what the guerrillas call their General Staff," the agent said. "I have been told that the General Staff is fourteen men and women but I have never met more than four, always the same four. These men convey the orders which it is my job to make operational."

"Make operational!" Adler snorted. "You don't even know when or how they are going to happen. You are a top commander, for Christ's sake, stupid, but you don't know what your troops are doing." Admiral Adler glanced at the other three men on the interrogation team, shaking his head. Of the three men one operated a tape recorder. Another operated a lie detector apparatus. The third followed the agent's present statements by checking them against a typed record of his previous statements.

"I pass orders and confirmations of logistics from a warehousing system to the city caches to five Army Corps Commanders below me," the agent answered patiently.

"But you don't know where these warehouses are or the location of the caches?"

"No, sir. But I know the five Army Corps commanders who do know. And I know how, when, and where to locate them."

"Stupid, stupid! We can't touch them yet. If we go near them, the leaders will go even farther underground. We want the leaders! How many times do I have to tell you over and over again—we must find the leaders!"

"Admiral—may I say one thing?"

"Speak up."

"Fuck you, admiral. Like double. I took all the

risks. All. You were playing bridge in some fifth-rate country club when I was being shot at in twenty-six degrees below freezing on a fucking side of a high mountain in western China. And right now—what? Who lives with the people who kill by preference—you or me, you little shit? Who can't sleep for worrying about being under surveillance by the smartest commanders you or the United States Army ever saw? You? No, not you. I know better than any of you that the fourth of July is getting closer and closer. But I can't do anything to save my country because they're too smart for all of us." The agent got up and said, "I'm going home."

Admiral Adler shoved the agent violently back into the chair. "You know what?" he said. "If you don't come up with real information the next time I see you, I'm going to give you back to Dr. Baum."

There were thirty-two days left.

15

February–March 1976

When all the guests had left what she laughingly called "the party for Kranak," Teel instructed Chelito to stiff Kranak every time he called: "Just tell him Miss Teel is too busy to come to the telephone."

It took Kranak four days of working on himself before he could bring himself to call her; he knew what he wanted from her and he didn't approve of it. He was a Lipan Apache. Suppose—just suppose, he told himself—the woman got so crazy in love with him that she decided to have a baby by him. How could he ever face the memory of his mother—which incorporated for him the historical meaning of his tribe —if he had cooperated in making a black or halfblack Lipan? It would be the world's most shameful anomaly. A Lipan Apache was the proudest and individually most unique thing a human being could be. What was a nigger? A nigger was exactly the opposite. The Lipans were at the top of the anthropological ladder. The niggers weren't even on the ladder. But, Jesus! Whenever he thought of her standing between the Secretary of State and the Chairman of the Joint Chiefs in that lavender dress and all those jewels he got a hard-on he'd have to close a window on to get rid of.

In cities Kranak always lived naked if indoors, winter and summer. He was a man. He would stand in front of his full-length mirror and study every inch of himself on view and he could do it for a half hour at a time and then do it again if he happened to be walking by the mirror. "Where is she ever going to find a man like this?" he asked himself aloud more than once.

He was five feet ten inches tall, not tall for a nigger basketball player, but he wasn't a nigger basketball player, he was a Lipan Apache—and that was tall for a Lipan. He had strong, well-proportioned shoulders, a very deep chest and long, thin muscular arms that never tired. His forehead was very broad; maybe broader than high, but he was a fighting man, not a school teacher. His mouth was enormous and garnished with strong, white teeth under a magnificent nose. His mother had said that no men anywhere had such noses as Lipan chiefs. The nostrils pulsated with every emotion. He quiffled them in and out as he stared at the mirror. He was fearless, he had always been fearless, he would always be fearless. His tribal name was Janamata which meant Red Buffalo. He was Lipan! He had enormous sexual powers! He had deep wisdom! His mother had taught him, *"Inday pindah lickoyee poohacante"*: "The people of the white eyes are wonderful medicine men." It was a matter of historical record—the cunning of the Lipan is only equalled by his skill and his audacity. A Lipan was trained from infancy to regard all other people as his natural enemies and to understand that the chief excellence of man lies in outwitting his fellows. Lipans had many, many wives because no woman was able to resist them.

She would be pleading with him very soon! For his brain strength! For his beyond-the-credible sexuality. Look at the size of that head! Look at the determination of that chin! The eyes might be somewhat small but they were exceedingly brilliant. What had happened to the days when a man could know where he stood with a woman, without all this coquetry of having some person say she was "too busy" to come to the telephone? The days when a man would stake his horse in front of a woman's roost and walk away to await the issue? If the woman wanted him—as he knew this black woman wanted him—she would come out after two days and take the horse to be watered, fed, and secured in front of his lodge or she would ignore the horse. At the end of four days the whole thing would be decided one way or the other. He had been calling this black woman sometimes twice a night for almost five weeks, so her actions had become an excess of coquetry. He had sent her flowers. He had sent her the perfume he liked. He had even sent her a Polaroid camera so she could send him pictures of herself, he had sent her some pictures of himself, stripped to the waist with his chest at maximum expansion, but all he had gotten in return was "too busy to come to the phone."

He decided that it did not matter that she was black (but he wished, in his heart, that he didn't know her black, black brother). She was a woman; a woman who commanded the respect and attention of really great men even if she were a square who had no idea she had a revolutionary for a brother. It was okay, he told himself—and what a pair of tits! With a whinny

of frustration he grabbed the telephone and dialed
Teel's number for the third time that night.

"Miss Teel, please."

"This is Miss Teel."

"What? Miss Teel?"

"Who is this?"

"This is Chandler Shapiro. Chandler Shapiro? The
friend of your brother's?"

"Oooh, the Indian!"

"That's right.'

"What can I do for you, Mr. Shapiro?"

"Are you free for dinner?"

"Dinner? It's a quarter to twelve."

"Is it? Well, we could have like a fashionable dinner."

Teel had watched him take charge for four years
in every weekly report she received from China. She
had chosen him for the top operational command over
all of them because he was a killer, a wrecker, and a
people hater. The kind of revolution she was going to
make would need all the monsters like that that she
could draw into it—but this one was a superlatively
trained monster. He was raw prejudice, amorality,
brutality and criminal instinct; unilaterally motivated.
What she had to find out—since he was the best of
all the worst she was seeking—was if she could control him outside theoretical conditions; if she, as the
Supreme Leader, would be able to force him to do
everything the way she wanted it done when the actual
operations got under way—or was he uncontrollable.
She knew she would never find that out in a drawing
room, so she decided to invite him into her bed to
provoke him into whatever unguarded madnesses she
could find for him there, then cut him down until she
knew she could control him.

"Well, no dinner, I think," she said into the telephone. "But why don't you come over and let me
read your palm or something?"

They locked in that night. It got better. Then it got
better than that until Teel began to worry that it was

interfering with Kranak's work because she knew it was beginning to interfere with her own.

In between all the fucking she talked to him in a faintly derisive way. That was how she read him. She gauged him as preferring to be mocked and, with skill, belittled by women.

"Were you a poor Indian, Shapiro?" she would ask him.

"Until I was fourteen we were very, very poor. All we had was the strength of my mother's tremendous pride that we were Lipan Apaches and not ordinary people, but I don't think I really had enough to eat until I was fourteen."

"What happened then? Did your mother shoot a buffalo?"

"My father owned a few thousand acres of desert property. They found uranium on it, I think."

"You think?"

He shrugged. "Maybe it was oil."

She decided to test him. "Is Shapiro an Indian name?"

"No."

"Your father was not an Indian?"

"He took the name because it is a paleface name. There were a lot of names he could have taken, I suppose—like Vanderbilt, or Astor or Edison—but he took Shapiro."

"Are you rich, Shapiro?"

"Oh, yes," Kranak said with pride. "I am very rich. Are you rich, Teel?"

"Well, you know," she said, "I'm a lawyer. We do all right."

He thought she thought he was the general manager of an export business. He thought she was merely a big-time lawyer and a power broker. Teel was beginning to feel hooked because she could not continue her life as a female in a male role without losing a few spangles. She could have been a lawyer, any kind of lawyer; she might even have been able to live as a politician and still maintain her balance as a female.

What tipped the scales and made her vulnerable was her attempt to carry out both of those roles plus the obsessive guise as Attila the Hun. Not that she "fell in love" like other females. She merely opened her spirit and agreed with herself to take on one more character: the loving and submissive mate to the man who was her lackey and her inferior in every way, particularly in scope, grasp, purpose (negative and positive) and vision. The female of the black widow spider undoubtedly has her softened moments which resembled Teel's. Then the male seems to contravene what the female believes she was put in place to accomplish and she widows herself with or without regret. Parting is sweet sorrow if there be power at hand when comes the morrow.

Kranak was a mess about the affair. He tried every ruse that occurred to his savage mind to dominate her. He became genuinely agitated and could fall into tantrums that seemed epileptic. He tried to crowd her, bully her. Once, he struck her and she broke the wrist of the hand that had hit her across the corner of a marble coffee table, turning it on its back and dropping all her weight on its elbow. While he whimpered, she told him she was throwing him out and nothing could get him back in. He began to whine. She said, "What kind of a Lipan Apache are you, Shapiro? You're afraid of pain and you're afraid to go without one woman. You're just shit, Shapiro. You and your mother and that Lipan Apache talk are all just a lot of shit." He mewed until she forgave him and let him go out to find a doctor. She had no respect for him except as a stud but while she could—as long as it was convenient—she clung to him.

16

April–May 1976

Enid Simms watched the romance happen, then grow. She watched through thick brick walls. Teel and Kranak were never seen together outside the house on 38th Street. They weren't like other lovers who went to restaurants or walked in parks. They stayed inside Teel's house and thought they were invisible, but Enid followed Kranak whenever she could. It was the only way she could be with him.

When Kranak could be with Teel as often as she would let him in, Enid became ill. She couldn't eat and she couldn't work. Enrique Jorge Molina was assigned to take over her department as a trained Freedom Fighter. Colonel Pikow sent three different doctors to see her. Two of them told Pikow she was very ill but that they didn't know what made her ill. One of them said it was his "general feeling" that Enid was dying, but he could not say why unless it was The Victorian Disease, a broken heart.

As a candidate for the presidential nomination Bart was able to persuade a great diagnostician from the Johns Hopkins Hospital in Baltimore to examine her in New York. The doctor said Enid's infection was deep within her mind.

Bart was campaigning hard. His national organization equalled the size of other candidates' campaign forces at the pre-election point. For the past seventy-eight days unsolicited money had been pouring in from all fifty states in one-hundred-, five-hundred-, and thousand-dollar bills, every contribution with a letter urging Bart to run, every letter mailed by the well-dispersed families who were a part of Mr. Palladino's interlocking national organization. Bart's fixed priorities were fully financed and more. The budget he carried in his wallet showed these appropriations:

DEPARTMENT	BUDGET
Administration	$317,000.
(Office) Administration	602,000.
Advertising	15,750,000.
Campaign Materials	1,700,000.
Citizens' Committees	4,800,000.
Political & State Support	
(Including "Research" Fees)	11,000,000.
Polling	1,250,000.
PR/Media "Assistance"	950,000.
Other Candidate Surveillance	1,400,000.
Direct Mail	2,900,000.
Telephone Campaigning	9,000,000.
Women, Minorities,	
Special Groups	3,500,000.
Speaker's Bureau	840,000.
Travel & Maintenance	1,200,000.
	$55,209,000.

Bart was running a dual campaign. Simultaneous with the intensive preconvention campaign going on in the fifty states, there was a concentration on the crucial-state strategy, which emphasized actitivies in: Pennsylvania, Michigan, Maryland, California, New York, Ohio, Illinois, Texas, New Jersey and Connecticut. All states were covered by television advertising, but the crucial states got an additional budget. All states were serviced by the Speakers' Bureau but the crucial states were saturated by it. The crucial states had telephone centers from which as many as seven and a quarter million households were called at an average of 16 cents a call. By late May Bart's prospects began to look as if they were unbeatable and he ordered a shift to a fifty-state strategy, sighting the target of a fifty-delegation sweep of the convention for a unanimous nomination on the first ballot. The "research money" he had spread among the State Chairmen and key delegates was definitely paying off. But he continued to run scared and spend hard because even when the polls showed him far ahead of the nearest contender, a percentage of undecided delegates was shown. So Bart Simms had to proceed with the startling understanding that there were some politicians and delegates who could not be bought, a factor that had shaken other politicians before him. He made a big point of having his support designed so that it was divided between Anti-War and Hawks/ Hard Liners on the upcoming war (wherever it was decided that would be set), so that he could appear to be uniting both extreme wings of the party and could, after election, move in either direction without seriously dislocating public opinion. He kept his own positions on such controversial matters entirely silent. He concentrated on endorsing the verities. Mother's Day, for one example, had never been celebrated as his candidacy celebrated it late in May 1976.

He spoke to Enid on the phone twice a day from whatever part of the country his organization had sent him. He could never reach her at night. She was never there at night. His first schedule break was over the Memorial Day weekend, essentially a warmaker's celebration. He was able to get back to New York to be with her. Enid looked ghastly.

"Now, Enid, listen to me," he said desperately. "You can't go on like this. The doctors say you have to rest but you are never here at night—and don't say you are here because——"

"I couldn't get interested in lying, Bart. Not to you."

"Well, anyway, dammit—where do you go?"

"I am living inside a Victorian novel," she said slowly. "A real weeper. I follow my lover just to be near him." She laughed bitterly. "It's true. I follow my lover every night, then when he goes inside to make love to his mistress, I stand out there, even if it's rain-ing, and torture myself with imagining what they are doing together. I do, Bart."

"But—"

"Everything is *very* real now. Daddy has come back. Sometimes when I follow this man I cannot have, I see, as he moves under a street light or past a store front, that he is Daddy and that he wants me to die. It is so real to me that at last I understand why Daddy killed himself. He did it to make me die."

"Who is he?" Bart was holding his sister's upper arms tightly.

"You met him. I pretended to him that I had told you all about him."

"*Who?*"

"Kranak. That unpleasant man at the black lawyer's party."

"How do you know him?"

"He was in China." Enid was livelier—lifelier—because she was talking about Kranak.

"Did he take you into China?"

"No."

"Who did? I have to know who did that, who tore us apart for every day of the rest of our lives!"

"The people who are going to make you President."

"Who? What are you talking about?"

"The agency. The CIA. Anything that ever happened to us they did. Only they could have taken me out of Hong Kong. They knew I was in Hong Kong and they had all the necessary power to take me out because of all the Chinese they brought opium to in Taiwan."

"That isn't true! That cannot be true!"

"What is the difference now, Bart dearest. I am dying inside a Victorian novel."

He stayed with her for the three days. He went with her when she followed Kranak to Teel's house. He stood with her through the dark, cold hours as she looked up at the high windows of the house, sometimes speaking to him but most often not.

Sunday afternoon at four fifteen he told her he had

to keep a political appointment. He went to Kranak's apartment, which was far east on 57th Street.

Kranak's apartment was messy. Kranak was wearing a blue towel robe over his usually naked body out of deference to the conventions of hospitality. He was barefoot. He invited Bart to sit down.

Bart remained standing. "My sister—you do remember my sister?" It was an agony for Bart to discuss Enid with this ruffian.

"Enid? Yeah. You bet." Kranak was wary. He didn't want to offend this man. He needed to stay real close to this man. They had to get along or maybe he'd be thrown right out some window, Gr-1'd.

"She's in love with you."

Kranak shrugged, then grinned with self-gratification. It was such an unkind grin that Bart decided he was going to hurt this animal before he left it here. Bart made himself continue.

"I don't ask you to understand this, but what she feels for you is confused by her with other unfortunate things in her life and—as a result—and I am saying that as a direct result of knowing you—she has become very ill."

"I never had a venereal disease in my life!" Kranak protested hotly, but carefully.

"Shut your filthy mouth!" Bart yelled at him. "My sister is dying. Doctors believe she is dying for the love of *you*."

"Come *on*, Senator. This is nineteen seventy-six."

"Yes. But that's how it is. That is it. She is dying because she loves you and you hardly know she is alive."

Kranak flapped his arms, letting the light plaster cast fall against his leg.

"Well, what am I supposed to do?" He shot a glance at the long mirror on the wall at his right and he had an indescribable urge to throw the robe off so he could see himself. He got a flash erection under the towel as he thought of looking at his body while someone else was in the room. He sat down abruptly next to a table and wrapped his arms around his middle. "It's like a corny opera and the guy in the next seat tells me it's all my fault."

"There is something you can do. You can call her. That could be a kindness. You can invite her out to dinner twice a month. That would be an act of human compassion. I'm not asking you to love her," Bart pleaded, "just that you acknowledge you care that she is alive."

Kranak saw the combinations at his fingertips and he saw the vault door open. This guy was freaked-out on his sister. The guy was helpless. There wasn't anything he wouldn't do for the sister, including taking him, Kranak, right up into the highest councils of FF/AFF movement and making him the same thing as a co-leader of everything this puling son-of-a-bitch wanted to happen. It was all a question of dominating him now, of twisting the knife in his sister's belly so that the brother would do anything to stop the pain. But he had to be sure at the same time.

Kranak sneered at him. "I think you know how we met," he said.

"You met in China. There is absolutely no need to talk about it."

The wasp of revelation stung Kranak's imagination. This was it! He was in! He was home free! There was no way, after the indoctrinations they got at those camps, for Enid to have told her brother about China and about him; therefore he was sitting in front of the power that had organized the camps and had put them all in there. All right. It was safe to make his first move. The leader needed him right now more than he needed the leader.

"Well, I'm sorry to disappoint you and Enid," he said as contemptuously as he could, "but I got a life to live myself and I can assure you it doesn't include her."

"Just for a few weeks," Bart implored. "Just get her out of this downspin."

"No," Kranak said harshly.

Bart said, "Agatha Teel is my lawyer. She is also the lawyer for a powerful figure in the Mafia. If you value Miss Teel's continuing friendship, and I have reason to believe that you do, I would advise you to reconsider my request."

Kranak got up, or started to get up, saying "Get the hell out of here." Having the advantage of total surprise, Bart moved with wondrous agility, considering his stiff leg. Galvanized by jealousy and frustration, he pinned Kranak's fractured wrist to the table, then, with a terrible blow from his stiffened other hand, rebroke the wrist, pulled the arm along the table toward him and fractured Kranak's lower forearm.

He jerked on the broken arm and pulled the fainting Kranak out of the chair, onto his face on the floor. Balancing on his stiffened leg, he kicked Kranak's ribs, smashing them on the right side, until eight were broken. He pulled a stool over beside Kranak's head, face down on the carpet, sat down heavily, and grabbing the hair on top of Kranak's head, as he had once grabbed the girl Louisa long ago, he spoke loudly to Kranak as he pounded Kranak's face heavily and steadily into the floor. "If—Enid—dies—from—you —you—will—die—too."

He flung Kranak's raw head away, wiped his hands on Kranak's towel, got to his feet with difficulty and left the apartment.

17

May 1976

Teel called Kranak the following night. She was curt. "Get over here at seven thirty," she said.

"I can't."

"I have to leave at eight o'clock, but I want to talk to you first."

"I can't. I had an accident. I slipped in the tub and broke my arm and my ribs and my nose."

"I know about that and I know who beat you up. Be here at seven thirty." She hung up.

To defy her Kranak did not arrive until twenty-five to eight. Teel saw him into a small sitting room on her main floor. She didn't offer him either a chair or a drink. She said, "You know about this. He told you. Well, get on that telephone now and call the girl. You're going to take her to dinner tonight and you are going to be very, very nice to her because I am going to have someone on you."

"What kind of a thing is this?" he said wildly. "You are my woman and you are supposed to be crazy about me so you send me out to stud with a insane broad."

"I am not your woman," Teel said. "You are a stud. You were my stud, but now I'm going to share you with the sister of a friend of mine. Dig, baby?"

"How can you talk to me like that?"

"Shad*dap!*" she said violently. "You are a little exporter named Shapiro who calls himself an Indian but who I personally think is one of the brothers trying to pass. My friend may be the next President of the United States—*do you have any idea what that can mean to me?*—and all my friend asks is that my stud take his sister out to dinner every now and then. So do it!" She looked at him with sudden frightening blandness. "And don't miss the point here, Chandler Shapiro, about what will happen to you if you don't do it."

He went to the phone table, opened the drawer under the phone and took out the phone book. Teel told him the name of the hotel. He dialed the number slowly, his face like a bronze mask. He would not take this from anyone. This woman knew the lifetime of training his mother and his tradition had put into him and yet she was able to humiliate him directly with flat orders that no one would even ask a nigger slave to do. Well, fuck that, he thought. I am not taking that. And I am also finished with this broad who would give up the kind of relationship they had just to turn a political advantage. Well, she is through. She is finished he thought as he dialed the number slowly.

Enid wasn't there.

18

January 1976

As each of Teel's national and regional commanders landed in the United States from China, some in San Francisco, some in Seattle, some in Boston, some in New York, and some in Miami, she put them under twenty-four-hour surveillance. The news Captain Maas had brought her four years before, that the

American government knew a group of people had been taken into China for training in revolutionary warfare, had sharpened her reactions to all her *own* people until, one by one, as they were proved otherwise, there would remain one traitor.

Within one week after Enid Simms arrived in San Francisco, Teel had isolated her from the rest of the commanders as the American government spy. From the moment Enid had left the plane, a team headed by the wiliest of Teel's Area Corps Commanders who had been standing in and preparing the organizations for the native commanders trained in China, Enrique Jorge Molina, a Uruguayan Tupamaro leader on loan to Teel, had photographed her at the pancake restaurant with the trendy man, had photographed Dr. Weiler, and, within four days, every technician who had worked in the wing isolated for Enid at the King de los Reyes Hospital in O'Farrell Street. They had gotten a floor-orderly and lab-technician rumor that Enid had had a faked appendectomy and had placed all the evidence in Teel's hands.

In the subsequent two weeks, the Molina surveillance team had followed Enid to the same "safe" apartment with transmitting wall limpets, recording four days of Enid's testimony under relentless inquisition, in which she had expanded upon a few details of the Teel organization but was unable to tell much more than that she was in charge of Intelligence operations for a movement called the Freedom Fighters/American Freedom Fighters and knew four members of its General Staff, said to comprise a total of fourteen people. She did not know the names of the American leaders who were over the General Staff. She was able to repeat the names of the people with whom she had studied at the War College in China and cite the Area Commands assigned to them, but those names had been changed, their passports changed, just as her own name and passport had been changed, so that she could not state who or where they were now. She only knew whom she got her operational orders from.

Teel telephoned Senator Simms, the former CIA agent who had been so long and so intimately involved with the agency, and asked him urgently to come to her house in New York that evening. That she would be asking him to pass a death sentence upon his beloved twin sister did not so much as occur to Teel. She wanted a few pieces of evidence confirmed so that she could be sure about which part of the government machinery had penetrated past her several shields. She had already decided, after San Francisco, then after she listened to the tapes of Enid in the "safe apartment" at 969 Park, that Enid was guilty, but it was equally important for Teel to know who Enid had been working for, because whoever they were, they were laughing at Teel. They had used Teel as their cat's paw, as if she were a fool, a simple-minded dupe who could be guided to do whatever they planned for her: to have the Chinese kidnap their own agent, to insure the safety of that agent inside China. Teel had done it all for them.

She and Senator Simms sipped Kirs. She said she was deeply interested in having him try to identify some photographs for her. She showed him photographs of the ranking technicians who had been with Enid at the King de los Reyes hospital and at the "safe apartment" at 969 Park Avenue.

"Why—they are all CIA, all three of them."

"Are you sure?"

"Quite sure. The tall one with the happy face is Youngstein. He is the Chief Psychiatric Officer in CIA Operations Division. This one with the Edward the Seventh beard is Dr. George Pappadakis, who is an astonishingly skillful neurosurgeon, and the man who looks like Benito Mussolini if Mussolini were to be played by Charles Boyer is the greatest living Pavlovian psychologist, *the* authority on reflex conditioning, Georges Ethilda Marton."

"I can't tell you how helpful that is, baby," Teel said, flashing the pearlies.

"How did you ever get pictures like that?"

"I can tell you this. In my kind of work, I get crazier clients than almost anybody can imagine. Come on! Let's get over to San Marco on Fifty-second Street and scarf up some of that osso bucco like the Queen of Italy used to make."

"I'm dead tired, Agatha. I thought maybe you might run up something here."

"Well—you bet yer bewts! What style—Italian, Japanese—maybe some Brazilian or Swedish?"

"Anything you think of that's light."

"You got it. Senator, I've been thinking about those papers we have in escrow at the bank. They must be a heavy weight on you."

He shrugged hopelessly, looking haggard.

"I want to be fair. Really—I do! Lookahere—I have a *very* big client who pays me a *fortune* of money every year and there is one vital thing that client has to know."

"What's that?"

"You find this out for me, Senator, and I am going to hand you those papers back."

"What, Agatha?"

"You been in on any meetings at the White House about a revolutionary movement that trained some convicts in China?"

"Yes."

"My client put a 'Must Know' on this. Must know from the highest possible source who the government agent was they planted with those convicts. You know?"

"I am on the Armed Services Committee. I think I can get that," he said quietly.

Teel was being thorough. She was sure about Enid but she had to be equally sure she had no other traitors in her revolutionary army to flush out.

Simms got up slowly, with exhaustion. "I don't think I can eat," he said. "I think I have to get over to my sister's and try to get a night's rest."

"You do just that, Senator. You got to stay strong.

This country is going to need you safe and sound in that White House."

Senator Simms left.

The team Teel had assigned for surveillance of the returnees from China had missed the U.S. Army Intelligence agent altogether. After Teel had cornered Enid, she set all her other commanders into free, unwatched movement. Her team had missed the agent because Army Intelligence was not as arrogant as the CIA. The Army had de-briefed their man in his own hotel, assigned to him by Teel's people. Then he was free to come and go, every subsequent de-briefing taking place in a different, always normal setting: a dentist's surgery, a tailor's fitting room, a public swimming pool, the barber's; not only different places, but always different interrogators, many of them brought in from Army and Air Force installations abroad and from ships at sea.

19

June 1976

In the morning of the twenty-seventh of June, Teel put out a Gr-1 on Enid Simms through Pikow, who passed the order directly to her executioners, by-passing all Area Command.

Pikow chose a brigade commander, a Princeton man with a very expensive habit, and his aide-de-camp, to carry out the operation. They were quiet, well-dressed men who could have been accountants making a house call. They were not *jagged* junkies but the sort of composed addicts one passes all day every day on the streets of any big city. They were in a state of perpetual fix, which was what had made them such efficient guerrillas. They had developed the Gr-1 into a science.

They flowed smoothly into the large hotel lobby, chatting an Ivy League sort of chat, and moved to the bank of elevators, which was out of sight of the main desk. They pushed the button for the floor that was two above the Simms apartment, went down the fire stairs to her door. Enid answered the door without delay. She didn't know the men, but if she had, she was given no time to object. The shorter man was upon her instantly with his hand over her mouth, moving her backward into the room while the other man shut the door and fastened the chain lock.

The taller man hurried across the living room to a window that faced the courtyard at the center well of the hotel. He opened the window, remaining well behind the glass curtains, then he turned to stare into Enid's horror-filled eyes; she knew the Gr-1 well as a training exercise. She struggled to find a leverage point to throw her attacker but he had been successful in keeping one foot, then both of her feet, off the ground.

The taller man grasped her wrist and ankle. The shorter man kept a grip over her mouth and one high on her thigh until the last moment before release from the swaying, swinging style which children use when they are about to douse someone in the lake from a boat dock at a summer camp.

They flew Enid far backward in an upward arc, then swung her smoothly forward to sail through the air, through the broad space of the opened window from the twenty-ninth floor. Her body followed her terrible scream down and down until it crashed upon the concrete pavement of the areaway.

The Central Intelligence Agency had lost their hold upon the country's leading candidate for the Presidency; the Freedom Fighters had lost a commander; but most of all Bart Simms had lost the only important part of himself.

20

June 1976

The government was torn into fragments of policy that
split the implementation of its directions, but the President held strongly to what he determined must be
done. The Pentagon wanted to arrest, then have Dr.
Baum interrogate the six guerrilla army commanders
and the four General Staff officers whose identities and
whereabouts were known and who—all of them—
were now under surveillance, but the Pentagon did not
want to attempt to separate the rotten apples from all
the apples in the barrel of the National Guardsmen because they said it was an impossible task, would require a gigantic diversion of effort and men at a time
when every single moment had to be spent trying to
run down the guerrilla ringleaders. If the separation
had to be made, they said it would be done in a purge
that would last from July 2 through July 4.

The Senate Armed Services Committee, the opposition party and the Vice-President wanted an immediate isolation and separation of the National Guard
traitors but were wholly opposed to the interrogation of
the guerrilla Army Corps commanders because, they
were convinced, it would render impossible any conceivable likelihood of uncovering the leaders before
the Fourth of July.

The President, his Cabinet, the Supreme Court and
the House Armed Services Committee opposed vehe-
mently any of the actions so favored. The President
told a combined secret meeting (and by some miracle

of fright secrecy was maintained) that if the Army's own secret agent didn't know who the leaders were, the subordinates surely wouldn't know, that any disturbance at that command level would jar the national leaders, that there was still time to interrogate those people, if all else failed, and to discover where demolitions and attacks were planned specifically, in time to prevent them. It was the leaders who had the money and the resources of organizing genius. They must get the leaders. Was that understood? *They must get the leaders before July 2!* The President agreed to fullest surveillance until the leaders were picked up.

At that combined meeting at the White House a compromise, as such, was accepted. The date for the arrest of anyone known to be a part of the movement of revolution was moved up from July 2 to midnight June 27. The arrests scheduled for that compromise date would include the National Guard insurrectionists, those Army Corps commanders who were known, the four General Staff officers and the Action Area commanders.

The White House compromise meeting was held on June 23, 1976. The President wanted to hold off arrests as long as possible until the Secretary of State delivered the ultimatum to the Chinese government, not only to keep the American guerrilla leaders from being alerted and escaping, but because of the dire consequences that could follow such accusations as would be made.

June 24 (Washington)/June 25 (Peking) 1976

The Secretary's visit to China was announced as a trade mission. The Secretary spent eleven hours with the Chinese Prime Minister, the Foreign Secretary and the Ministers for Defense and Air, slowly and grimly revealing his information. He gave dates, training sites, names of trainees, names of training camp and War College officers, the positioning of trainees following their graduation in China, their military, political and guerrilla objectives as specified in the Chinese course of training. Every fragment of fact that Dr. Baum, the three colonels and the other interrogators had been able to extract from the Army's plant on his return, every scintilla or action/counteraction that the CIA technicians who had designed Enid Simms's memory had been able to extract from her, had been marshaled before the Secretary in his thick, black looseleaf case books.

There was no response, because there could be no response, from the Chinese. They did not attempt to bluster or to minimize. They waited for what he had most surely come to tell them.

He demanded to be told the names and locations of the ringleaders. He demanded to be told the sources of such gigantic financing. He wanted those facts at that meeting, without recess. He wanted the names of the ringleaders above all else and he wanted them instantly while there was still time to act. He wanted the names, ranks and whereabouts of all Chinese, or foreign guerrilla, or Communist or Socialist advisers who had assisted the movement, and he wanted their immediate whereabouts whether they were inside or outside the United States. If they were, any of them, inside China, he wanted them delivered to him for return to the United States for trial and execution.

The Chinese had been silent for what might have been two hours of the Secretary's colloquy. It was at that moment that the Chinese Prime Minister made his government's answer.

"We regret this disaster which your country faces," he said. "But we have no such knowledge nor had we any such participation. We are unable to offer you any assistance."

The Secretary was dazed and limp with sweat. He stood at the end of the table in his shirtsleeves. "In that case, you are making a terrible mistake," he said. "If —and I lay this down in front of you as the most prodigious *IF* history has ever known—*IF* this guerrilla war

begins in those thirty cities of my country—I said *IF*—
then we will systematically destroy China. We will destroy you from north to south, from east to west. Your
population of seven hundred and fifty million people
with their density of seventy-nine to the square mile
will be reduced to ten million mutants when we finish
with you. That is the message, and the assurance, from
the President of the United States. Think hard."

June 28 (Peking)/June 27 (Saskatchewan) 1976

In the loveliest part of summer, while China was transmitting its instructions over the top of the world to
northern Canada for re-transmission to southern Que-
bec by courier, then across the border to a private airport twenty-six miles south of Massena, New York, to
Teterboro Airport in New Jersey, the 11,300 employees of the National Security Agency had been reorgan-
ized and redeployed and were at work in and around
the longest unobstructed corridor in the world, 980 feet
long, 560 feet wide, working day and night shifts in the
total 1,400,000-square-foot area of the agency at Fort
George Meade, Maryland, utilizing sixty-three on-line
computers, eighteen miles of conveyor belts that
moved document trays from sub-station to sub-station
at the rate of 100 feet a minute to conduct the "deepest" analyses of the 83,000 individual American citizens and 214,800 aliens whom the CIA had had under
surveillance in the past six years in the United States
and abroad. The machines and men sought out convicts who had been sentenced for armed robbery to
American prisons who had also been enlistees in the
U.S. Army or who had been radical organizers in those
prisons. They checked out the records, measurements
and photographs of tens of thousands of female prisoners serving time for armed robbery over the previous
ten years in all states working against the best descrip-
tion their secret agent could offer to the interrogation
teams during his de-briefing. Under identical analyses

were the attenuated "action/active" and "Hidden Ball" files of the Federal Bureau of Investigation: reports on 883,400 U.S. citizens and 319,000 aliens. The "Secret Only" Movement Reports compiled on 721, 932 U.S. Citizens and 3,279 aliens by U.S. Army Intelligence were in the trays and under analyses to pull the pictures of the guerrilla Army Corps commanders and mug shots of the Western Action Area commander.

Every American or alien resident in the United States who had traveled in eastern Asia since 1966 was being sifted out and his travel patterns examined minutely. Those files set aside for further examination were immediately checked against "density" files on the personalities/interests of the people represented. If there was any indication of eccentric Asian travel pattern, political, criminal or "reasonably alarming" information such as real or casual linkage of such a person with any of the known officers of the guerrilla movement, these people were to be arrested on June 28, 1976, in the trans-national roundup beginning at 12:01 A.M., that date. The records of every National Guardsman in present active service were studied for (1) slum origins; (2) narcotics addiction; (3) former or present street gang membership, and all Guardsmen matching those indictments were to be disarmed and arrested.

The President suspended habeas corpus. As the incriminating files were segregated, excluding the projected arrests of National Guardsmen, the Army was able to make provision for the arrests of 31,641 suspects and their detention for questioning in fifty-eight "camps" around the country beginning on the first minute of morning, June 28. Interrogation teams working with Action Manuals developed by Dr. Lothar Baum, U.S. Army Intelligence, were drawn from the CIA, FBI, NSA, Army and Air Force Intelligence: 917 men and women selected from psychological profiles indicating "non-revulsion to inflicting hardship where necessary."

Teel's name and record was among those segregated

for action because she had once traveled to Asia in "an eccentric pattern," she had political and criminal connections as a trial lawyer, in a most active manner, she showed "reasonably alarming" linkage by being the sister of Jonas Teel, an officer, they thought, of the guerrilla movement. Her file was "further segregated" and stamped boldly FOR EARLIEST ARREST 28 JUNE 1976, which also meant that she would be accorded the "deepest" interrogation and de-briefing.

The President took the decision to move the army into the cities on the morning of June 28, to guard bridges, tunnels, sewer and electrical mains, hospitals, churches, schools and places of public assembly and to patrol rooftops with/by snipers carrying rifles with telescopic sights. The troops were to go in wearing civilian clothing having luminous armbands and were to be referred to as Youth Corps Volunteers "on urban maneuvers," with the cooperation of television, press and radio outlets. Until the second of July, excepting rooftop patrols, these troops would be supplied with small arms only. The President and the army leaders were fairly certain that there would not be anything to shoot at even if action began. The guerrilla tactic would be to remain out of sight; striking and mingling. Other than making formal shows to reassure the public when the action began, with armed patrols of two men each, fifteen feet apart, it was not yet certain how the troops should be deployed.

Ten days remained until the Fourth of July.

1:37 P.M., June 27, 1976

The Canadian courier for the Chinese government delivered the pouch to Colonel Pikow at 1:37 P.M. on June 27. When Colonel Pikow read his orders, he began to call Teel at every known contact area. He reached her at 2:41 P.M. at the Tombs Prison where she was visiting a client whose trial for murder would begin on June 29. In their short telephone conversation Colonel Pikow conveyed the three Code Color words, which indicated maximum danger. Teel left the Tombs without returning to the prisoner. She and Chelito took the subway all the way uptown to 155th Street and Eighth Avenue, riding in different parts of the subway car and leaving the car by different exits.

Teel reached the bunker at 3:27. She entered as she always entered, through the adjacent tenement building. Chelito went in through the junkyard, an entrance that had been carefully designed but never used. Colonel Pikow was waiting with a tall, blond Scandinavian-looking man.

"This is Bo Lundquist," Colonel Pikow said abruptly. "He has been on sleeper duty in the Greater Holden area of Saskatchewan for four years waiting for the fail-safe message that came in yesterday. There is proof of a traitor. We have had that confirmed to my government."

"Who?" Teel was distant and calm.

"Unknown."

"How was this confirmed?"

"The American Secretary of State who returned today from what they called a trade mission to Peking, revealed to the Chinese government the American government's knowledge of the most intimate details of our battle plans for the first three weeks of the campaigns."

Teel sat down.

"Where is Chelito?" Colonel Pikow asked.

"I missed her when I left the Tombs. Will she be in trouble if she goes to my place to wait for me?"

"I don't know. I don't think so, but I don't know. The American government will not go into a total alert until after midnight tonight."

Teel spoke to Lundquist. "Tell me how you got the Peking message and what the orders were."

He was hesitant. "I was in my house. It is in the woods three hundred miles above Indian Head, on Lake William in Greater Holden. I am known as a trapper there. I wait for the midnight signal from Peking which has always come in as a test transmission.

The message was in Chinese and in code. It was for Colonel Pikow's eyes only."

Teel turned to Pikow. "What was the message?" she said.

"The war must be called off."

"That is the *sub*stance of the message, Peek. What was the message?"

"The Americans had a plant in Tsinghai from 1971 on." He was unnaturally tense.

"What else?"

"The Secretary of State demanded that the Chinese government immediately persuade the American guerrillas to abandon war plans."

"Yes?"

"My government denied any knowledge of or implication in any war plans by American guerrillas."

"And——?"

"The Secretary of State then made the following statement." Pikow took a slip of paper out of his outside breast pocket with a pair of eyeglasses which Teel had never seen him wearing before. His hands shook badly as he put on the glasses. He read from the paper. " '. . . we will destroy you from north to south, from east to west. Your population of seven hundred and fifty million will be reduced to ten million mutants. . . . That is the message and the assurance of the President of the United States. Think hard.' "

The two men stood facing Teel, who sat in an armchair. "I want to be sure," she said to Pikow. "What is China's answer?"

"What is the *answer?*" Lundquist asked incredulously.

"The only answer," Pikow said. "There can be no war of any kind. Not here and not in China."

"All right," Teel said. "I accept that." Pikow slumped into a chair.

Teel got up heavily. She looked old just then. "Peek, tell me somethin'. What was in the orders if I told you I wouldn't call off the war I worked so long and so hard to get?"

He stared at her longingly and sadly. "Mr. Lundquist would kill you," he answered simply.

"Well, anyhow," Teel replied, "I am glad it wouldn't have been you who had to do it. And I'm glad it isn't me. *Los dos, Chelito!*"

The long flying knife hit Mr. Lundquist at the center of his chest, its force knocking him backward off his feet where he lay jerking spasmodically. Colonel Pikow stood up slowly and unsteadily, staring blankly at Teel as Chelito came out into the room holding a gun.

"Do it well, Chelito," Teel said softly. "*Es muy hombre.*" Chelito shot once.

Teel turned away and walked to the telephone at her desk. She dialed a long distance number. "Senator Simms?" she said into the telephone. "This is Agatha Teel. Do you have that name for me?"

"I have the name," Simms's voice said. "I got it forty minutes ago from the chairman of the Joint Chiefs of Staff."

"What is it?"

"My sister is dead, Agatha. You hardly knew her, but she was everything I had in life and she killed herself because of a man."

"I am deeply sorry to hear that. What terrible news for you. What is the man's name?"

"I will tell you his name if you will invite the man who drove my sister to suicide to your house at ten o'clock tonight."

"All right."

"Thank you."

"Who is the man you want at my house?"

"It will be easy for you. He's a man we met at one of your parties."

"Who?"

"A man named Chandler Shapiro."

"I'll have him at my house at ten, Senator." She hung up.

Teel, Jonas, and Chelito manned telephones in the bunker, not even taking time to dispose of the two bodies, and began to call the guerrilla Army Corps commanders across the United States, to get them into New York and out of danger. As they reached each one, Jonas got on the line and ordered them to reach and warn every National Guard regimental guerrilla unit leader before eleven o'clock that night and to have all of them "change cities" and go underground. The organization would get money to them in three days' time. He ordered the guerrilla Corps Commanders to New York.

They were able to reach Anderson, Weems, Gussow, Buckley and Reyes. They could not reach Winn, Dawes, Duloissier or Enid Simms. At 9:25 Teel told Jonas she had to go downtown, but that he had to keep calling the missing, except for Enid, of course.

"Get them into New York *tonight*," she said. "I want them safe in this bunker. Tomorrow morning is going to be worse than hell. Make them charter if they need to. Get them here *tonight*."

"What you gone do, Ag?"

"Shit, honey—where's the itch, the government got a right to get hip. So they did. That's what makes tennis players. You need a good crafty enemy in the other court. Well, they got hip and we cain't get our war started on the Fourth of July, nineteen hundred and seventy six and maybe not for four more years—but we're okay. We're near to bein' intact so we gone regroup. That's all. We got the gold an' we gone regroup."

"Then why you goin' downtown?"

"Don't you think we got to settle things with the traitor?"

He nodded grimly.

9:50–9:56 P.M., June 27, 1976

Bart arrived at Teel's house on 38th Street at 9:50 P.M. Chelito came down to the main door and led him into the elevator. They rode up two floors to the main living room.

Teel was waiting for him, seated on a long yellow sofa covered with striped silk in the Victorian manner. In the chill of her air conditioning she wore a long dressing gown of white-dyed beaver with deep sleeves. She asked Bart to sit down. He pulled up a chair facing the elevator. Chelito sent the elevator down to the main floor and took a seat in the shadows on the far side of the room.

"Will he be here?" Simms asked.

"Any minute now," Teel said. They heard the sound of the elevator rising.

Simms said, "Here he comes." They watched the light of the lift car slowly fill the opaque glass area which was the elevator door. The elevator door opened. Kranak strode into the room with a cocky macho walk, the man who had been invited to bed by popular request. He stopped short as he saw Bart rise out of the chair.

"I would like to introduce Colonel Lucius Purcell of U.S. Army Intelligence," Bart said. "He is that agent you had asked about. I hold him responsible for the suicide of my sister."

Bart took the single-shot Liberator out of his side pocket as Kranak pulled at his pistol, using his one good arm. They both seemed to fire at once, but Kranak was faster. Kranak's bullet went through Bart's left eye and out the back of his head. Bart's bullet hit Kranak high in the chest, shattering his collar bone.

Chelito threw the knife at the instant the bullet slammed Kranak around toward her, so that, instead of taking him through the chest, it slammed into the base of his throat causing gobbets of blood to cascade like an obscene fountain as Kranak fired at Chelito, hitting her dead center in the face as he came out of the chair with a pistol.

As Kranak fired, Teel drew her gun out of her deep sleeve, put out the room lights with her other hand and shot at him as he stood swaying in outline against the back lights of the elevator. She missed him. She was knocked to the floor with the shock of his bullet slamming into her. Kranak turned and lunged into the open elevator, his back to the dark room. Teel fired again. Her bullet passed through his left lung. She could hear the elevator descending sedately.

Kranak clung to the building wall and made himself move toward the lighted public booth at the corner of Park Avenue, the knife handle protruding from his throat, screaming to himself inside his head that he was a Lipan Apache and that one Lipan could do what would make fifty Navajo quail.

Admiral Adler picked up on the first ring.

"Purcell," Kranak gasped into the phone. "Booth—thirty-eighth—Park."

"Are you hurt?"

Breathing whistled the answer.

"Did you find the leader? *Do you know the leader?*"

At last Kranak revealed the secret of the case he had been trying to build to prove the truth of his knowledge; defying Dr. Baum to prove otherwise. He was a Lipan Apache saving his nation. "Senator Hobart Simms," he said, then hemorrhaged into death.